THIS VIOLENT LIGHT

BREE WILDE

To those who cried because
*Klaus was **not** Caroline's last love...*
I wrote this for you

*(I promise not to f*ck it up)*

CONTENTS

Prologue   1

1. twenty years later   7
2. bad, bad things   16
3. the sweetest blood   29
4. tell me what you want   37
5. not if you're involved   48
6. the last descendant   60
7. I suggest you cooperate   71
8. all of you, monsters   83
9. nod if you understand   94
10. give me something   103
11. one of everything   114
12. don't you dare   124
13. a red billboard   133
14. don't even think about it   141
15. give me a little credit   151
16. don't let them move   161
17. we've both done things   167
18. you kissed me first   176
19. don't rush me   186
20. so pretty when you beg   197
21. mortal emotions   203
22. say the word   210
23. I warned you, Master   216
24. it's a relief, truly   224
25. the most beautiful thing in the world   235
26. maybe Oskar was right   246
27. sacrificial lamb   254
28. the great and fearsome Sebastian Vulce   263
29. that's it, little witch   275
30. one month later   282

Acknowledgments   289
About the Author   293
Also by Bree Wilde   295

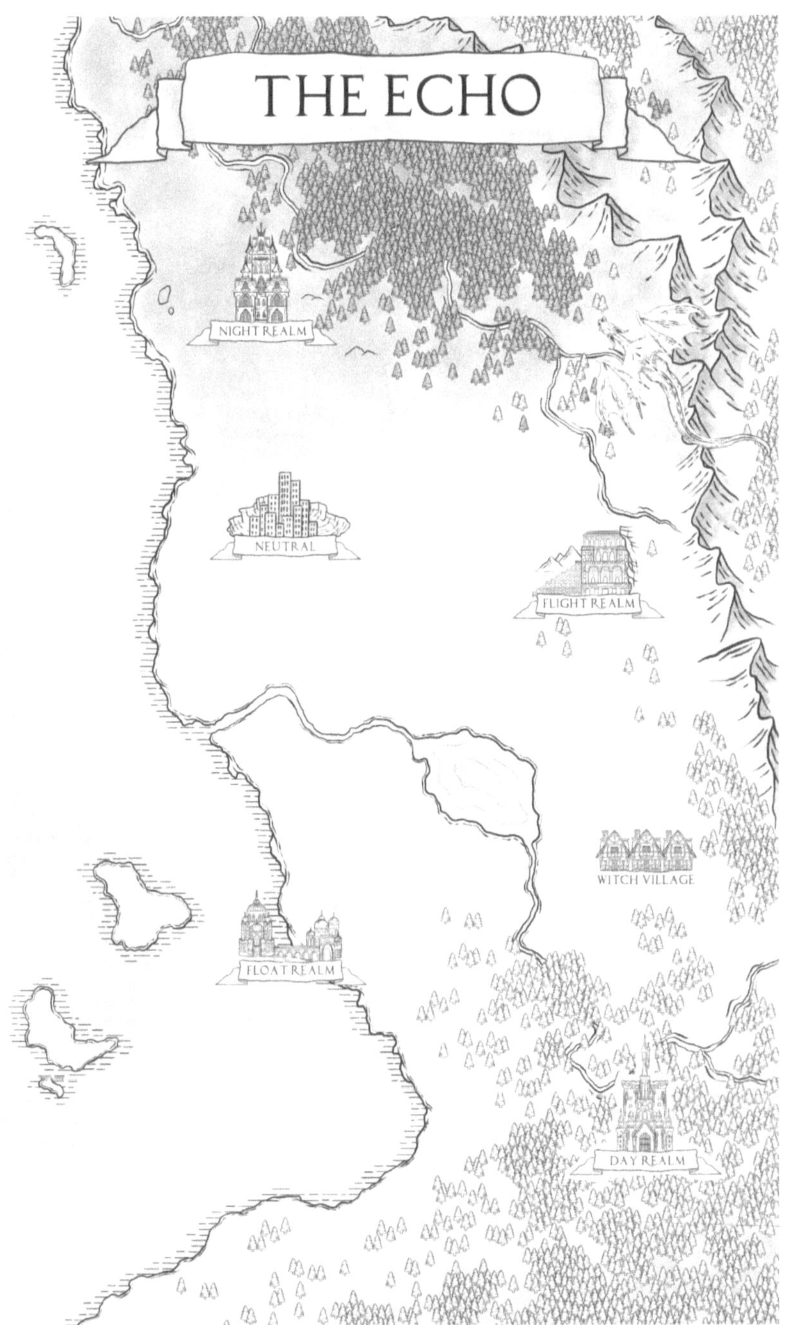

THE ECHO
NIGHT REALM
NEUTRAL
FLIGHT REALM
WITCH VILLAGE
FLOAT REALM
DAY REALM

PROLOGUE

Sebastian

It is a coward's end.

In all my years of rule and all those nights of paranoia, I never imagined losing like this. If I fell, I believed I would at least be bloodied, beaten to the bone, in the midst of a violent battle. Instead, I stand in the dusted shadows of my manor, carefully peeking between mismatched curtains. They're blankets, technically. As soon as darkness fell last night, we stripped all the beds in this place and haphazardly hung the multicolored quilts over each and every window.

Now, with the sun high above the Echo, I watch the world go on without us.

Through the curtains, I catch glimpses of the gathered crowd. Men and women, even children. Humans and witches, fae and harpies. They're all here to taunt us, to mock the great and fallen rule of their vampire king. Near the center, a human tips her head back, cheering along with the crowd. She stands on the lawn of *my* manor, her throat exposed, jugular begging for my teeth.

I would kill her first, I decide. If I wasn't trapped in these shadows, victim of the witches' petty hatred, I would drain the blood from her body. Then, I'd do the same to the men and the children and anyone else I caught before they escaped the Night Realm.

I'd engorge myself to death, just to ensure they pay for their sins.

"Master."

I startle, turning to look at one of my long-time followers. Oskar Duluth is younger than I am, but he's trapped in an elderly body. Silver hair, wrinkles at the corners of his eyes, and spots from years of sun exposure. They're afflictions from his mortality, forever frozen on his skin.

If he stepped outside now, he'd fare far worse than sun spots.

"You are the only man capable of surprising me," I tell him. I'm not sure why. I typically keep weaknesses to myself. It must be the hunger. I haven't fed since the witches cursed us two nights ago. Condemned us to this darkness.

I glance down the hall, opposite the direction of Oskar. Three corpses litter the elegant marble, their bodies caught in sunlight and scorched to the bone. The smell of death permeates the air, and the stench will inevitably linger for decades.

When I return my gaze to Oskar, his bloodshot eyes study me. He's as hungry as I am, but like always, he's less affected. More controlled. He doesn't acknowledge my confession, and I pretend I didn't make it.

"Freja?" I ask. I heard she was one of many caught in the sun without a place to hide. Oskar spent the last two nights looking for her among the bodies. This is the first I've seen him since it all began.

He swallows hard and stares at the heavy drapes, rather than replying. It's answer enough.

"They will pay," I say carefully. I never understood Oskar's affection for Freja. She was his wife before they turned, and it's the only reason I imagine he loved her now. Vampires aren't meant for love or romantic titles. We feast. We fuck. We do as we please.

No, I've never understood Oskar's affection, but I've known him long enough to acknowledge it exists.

"Perhaps tonight, once the sun sets, we will find their villages," I say. "Burn them to ash. Do to them as they've done to us."

Even as I speak, I know it's a foolish idea. The witches are smarter than I often credit them. It's the reason we're in this mess in the first place. And, temporary as I expect this to be, it's a reminder not to underestimate them.

I can't afford to tear across the Echo with a half-formed plan to murder every coven we find. If I fail, it will inevitably bring more unease amongst my followers, and right now, that's not something I can afford.

I sigh. It will likely be days before we put an end to this. For now, we are trapped during daylight hours. Quiet, hushed, ashamed. We are caged animals, locked away by mere mortals.

"The responsible will pay," I say. I look over my shoulder at Oskar.

He stares blankly through me, to the point I don't expect him to respond. When he does, my attention has already drifted back to the slit in the curtains.

"Yes," he finally agrees. "They will pay."

We remain in silence for several minutes. Just when I'm readying to leave, to force myself to plan, rather than simply wallow, it strikes.

A raging heat spreads through my chest, then deeper,

burrowing into my bones. I feel it everywhere, a tortuous burn, like a flame loosed inside my veins. It explodes beneath the skin, infecting each organ like a rabid parasite. Stomach. Lungs. Brain. I'm positive the sun has somehow broken through the curtains, that I'm being burned alive where I kneel.

"Hells," Oskar gasps. It's barely a whisper as he falls to his knees, both hands clasping his sternum.

It lasts seconds, minutes, hours. I can't be sure. Time ceases to exist. *Everything* but this roaring pain disappears, until I find myself begging for death.

Then, it stops.

All at once, the pain vanishes as abruptly as it appeared. It feels as though I've pulled a curtain around my insides, protecting them from invisible sunlight. I gasp for breath, an instinct I thought I'd forgotten. Only now do I realize I've fallen, face flat to the marble.

The sour stench of urine surrounds me.

"Fuck," Oskar mutters. "I think I pissed myself."

"Those cunts!" I roar. I shove to my feet, legs buckling as I rise. "I don't know what they're doing—or how—but it's them. Those fucking witches are trying to kill us!"

"Maybe it's the curse breaking," Oskar offers weakly. "Maybe it's done."

It's a stupid, childish hope, but I act on Oskar's theory anyway. With my shoulder propped against the wall, I slide my hand between the curtain and the window. Sunlight falls over my skin, and the hellfire I felt moments ago is back, scorching my palm into thick welts.

"Cunts!" I scream. I clutch my hand to my chest, glaring at the rapidly forming blisters. Back in the shadows, I'm already healing. The pain disappears, but the anger only pulses faster. "Round the inner circle. Meet me in the theater."

"Master," Oskar says. He's knelt to the side of his piss, staring absently toward the window. "Do you think they've sealed it?"

Oskar is the only vampire in my manor who was born with witch blood. It's rare for full-bloods to survive the transition. Both he and Freja were born into covens, and they'd worked their way into leadership roles, only for it all to be torn away. A random attack left Freja turned and disoriented, disowned by her kind. Oskar brought her here. He'd begged us to save her, to change him too, despite the risks.

In exchange, Oskar told us everything we needed to know about the witches. Their loyalties, their practices, their *weaknesses*. Freja never played a part, but Oskar was largely the reason we stole power as quickly as we did.

"Sealed," I repeat, looking down at him. "You've never mentioned this."

"It's an ancient craft," he says, still gasping for breath. "Not something I've ever seen. It's supposed to be near-impossible. If they did it, if they pulled it off, our chances of breaking the curse just disappeared."

"You're wrong," I say. I don't let his words settle into my brain. I shove them far, far away, deep into the recesses of my mind.

I step closer to the curtain, carefully viewing the street from the safety of shadows. They're all still there. Grinning. Proud. Viciously pleased with themselves.

The streets should be empty. Only days ago, they were. People were terrified. They knew their place: far below us on the food chain. So far below, I ruled with reckless fists: violent, but loose enough to let power slip right between my fingers.

I glare at those fragile creatures, at their foolish celebrations. So breakable, so arrogant and sated.

"I will kill them all," I hiss. "As soon as I'm out of here, I'll kill every single one."

1

TWENTY YEARS LATER

SEBASTIAN

"How's it feel?" I ask. I lean against a granite statue of myself, watching breath turn to fog.

This courtyard was once forgotten and neglected, but in the years since the witches' curse, I've brought it back to life. Thick vines now curl over the manor's stone walls and brush against the uneven cobblestone. Fruit trees and floral bushes frame the main square, and a massive stone table claims the western corner. This damned statue stands proudly at the center.

It's undoubtedly arrogant to have a statue of myself in the yard, but I knew it was only a matter of time before a snot-nosed human destroyed it out of spite. I'd stolen it from the neutral territory years ago, dragging it from the public square in the dead of night and planting it here. I thought it might have a comforting presence, a promise of the power I'd had once, and would again.

Instead, it's mocking me. Standing twice my height, it maintains an air of confidence I haven't held in over a decade. Now, I stand at its base, shivering in this ridiculously heavy coat.

Vampires aren't meant to shiver. We're dead, for fuck's sake.

Magic always comes at a cost though, and this sunwalker spell is proof. It allows me to stand in the direct sunlight, to feel the gentle warmth of day without the skin-blistering heat. But I'm different too. Weak. Horridly mortal, with soft flesh and a beating heart.

A flimsy knife would puncture my skin. It would likely *kill* me.

"It's strange," Theo says. It takes me a moment to remember what I asked.

While Oskar and I lounge in the middle of the courtyard, Theo lingers near the manor's entrance. The double doors remain open, as if arms ready for an embrace, and I imagine Theo left them this way on purpose. He could reach the safety of shadows in two steps if need be.

"Good strange?" Oskar asks. He lights a cigarette and pops it between his lips. The stench of smoke devours the fresh air, until it's all I can taste.

"Very good," is Theo's reply. Despite the frigid air, he removes his sweater and smiles as the morning light touches his bare skin. He bows his head toward me. "Thank you, Master."

"It was earned," I say.

It's true. Of the five hundred and some followers who live here or in the surrounding settlements, only the best are awarded sunwalker spells. They've been with me the longest or proven the worthiest, and after twenty years, only five have claimed the honor.

Oskar. Milas. Beatrice. Amelia. And now, Theo.

Within minutes, the others arrive, all wearing black leather and bloodied smiles. Beatrice attempts to wipe her face, but the others wear their breakfast proudly, eyes dark with satisfaction.

Theo tugs his shirt back in place, scowling when Milas whistles at him.

"Don't get dressed on our account," Milas calls. He stretches an arm around Amelia's shoulder, tugging her against his side. "Personally, I think we should all get naked. Why don't you start, Amelia?"

Amelia smacks him playfully on the back of his head, but Beatrice smirks at me, like maybe there *should* be a new dress code.

"Another time," I say, winking at her. Then, glancing between all of them, I add, "I hope you were subtle. That's not exactly the best example for our newcomer."

"Wait, was that...is that *fresh*?" Theo asks. He starts across the yard, movements staggered and awkward. He frowns as he jogs, adjusting to his drastically weakened muscles, and I hold back a laugh.

"Always," Milas drawls. He strokes Amelia's arm, and she quickly shoves him off, glaring. Unbothered, Milas continues, "We came across a fisherman by the river. Completely alone. Too good to pass up."

Fresh blood is *always* too good for them to pass up, especially when hunting is involved. There's something inexplicably different about drinking in the wild, rather than from the wrist of an occupational bloodletter.

"Don't worry," Beatrice says. "We were discreet. I cleaned up after us."

"I know," I say. It's the truth. Beatrice is my most level-headed follower, and she's quick to shoot me a reassuring smile now.

She steps closer, surrounding me with the intoxicating scent of fresh blood and her sugary perfume. I trail my fingers over her ribcage, down to the flare of her hips. Her dress ends several inches above her knees, and I tease the hemline.

"Hells, I'd love to fuck you in this," I tell her.

Oskar clears his throat beside me, but the others barely react. The old man is the only one easily offended. The rest of us? We're always ready to feast, flirt, and fuck. Typically in that order.

"You probably will," she says breezily. Then, she saunters across the courtyard, swaying her hips as she walks. Amelia meets her partway, linking their elbows together.

"You deserve better. Both of you," Oskar says. He drops his cigarette butt on the cobblestone and smashes it with his heel. "Games like this don't end well."

"I disagree," I say. "I think this will end with Beatrice bent over my desk and my cum between her legs. A perfect ending, if you ask me."

"Or perhaps it will end with your severed cock on *her* desk," he argues. With slanted brows he leans closer. "Truly, Sebastian. Love has driven people to madness."

"What's love got to do with fucking?" I ask, unable to keep the smile off my face.

Oskar doesn't reply. He only sighs, as if I have simultaneously disappointed and exhausted him.

I laugh and slap him on the shoulder.

It's been twenty years since Freja died, but Oskar still pines for her. It's a sentiment I don't understand and don't particularly care to. His affection for her has left him lonely and sore, and yet, he's convinced I need that sort of debilitating love for myself.

No. Thanks.

"You have the brain of a witch and the instinct of a vampire," I say. "But that heart of yours is bloody human."

Two hours later, the courtyard's table is covered in parchment. Only glimpses of stone are visible between faded maps, torn grimoire pages, and more than one stolen letter. We've spent most of this session getting Theo up to speed. Even though he's been a follower for twelve years, he's never had access to information like this.

As we near a close, he has a hand on either temple, massaging slowly. I can't decide if he's trying to rub the information into his brain or if we've given him a terrible headache. Either way, it's clear we've covered enough for today.

"We'll pick back up next week" I announce. I stack the papers nearest to me, and Milas does the same on his end. Looking to Theo, I add, "Plan to meet with Amelia before you go into daylight alone. She'll walk you through everything you need to know."

Theo nods, his fingers still pressed against his forehead.

"And for now—"

I don't get the chance to finish. A hideous burning sensation bursts through my chest. It's fast and harsh, fluctuating in intensity. It feels like bubbles of scalding heat are popping beneath my rib cage. I hunch forward, but it doesn't help. There is nothing to do but feel the shocks of heat and heave uselessly for breath.

"What the fuck..." Beatrice groans and slumps against the table, her head thumping as it meets stone. She's passed out, and Milas isn't far behind her. He moans incomprehensibly, hands wildly clutching his chest and stomach.

Whatever is happening, we're all feeling it.

"Do you..." I say. It takes every ounce of my conscious effort to get those two simple words out. I want to know if the others recognize this blistering heat. I am certain I've only felt it once before, twenty years ago. I was sure I'd never feel it again.

As with the first time, the pain stops suddenly, moments after I decide I'd rather die than feel it. We are all left choking for breath, and by the time I've straightened, Theo is already fleeing for the doors. He thinks this pain comes from the sun. He wasn't yet turned when the witches attacked twenty years ago. He doesn't understand...

"The curse," I spit, still gasping. I look at Oskar, who has one hand to his throat and the other tight on the table's ledge. "Oskar, has it ended?"

"I don't think so," he whispers. He rubs his chest, eyebrows dipping low. "But something happened. Something *big*."

HOURS LATER, long after the burning sensation has faded, I remain alone at the courtyard's stone table. I dismissed the others and sent most of the parchments with Oskar. Now, I have only curse-related texts spread before me. Years' worth of symptom tracking and a variety of theories and failed attempts at freedom. It's pathetically little information, most of which I memorized long ago. I read it again anyway, searching for answers while I wait for Cora to arrive.

I smell her long before she appears in the courtyard. Witches reak. It's a defense mechanism, and a damned effective one. Their blood is magicked to smell of death: rancid and foul, like they've gone rotten. They taste even worse.

"Sebastian," Cora says. She sashays across the cobblestone, rolling her eyes as she passes my statue.

She's a scrawny little thing, but her features are big. Large eyes, thick brows, puffy lips. Her black hair is slicked into its typical high ponytail, fastened so tight it pulls at her forehead. Her brown eyes survey me as she approaches. She looks unimpressed, as usual.

"Cora." I rise from the table. She's written a few of these texts herself, and she's read the others nearly as many times as I have.

"Your followers are nervous," she tells me.

"I know," I say. "Any chance you know what this means?"

Cora is the only witch willing to be in my presence. She's somewhere around thirty now, but she was fifteen when we met. She'd been sentenced to death for practicing dark magic, and only a chance encounter with *me* (of all things) saved her life. Unlike her own kin, I do not fear her darkness.

Cora has lived here ever since. She's given six sunwalker spells and invaluable insight to her people's ruthless curse. She pretends it's to repay me. I pretend to believe her. We both know it's because she hates her people as much as we do, because her heart is as black as ours.

"It could be many things," she says. She reaches the table and sits opposite me, crossing her skinny legs. She's wearing a simple black frock, buttoned to her throat, and thick tights. Like all her clothing, this ensemble is loose and ill-fitting.

I lean against the ivy-covered stone behind me, mostly to escape her pungent scent. Once again, Cora knowingly rolls her eyes.

Despite her small size, she exudes confidence and ease. I could kill her before she realized I moved, but she doesn't show an ounce of fear. Probably because she knows I'd be a fool to kill our best—and only—witch ally.

"The witches cursed you to burn in the sun," she says after a long pause. "It's a difficult spell. Hard to conjure, harder to break. As some of your followers can attest, the curse remains true."

Cora pulls the stack of parchments toward herself, skimming until she finds the one she wants. It's the first piece she wrote for me: a breakdown of the curse, as much as her childhood self understood it. And it was...*heavy*. It required power from multiple familial lines, human and animal organs, and the very life of their beloved leader. Walter Pruce gave his life —willing or unwilling, depending on who tells the tale—to seal the sun curse. He was the last of the formidable Pruce line, and according to Cora, only his blood can undo what's been done.

"It has to be something with the seal," I say. Without meaning to, I press a hand to my chest. "The only other time we felt that burn was when they sacrificed the leader. He died, the curse sealed, and we *all* felt it. Now we've all felt it again..."

"I wonder..." Cora says. Her words fade as she starts to read, thick brows scrunching toward her nose.

She reads the text once. Twice.

Eleven times.

So many times that the sun sets, darkness falls, and the manor awakens. My followers call to each other as they leave in droves, laughing and scheming. Soon enough, the Echo will be crawling with vampires, out for a long night of fucking and (likely failed) feasting. Unfortunately, the Echo has long learned to stay indoors once the sun falls.

"Cora," I say finally. It's been hours of silence, and I can't bear to read these texts a single time more. "I am a patient man, but you have to give me *something*."

"Walter Pruce," she says without looking up.

"What about him?"

"They sealed the curse with his blood and then killed him. Right? Without his blood, the curse cannot be fully broken," she says. She's told me this many times, but I've yet to fully accept it. There *has* to be another way.

Cora scratches her brow, glancing at me, then back down.

"What if he wasn't the last of his line? What if...what if there is another?"

"Impossible," I say. It takes every ounce of control not to scoff. *That* is the grand explanation she's been cooking up these past six hours? When Cora doesn't respond, I continue, "They picked him because he never took a lover, Cora. Never had children. He's been dead twenty years, so I imagine that hasn't changed."

"What if they were wrong though?" she argues. Her voice hushes, and she leans close. "What if he had a child, all those years ago, and they just didn't know it?"

"Impossible," I repeat. "The witches would have known. And they would have murdered his child too."

"But what if..." she looks at the text again. "What if the child was born, not here, but on the outside? What if there is a Pruce child in the human world?"

Chills skate up my arms, no longer from the cold. With night over us, I have returned to my natural form: deadly and invincible. Yet I feel more unsteady than ever.

"We would have known by now," I say. "Even on the other side, the magic would have sensed it. The seal would have failed."

"Maybe," Cora says. "Or maybe the child was so far away, the Echo couldn't sense it. Walter Pruce was known to travel in the human world. It is possible he impregnated a human without knowing—or at least without telling. The child could have been raised elsewhere. Perhaps now...that same child is near."

"Unlikely," I say. Because I can't risk believing—*hoping*.

Cora's throat tenses as she swallows.

"Unlikely," she finally agrees. "But *not* impossible."

2

———

BAD, BAD THINGS

GRACE

If I weren't desperate, I wouldn't take the apartment. It's not bad, necessarily, but it *is* wrong. I've spent my entire life striving for sunshine and warmth, bright colors and easy laughter. This is...earthy. The girl—Tessa McDowell—is wearing black skinny jeans and a matching tank top. Her hair is messy, thrown in a bun, and her face is without a stitch of makeup.

The apartment fits her vibe perfectly.

One glance at my pink mini skirt, eyelash extensions, and glittering phone case, and it's obvious I don't belong.

Yet, here I am. Studying the dark wood furniture and the large bookshelf that's overflowing with antique novels. I wonder if she actually reads them, or if they're just for show. It could be a sign she's pretentious. One of those, *classic fiction is the only acceptable literature* kind of people.

Forget what I said earlier, this place *sucks*.

There are too many plants and sage-scented candles and a freaking fish tank in the corner. Who has a fish tank? It's not even the cute bubble kind. It's a full-on rectangular fish tank with dull brown guppies and a miniature shipwreck.

Mom would hate this place too, and she'd be horrified to know I'm even considering it. She'd tell me to stay in a hotel until I find a better option. If she wasn't dead, I might do that.

Since she *is* dead, I'm stuck settling for one of the only month-to-month rentals I can find. This one might have somber colors and a vintage rug that looks like it was dragged in off the street, but it's cheap and Tessa—though weird—looks harmless.

"I'll take it," I say.

"Really?" Tessa asks, arching an eyebrow. She leans against the wall between the fish tank and the bookshelf.

"Yup," I say. I tighten my purse to my side. "As long as you're not in a cult and don't throw sex orgies in the living room, I'll take it."

"Not in a cult," she confirms. "I'll keep all orgies in my bedroom."

I can't tell if she's joking, and I decide it's better not to ask. Instead, I dig the first month's rent out of my purse. Tessa crosses the room, counts the cash, and jerks her chin toward the empty bedroom.

"You can move in whenever," she tells me. She plucks a key off the well-worn counter and holds it toward me. "Rent is due on the first, and if you're late by more than a week, I'm kicking your ass out."

"It won't be a problem," I say, and so long as I get the shitty Target job I interviewed for this morning, it won't be.

IT TAKES NEARLY a week to fully settle into Tessa's apartment. I didn't bring much stuff from South Carolina. I drive a beat-up Camry, and there was only so much space for my personal belongings. Definitely no room for a rug or a bed or a desk. Luckily, I was able to find a few gently-used items from a nearby thrift shop. With ten minutes of flirting, I was able to convince two of the workers to deliver the four-poster bed and the antique dresser. They're both hideous, but I don't plan to use them for long.

I *did* buy a brand-new mattress though. I've gotten better about shopping second-hand, now that I'm poor and all, but I draw the line at dirty mattresses.

I'm sitting on said mattress now, surveying my bedroom. It's sort of a masterpiece, if I do say so myself. I've got a few art prints to cover the beige walls, a beautiful fluffy rug to hide the scratched hardwood floors, and a couple houseplants to decorate the elongated window. Directly across from me, a standing mirror reflects me and my hot pink quilt.

I collapse back into the overstuffed pillows and pull my current project onto my lap. It's a stack of Mom's old letters, most of them from my father. He skipped out on us when I was only four years old, and though Mom insisted he would never leave us, I always assumed she was in deep denial.

A lot of women assume their husbands would *never* cheat or leave or end up being a raging asshole. So, despite what Mom believed, I always figured my dad was a deadbeat loser. I never asked about him, and Mom eventually stopped trying to enlighten me.

I didn't know who he was, where he was from, or what happened to him. Before Mom died, I didn't really care. Good riddance, I'd always thought.

Then I found these stupid letters. Dozens of them over a ten-year span, all sent from an Aberlena, Washington address. They're all sweet and loving, and maybe that was why I started digging deeper into the mystery of my father.

Walter Pruce.

A man who never existed, according to the results of Mom's police report. He'd used a fake name, obviously.

My current theory is that Walter Pruce has another family here in Aberlena. That he either decided to pick them over me and Mom *or* that he died in a car accident and that's why he never came back.

I'm still flipping through the letters when my phone lights with a video call. I glance at the caller ID and restrain a groan. If I don't answer, I already know she'll call until I do.

"Hey, Lib," I say. I push the letters off my lap and settle deeper into the pillows.

My best friend Libby has wavy black hair, flawless dark skin, and unfairly full lips. Right now, she's decked out in a full face of makeup, complete with sparkly eye shadow. She's ready for a night on the town, and my stomach pinches with jealousy. I should be there with her, wearing a low-cut top and not this ratty sweatshirt.

"Ew," is her immediate reaction. I can't decide if she's talking about me or my surroundings. Her nose crinkles and she leans toward her camera. "Jesus, Grace. Where *are* you?"

Guess that answers that question.

"My new place," I say. I shift until the dingy walls are out of sight, and my face is surrounded by nothing but frilly pink pillows. "It's really not bad, but it doesn't matter. It's only temporary."

Libby doesn't reply for a long moment. She's still staring at me with a mixture of confusion, disgust, and pity.

"You should be here," she says, echoing my sentiments from a minute ago. "Literally, Grace. Just *look* where I am."

She pans to her surroundings: a sleek and modern apartment with immaculate white walls and tasteful decor. Through the floor-to-ceiling windows, New York City glitters, taunting me.

"I'll be there in a month. Two months at the most," I say. I can't keep the desperation out of my voice, and not for the first time since arriving in Aberlena, I question if I've made the wrong choice.

"I don't know why you're chasing down some loser you don't even know," she says. With a heavy sigh, she returns the camera to her face. "You're putting your life—a fucking NYC adventurous life, might I add—on hold for a deadbeat sperm donor."

"Yeah, I know," I say. And I do. Despite what most people assume (either because of my platinum hair or my unyielding love of pink), I'm not an idiot. "I can't explain it. I just...I want to know."

Libby doesn't reply, and I don't blame her. If she had been the one to ditch our New York plan, I would've thought she was insane. We were both supposed to go to New York, live in her cousin's sweet high rise apartment, and get jobs at any fashion magazine that would hire us.

"Only a month or two," I say again. "Then I'll be in New York, and you can talk me up to your snazzy fashion boss and get me a job."

Libby snorts. "I think that requires me to *have* a snazzy fashion boss. I haven't landed a single interview."

My chest relaxes as we shift the conversation to lighter topics. I'm an eternal optimist, but I'm also a bit of a pushover. If anyone talks down on my ideas for too long, I'll inevitably fold and give up. This is one of the few times I'm determined not to let that happen.

"It's only been a week," I say. "And besides, you're in New York with a free place to crash. You better enjoy it. Let me live vicariously through you. Go to all the swanky clubs and convince hot guys to buy you drinks."

"Trust me, I will," Libby says, grinning. Nearly as fast, her expression shifts to a deep frown. "I'd feel better if my best friend wasn't clearly falling into a deep pit of despair. I can't remember the last time I saw you in sweats on a Friday night."

"There aren't exactly swanky clubs here," I point out.

"There are absolutely bars and places to dance though," she says. "You're in a freaking college town. That *you* decided to banish yourself to, in case you forgot. So change out of that hideous sweater, grab your weird roommate, and go shake your ass at whatever bar you can find."

"I like this sweater," I say. When Libby only arches an eyebrow, I let out a heavy sigh. "Fine, I'll see what I can figure out."

"Good girl," she says. "And remember: safe sex is great sex!"

"I won't be—"

Libby hangs up before I can finish my protest.

"To my first week in Aberlena!" I announce. I raise my vodka shot above my head, frowning when half of it sloshes onto my bare arm. Across from me, Tessa snorts. I don't even care. I'm just happy (and really, really surprised) she agreed to come out with me at all.

I throw back my shot and Tessa sips her beer. She doesn't *do* shots, apparently. No, cool girl Tessa drinks the darkest beer she can find and maintains the world's most intense grimace as she watches the drunken crowd around us.

Shit.

I'm being judgemental. That is basically the opposite of girl power. If she wants to drink yucky beer and wear a boring outfit to the bar, that's *her* prerogative.

"Are you going to the college?" Tessa asks. She leans her elbows against our table. We're near the back, at the only open table we could find when we arrived thirty minutes ago. Barco's, according to Tessa, is the only decent bar in Aberlena. The rest are overridden by college students. She'd told me this, as if going to college was the equivalent of being a cockroach.

And now, she's asking if I'm one of those cockroaches.

"No," I say. I signal the waitress for another shot. It will be my third, and I know better than to drink this hard this fast. Still, it's clear Tessa won't be matching my freak tonight. She'll probably want to leave in twenty minutes, and I'd at least like to feel drunk before that happens.

"You here for a job opportunity?" she asks. She sounds skeptical at this one, as if the thought of *me* getting a job offer is ludicrous. To be fair, she's not exactly wrong.

I've got an unfinished business degree and zero relevant work experience. I was partway through my junior year of college when Mom's health tanked, and my temporary leave from college turned into a permanent one.

"I'm looking for someone," I say. I'd promised myself I wouldn't tell people what I was doing here. I knew it would draw pitiful looks.

What kind of grown woman goes looking for a father who clearly abandoned her?

I've had that thought often.

"My dad," I say. I'll blame the alcohol for my loose lips, but honestly, I've never been great with keeping secrets. "Or my sperm donor, as my friend Libby calls him."

Tessa doesn't say anything. She looks like she wishes she'd never asked. Her eyes hone in on her half-empty beer (still her first one), and she traces the condensation with her finger.

Jesus, Grace. Way to kill a mood.

Not that we'd been having a spectacular time before that confession. Still, if I had any hope of Friday bar nights with Tessa becoming a habit, I think I just squashed it.

"Well, I hope you find him," she says. She keeps her eyes on her beer. "He sounds like an asshole though."

I let out a surprised laugh that turns into a snort. For the first time, Tessa gives me a genuine smile. She echoes my laughter and takes a generous chug of beer.

We sit in silence for a few minutes. I check my phone notifications, and Tessa leans back in her chair, surveying the crowd. Once I've replied to Libby's sixteen texts, I place my phone back on the table.

"Okay, so what about you?" I ask. "What's your—"

"You still haven't noticed," Tessa interrupts. She's smiling at me, but it's a reduced version, lips just barely tilted.

"Noticed?" I repeat.

"That guy has been staring you down since he walked in," she says. Her eyes spark with amusement. "The second you look at him, he's going to come over and offer to buy you a drink."

"I doubt that..."

I follow Tessa's gaze across the room, where a man occupies a booth. He is ridiculously attractive. Dark blond hair, hard jawline, a small scar on the side of his forehead. He looks dangerous and delicious, and far more likely to choose someone like Tessa over me.

She's not lying though. His eyes, a deep shade of green, are focused intently on me. I squeeze my legs together and snap my gaze back to Tessa.

"Oh my god, he's beautiful," I hiss.

"Beautiful?" she repeats, arching an eyebrow. Her attention flickers from me to him. "He *is* good looking, but I don't know. Something seems...weird about him."

"What? That he's looking at me instead of you?" I snap. I immediately feel like a jerk, and a hot flush flares over my cheeks. "Sorry. I don't know why I said that."

"Relax," she says, rolling her eyes. "I'm not interested in your creeper. I'm just saying...Think about it, Grace. He's alone at a bar, just sitting there. He doesn't even have a drink. And he's too handsome. Like, suspiciously handsome. Why hasn't anyone else approached him, huh? Because, Grace. Bad, *bad* vibes."

I'm nodding along to Tessa's crazy words, all the while wishing he'd come do bad, *bad* things to me. The man holds my gaze, and the tip of his mouth tilts into a dangerous smirk.

"Just, if you're determined to fuck him, do it at our place," she continues. "I feel like if you go with him, I'll never see you again."

"I knew you liked me," I say, grinning at her.

"I like your rent," she corrects quickly. She casts another sideways glance across the room. "Called it."

The mystery man is no longer in his booth. He's partway to us, eyes locked confidently on me. An eruption of pleasure dances through my stomach. I don't think a man's ever looked at me like he is now. Like he doesn't just want to sleep with me... like he wants to devour me whole.

"Act natural," I hiss at Tessa. I snatch my empty shot glass from the table and twist it between my fingers. I stare at it, rather than the man, as if it's the most fascinating thing in this room.

"I'm not the one being weird," Tessa says. She grabs the shot glass from my hand and returns it to the table. "Chill the fuck out, Grace. He obviously wants you."

I breathe a heavy sigh through my lips, centering myself. She's right. He's coming toward our table like a man on a mission, and from the looks of it, *I'm* that mission.

I'm not some inexperienced virgin. I had a few boyfriends in high school and a lot of hookups in college. I also know I'm relatively attractive. I've never had a hard time getting a guy into bed, and from the way this man is staring, he wouldn't protest one bit.

And yet...I'm a fidgeting mess by the time he reaches our table. He's that good-looking, and by his easy confidence and arrogant stance, he clearly knows it. He smirks at me, green eyes dancing.

I glance at Tessa, but rather than melting into a puddle like I currently am, she lifts an unimpressed eyebrow.

"Hello, beautiful," the man says. He has a strange accent that makes his words even more intoxicating. That, mixed with his intense gaze, makes me forget how to speak. I gape at him, mouth parted.

"I'm Tessa," my roommate says.

When the man doesn't respond, and I only stare, Tessa kicks me under the table.

"Grace," I finally blurt. "My name is Grace."

"Beautiful," he repeats. His smile is slow, but it changes his entire face. "I'm Sebastian."

I swallow. I've always been a big talker. Mom said it was the curse of her side of the family. We love to talk, and we never know when to stop. I *really* wish I could channel some of that energy now.

Instead, I'm just staring at him, mouth slightly agape. I must look *ridiculous*, but Sebastian only smiles at me. I've never met someone named Sebastian. It's old-timey and should be dorky, but on him, it's anything but.

Right now, I know with absolute certainty, or at least ninety-eight percent, that this man is my soulmate.

"Care to dance?" he asks. His voice is deep and gravelly, and that accent...it should be illegal for the ways it's messing with my head.

"Um," I glance at Tessa. She's back to sipping her beer, but she's clearly hiding a smile. "Yes. Yes, I would love to dance."

Sebastian extends his hand toward me. His fingers are long and pale, but strong too, like they're accustomed to work. If I'm lucky, I'll know exactly how strong and capable they are by the end of the night.

I place my hand in his, briefly shocked by the cool touch of his skin. I shoot a parting smile to Tessa and slide off my stool. When I look back at Sebastian, I'm expecting that same, flirty smirk. Instead, his face is scrunched, displeased, as if he's just noticed something about me that he hadn't before.

My nose, I decide. He must have noticed my nose is weird, a little too long for my face.

I swallow and try to shake off my insecurity. It doesn't matter. It's taken root now, even as Sebastian's disgusted expression melts back into the smooth one from before. I can tell he's faking it now. If I look hard enough, I can spot the grimace lurking behind his handsome smirk.

I'm so distracted, I don't realize my heel is caught on my chair until I'm reeling forward. My hand slips from Sebastian's and I pitch straight into his chest. I instinctively reach for him, only for him to lurch out of the way, as if my touch is poisonous.

I fall to the sticky floor, knees striking hard enough to bring tears to my eyes. I remain on my hands and knees for a strained moment. A scorching blush stains my cheeks, until all I can feel is that unpleasant heat.

I force myself to look up, and Sebastian is still a foot away. He looks as surprised as I feel, and yet, he doesn't move to help me. It's as if I've transformed into a vile rat.

Maybe you are, I decide. *Maybe he's realized you're ugly up close and—*

"Move, asshole," Tessa says. She shoves Sebastian out of the way, shooting him a scathing glare. Her expression remains hard, irritated, as she peels me off the floor.

"Grace, are you—"

"Uh-uh," Tessa interrupts. She steps sideways, as if to block me from his view. She's too short though, maybe five-two where I'm five-nine. "Nothing from you, *Sebastian*."

She says his name like it's a foul curse.

"I'm fine, Tessa," I say. Still, I can't keep the heat from lingering on my cheeks. "I just tripped. It's really okay. It's not like he tripped me."

"No, he just let you fall on your face," she says. Her nose scrunches, and she casts another glare his way.

"That's a bit dramatic," Sebastian says. He steps closer, towering over Tessa. He's only a few inches taller than I am, maybe five-eleven. And yet, he holds himself as if he's a giant, as if he could destroy both of us with his bare fists. "She said she's all right."

He extends his hand toward me again, and I start to reach for it, only for Tessa to slap his wrist.

"She's not interested," she says.

My mouth gapes in shock, but I'm too stunned to say anything. Libby would *never* chase off a hot guy. She'd know my pride isn't all that important to me. Who cares if Sebastian dropped me on my face? He's hot. He probably didn't mean to lurch away from me like I was a nasty insect. And if there's a chance he still wants me...

"Grace," he starts. His deep green eyes search mine. "Just give me one dance, and I'll—"

"She's not interested in assholes," Tessa repeats, firmer this time. "Go find another girl to fumble."

With that, Tessa tightens her grip on me. She leads the way out of the bar and onto the moonlit street, where she orders a car. I do my best to stay steady on my feet. The three shots have caught up to me, all at once, and I realize I never even got my fourth.

"Sorry," she says after a long pause. "I didn't mean to cock-block you or anything. I just...you deserve better than that."

I'm not sure I do, but I don't say that. Instead, I link my elbow through hers and force a smile.

"I knew you liked me."

"Maybe a little."

When our car arrives, I risk a glance over my shoulder. I'm not surprised to spot Sebastian still in the bar, but I *am* surprised to find his eyes on me. He stands near the window, frowning as I get into the car.

Tessa was right to pull me away, and yet, I feel an inexplicable urge to return.

3

THE SWEETEST BLOOD

SEBASTIAN

I sit with my back to the ivy-covered wall and my elbows propped on the stone table. The sun shines into the courtyard, and despite the chilled air, I feel overheated. I'm suffocating, I think, surrounded by the memories of Grace and her smell and the glide of her skin against mine.

Wrong. It was all wrong, and I still can't make sense of it. If she had been what I'd expected, what she *should* be, last night wouldn't have been a problem.

Instead, I'd let her—quite literally—slip through my fingers.

"Where's the girl?" Cora asks as she enters the courtyard. As always, she's wearing thick leggings and a basic frock, both black. Her thick eyebrows slant at the empty space around me.

I'd asked Cora to meet me this morning in full anticipation Grace would be here too. Willing or unwilling, she should be here. I can't quite articulate why she's not.

"Assuming you messed up then," Cora says as she settles into the place across from me. She's the only one brazen enough—or perhaps stupid enough—to talk to me this way.

I grab the front of her shirt, so fast it startles her. Her dark eyes widen, as if suddenly reminded of the fact I could really, truly kill her. Drain her of blood until she is nothing but fragile bone and ripped flesh.

"Master," she whispers.

If my head weren't a jumbled mess, I might let her grovel. My nerves are shaken since meeting Walter Pruce's daughter though, and for once, I don't care to have my ego stroked.

"You *stink*," I tell her. She's half over the table now, frozen in my grasp like a terrified rabbit. I can feel her heart beating through her chest, unsteady and violent. Her expression doesn't change as I draw her closer and press my nose to the collar of her dress. "Fucking vile. It's pungent, revolting, distracting. I've never smelled anything quite as terrible as a witch."

I release her, and Cora snaps back to her seat, visibly trembling. Her eyes remain wide and her movements rigid, as if she's forcing herself not to sprint from me, back to the safety of her quarters.

"Witches reek," I say. I slump back to the wall, closing my eyes. I can still smell her stench, the sour odor of expired meat. It's worse than usual right now, each violent beat of her heart stirring her blood until it's all I smell.

"Yes, Master," Cora says.

She wouldn't normally agree. The Cora I've grown to tolerate over the past dozen years would typically have a smart retort. Now, she's just staring, insides raging with terror, outside too frozen to move.

I should remind her I won't kill her, but I don't. I only clench my fists, lip snarling as I speak.

"Amelia got the wrong woman," I say finally. "Whoever that woman was, she's not the one we need."

Even as I speak the words, I doubt them. I'd read up on Amelia's research. Grace might have a different last name than Walter, but there are too many coincidences for her to not be his. She's from the East Coast, raised by a single mom who once reported a nonexistent man missing. Most damning, she arrived to Aberlena the same fucking day we felt our chests catch fire.

There's no way she *isn't* the woman I need. And yet...

"Why do you say that?" Cora asks. She's absentmindedly holding the collar of her dress, right where I'd grabbed her.

I study her face before replying. I can see it in her expression: she knows Grace is the right person. She knows *I'm* the one who's wrong.

"She smelled..." I trail off, searching for the right word, but none of them seem right.

Good.

Delicious.

Incredible.

Fucking perfect.

"She did not smell like a witch," I say finally. I straighten my fingers and study my palm. I'd had her hand in mine, and if I hadn't gotten distracted, I would have dragged her all the way here.

Instead, I'd found myself inches from forgoing everything I've ever wanted. Forget the curse, forget lost power, forget everything but the sweetest blood I've ever smelled. I was ready, in that moment, to lose it all if only I got to taste her first.

Cora doesn't look alarmed by my words. In fact, they seem to put her at ease. She drops her collar, placing both hands on the table. Her breaths become steady, pulse slowing with each inhalation.

"She's not of the Echo," she says.

I lift an eyebrow, a silent *so* to encourage her to continue.

"Witches aren't born with sour blood," Cora says. A small smile tugs at her lips, as if, despite everything, she enjoys having this knowledge over me. "It's a spell, like any other protection we have. They cast it while we're in the womb or shortly after birth. Grace was never here."

"Walter didn't think to protect his own daughter?" I press.

Because surely, no man would be foolish enough to leave his daughter vulnerable. Especially not one who smells so irresistible.

"I think it's clear Walter Pruce didn't want Gracie anywhere near us," Cora says. She stretches her fingers across the table, looking at the small scars on her knuckles, rather than at me. "Smart man."

"Clearly not smart enough," is my only response. I shove from the table, striding through the sunlit courtyard. "We'll meet here again soon."

"Will she be here next time?" Cora calls. She's taunting me, and it soothes the tension in my chest.

I'm not good at forming relationships, alliances. It's part of what got me into this fucking mess in the first place. Oskar loves me as a father might his son. Beatrice enjoys my cock more than my mind. And the rest of my circle fears me too much to be considered friends.

Cora might be the closest thing I have to a true companion. I'd rather not have her hate me.

"Cora," I call, pausing at the center of the courtyard. My statue towers over me, and I study its stone features, rather than looking at her. Several seconds pass, until I'm fidgeting, but the words still refuse to come.

"I know, Master," she says finally. "I know."

I nod, not looking back. And then I'm off, ready to finish what I've started—once and for all.

"Perhaps I could accompany you," Beatrice says. Her long legs easily match my fast strides, her heels clacking against uneven cobblestone. Our side of the Night Realm is always quiet at this time of day.

The sun curse forced change here. With the vampires locked indoors, the werewolves grew bored of our sparsely-populated towns. They started spending more and more time elsewhere: their own civilizations to the north, the neutral territory to the south, and even the Flight Realm to the east. They'll come this way once night falls and my kind comes out to play, but for now, we're alone.

"Maybe if I come with you—"

"No, Beatrice," I say, cutting her off.

I'm not surprised she's asking. I figured it would come up in our thirty minute walk to the neutral territory. She claimed she needed to visit the Paragon anyway. I didn't believe her then either.

It's been three days since my disastrous attempted abduction, but I finally have a plan. I don't bother specifying this out loud, but Beatrice's presence would absolutely ruin it.

"Since you're here though," I say, glancing at her. She's wearing a more feminine dress today, with a high neckline and lacy tights. The outfit is a blend of deep purples and soft violets. Her dark eyes cling to mine, hopeful. "Tell me about our next group of initiates."

"Oh, sure," she says. She blows out a heavy breath. "I easily picked twenty recruits, and I think I'll be able to add another ten. I know you want forty, but..."

She trails off. This time, her attention stays straight ahead. We've walked far enough to leave the largest estates out of sight. Now, we're surrounded by a strip of vampire owned stores. Stone building after stone building promises one service or another, ranging from *the best bloodletters in the Echo* to *one-hour venom extraction* and *walk-up fang cleaning*.

At nightfall, they'll all come to life. Heavy music will thump through most buildings, and drunken vampires will arrive to party, hook up, and forget their shitty reality.

"I don't want forty," I say. "I *need* forty. That means you'll find forty, understood?"

"Yes, Master," she says. Though I don't look at her, I can see her sharp nod from my peripheral. "It's just hard to find vampires willing to work, to fight."

"Good thing we're about to give them something worth fighting for."

Ten minutes later, we reach the divide between the Night Realm and the neutral territory. Despite myself, I hesitate. It's likely not long enough for Beatrice to notice, but I hate that *I* notice.

There wasn't always this sharp divide between each territory. Once, the Echo was a unified kingdom, and the vampires ruled it all. It was the witches who destroyed everything.

They started by placing these dividers. Deep black lines that scorched the ground, cutting through anything in their path. Grass, dirt, stone, it didn't matter. A black line spread through the Echo, separating us into respective territories, making it more difficult to travel between them.

The Night Realm.

The Day Realm.

The Flight Realm.

The Float Realm.

And then, of course, the neutral territory. This is where the academy educates our youth, where the council conducts its meetings, where the filthy, alluring humans live.

Injury to any supernatural creature is forbidden here. Much as I'm tempted to kill a couple witches as we pass them, I don't. Any supernatural who attempts to harm another supernatural faces the consequences, quite literally.

Stab a witch. You'll be the one with a knife wound in your side, blood pouring over the floor.

Strangle a harpy. You'll have a crushed windpipe and a bruised throat.

Murder a fae. You'll be the one lifeless, crumpled to the stone while they go about their day.

I force myself to cross the line, and Beatrice again keeps an easy pace. She's still talking about the initiates, highlighting a few with extraordinary potential, but I've stopped listening.

Now, I'm busy studying the neutral territory.

It looks more like the human world, like Aberlena, than anywhere else in the Echo. Where the Night Realm is characterized by daunting estates, magnificent stone structures, and elaborate fountains, the neutral territory is overrun with stucco buildings and small storefronts. Here, everything is labeled and neat and orderly. The homes have numbers. The streets have signs. They've even got rules posted outside their parks and shopping centers.

The neutral territory is undoubtedly the least interesting place in the Echo, save for the fact it houses the Paragon. A beautiful and impenetrable building, surrounded by massive pillars and covered in stone gargoyles. It is the mirror image of Aberlena University and the only known door between the Echo and the human world.

Here, one can travel between the two as easily as crossing a bridge.

I jog up the steps, pausing beneath a particularly anguished gargoyle. His face is frozen in dismay, eyes wide and unseeing. I force my attention away from the man, to Beatrice, who stares at me with her bottom lip pouted.

"It might be better if—"

"Get me forty," I say, cutting her off. "And ready them for war."

I don't give her the chance to reply. I leave her standing beneath the gargoyles and duck into the Paragon Building.

4

——————

TELL ME WHAT YOU WANT

GRACE

I've always loved high heels. There's something empowering about them, and not just for the added height. Every time I wear them, I feel like I'm shouting to the world: *that's right, I can do it better than you, and I'll do it wearing these six-inch platforms!*

Despite today's red-bottom heels, I don't feel at all empowered. I just finished my second interview of the day, and I am confident I won't get either job. The first—a position at the local paper—was a long shot, and I crashed and burned accordingly. The second one though—a cashier position at a nearby grocery store—should have been easy. I figured they'd offer me a job on the spot.

Instead, I fumbled my way through an interview with a guy years younger than I am. The whole time, he kept raising an unimpressed eyebrow. At the end, he said something along the lines of, "we'll let you know either way."

Either way?

Yeah, I definitely won't be getting the job.

My heel catches on the sidewalk, and I stumble. I curse under my breath, then glance over each shoulder to make sure no one saw me. Shifting my bags in my arms, I continue walking toward the apartment. To make up for the awkwardness of Friday night, I promised to take Tessa wherever she wanted for dinner.

Naturally, she didn't *want* to go anywhere. She wanted takeout Chinese food, hand-delivered by yours truly. So I've got two hefty bags of teriyaki chicken, fried rice, broccoli and beef, and a large container of egg drop soup. It smells delicious, but I'm pretty sure at least one of the containers is leaking, dripping as I make my way across town.

My phone buzzes in my purse, and I have to shuffle the bags again to answer it, putting Tessa on speaker.

"We are *so* even," I tell her before she can say anything. "I am currently walking the least-maintained sidewalk I've ever seen, and this food weighs about a million pounds."

"Did you get the egg rolls?" she asks.

"Yes," I say. "I got the egg rolls and the soup and the rice and the noodles and whatever the hell else was on your list. It's your fault if I can't afford rent this month, by the way."

There's a momentary quiet.

"The interviews didn't go well, I take it?" She's mocking me. I might not be able to see her, but I'm quickly accepting that my new roommate is sarcastic, blunt, and a little bit mean.

I shouldn't like her, but of course I do. I like everyone, and I'm pretty sure that'll get me killed someday.

"You can pick the movie," she says when I don't reply. "Even if it's one of those stupid romantic comedies."

"Rom-coms are *not* stupid," I say. "They're a staple of modern entertainment, and if you don't see that, maybe *you're* stupid."

Tessa laughs. In the background, I can tell she's turned on the TV. It sounds like she's watching yet another horror flick. What she sees in those, I'll never understand.

"All right, well I'll be back in less than five," I say. "So turn off your Frankenstein movie and pull up *Legally Blonde*. It's time for you—"

I cut off.

I have the inexplicable sensation that I'm being watched. I tighten my hold on the takeout bags before doing a slow rotation, taking in the streets around me. Winters in Aberlena are bleak and dreary, so it's not unusual for it to be dark at five fifteen in the evening.

It *is* unusual for me to feel unsettled by that. Aberlena is a small town, and though I haven't checked, I bet it's got one of the lowest crime rates in Washington.

I study the shadows of the nearby subdivision. There's no one here, and certainly no one who's watching me. I'm completely alone.

"Hello? Grace?" Tessa asks. "Did you hang up on me? Because if you did, that's a real bitch—"

"I'm still here," I say. My voice shakes, and it's honestly embarrassing. If Tessa knew I was out here freaking out over *nothing*, she'd roast me. And yet, I still find myself saying, "I thought I heard something. Stay on the phone with me until I get back. Okay?"

"Heard something?" Tessa repeats, her voice drawling. "You're literally outside, Grace. You're probably hearing all sorts of new sounds. Cars and birds...maybe even people."

I tune her out and start walking again, keeping the bags close at my sides. The apartment building is visible. Less than three minutes, and I'll be home. Tessa will make fun of me for being scared by the outside world. She'll tell me I got something about her order wrong. We'll watch Legally Blonde, and everything will be fine.

My heart thumps harder, faster. The hairs on my arms and neck prickle, until I stop walking again. No one there.

Of course no one's there. I'm just freaking crazy.

"If I have to stay on the phone, you at least have to entertain me," Tessa goes on. "Otherwise—"

I don't hear the rest of what she's saying. One moment, I'm clutching my phone and these stupid bags of takeout, and the next, I'm empty handed.

The Chinese food splatters across the sidewalk, and my phone is simply *gone*. I stare at my hands in shock, blinking rapidly from my trembling fingers to the broken boxes at my feet.

I lift my gaze.

Sebastian stands five feet from me, his handsome face tilted in a mix of frustration and amusement. He holds my phone in his hand, and with a taunting grin, he hangs up on Tessa.

"What—"

That's as far as I get. The word hangs in the air and silence swells around me. Sebastian, the random hot guy—the *asshole*—from Barco's has my phone. He has my phone, and he just threw all my takeout food across the sidewalk.

"That was expensive," I snap. It's an instinctual response, but my confidence is fleeting. I take a small step backward, stomach dropping when Sebastian echoes the movement, only stepping closer. "Were you following me?"

He doesn't immediately reply. He puts my phone in his pocket and again steps toward me, dodging the spilled Chinese food. His eyes are narrowed, calculating. He looks like an animal, like a starved predator who has stumbled upon vulnerable prey.

I swallow, and his gaze flickers to my throat, as if he's heard it.

"What do you want?" I ask. I take slow steps backward, eyes flickering at my surroundings. We're alone right now, but this isn't an isolated area. Anyone could walk by, so he wouldn't risk attacking me.

Right? Right. Absolutely.

I'm still searching for help, for an escape, for anything, when I step off the curb. I wasn't paying close enough attention, and my entire body lurches. The heel of my shoe snaps and I flail for the ground.

Only I don't hit it.

There's a dizzying blur of movement. It's too much for me to process. Sebastian. Wind. Flashing colors. A jolting drop in my stomach.

I don't realize I've closed my eyes until I stop moving.

I blink, cracking one eye open before the other. My heart pinches as I take in my surroundings, which have inexplicably changed. Only moments ago, I was a few minutes from my apartment. And now, without taking a single step, I am blocks away. I can see the Chinese restaurant from here, its neon sign flickering against the dark sky. I'm almost back to the grocery store where I interviewed.

I shift my attention to Sebastian. He isn't touching me. He stands the same distance as he was by my apartment, but it's clear *he* did this. He magically transported us, and now, he's staring at me with the same amused expression from before. He thinks this is funny, I realize. He's just done an impossible magic trick, and he's waiting for me to ask him how he did it.

I should ask. Because, *really*, how did he do that?

Instead, I straighten my top and skirt. It takes all my concentration to keep level footing, seeing as my left shoe is now missing its heel. I cross my arms and glare at him. As casually as I can manage, I evaluate our new location.

The restaurant and its surrounding buildings are too far for anyone to see us. There's an empty park behind him, complete with a slide and a jungle gym. On the opposite side, there's a sprawling subdivision, blocked by a solid wooden fence.

My best chance is the Chinese restaurant, I decide. If I can manage to get out of these shoes—they're latched around my ankles, unfortunately—I might have a chance. I'll take off as soon as he lets his guard down, and I'll just pray his magic trick was a one-time thing. If it was, I *might* have a chance of outrunning him.

If that fails (which feels very possible, to be honest), I'll scream as loud as my lungs allow. Then I'll scream even harder.

"Tell me what you want," I say. It sounds demanding, confident, but Sebastian only smiles at me. Despite his attractive face, the smile doesn't look quite right. It's too predatory, as if he's not truly human.

He steps closer, and I force myself not to move. Instead, I take off my broken heel. Once it's discarded on the sidewalk, I start on the next. The whole time, I keep my shoulders relaxed, my face impatient.

This is fine, I'm trying to convey. *Say what you want, and then I'll be on my merry way. I'm not going to run. We're not going to have any sort of altercation.*

"Your father," he says. "What's his name?"

I freeze, fingers paused on the latch of my right heel. When I look up at him, Sebastian is two feet away, staring at me with a strange expression on his face. It's the first time he hasn't looked predatory *or* mocking. There is only open, gaping curiosity.

"I don't have a father," I say. I can only hope he doesn't notice the way my words shake, the way my heart pounds loud enough I can almost hear it.

There's no way anyone in Aberlena should know I'm here looking for my father. It's got to be a trap, some sort of manipulation...

"Say his name," Sebastian demands.

I lick my lips, but my entire mouth has gone dry. I blink at this strange, mysterious man and wonder if I've had it wrong this entire time. Maybe there *is* a reason he approached me at the bar. Maybe he already knows who my father is, and maybe it's because...

"Are you my brother?" I blurt.

To my surprise, Sebastian laughs. It's deep and warm, a pleasant sound that doesn't match his cold demeanor.

"No," he says. His mouth twitches, but he doesn't release a full smile. "And thank heavens for that."

"What're you going to do?" I ask. My stomach bottoms out, and I glance again at the Chinese restaurant.

No one is thankful they're unrelated *unless* they plan to do terrible things to you. A few nights ago, I loved the idea of Sebastian doing exactly that. Now, I can only hope he never gets the chance.

"Your father's name," he repeats. He takes a small step away from me, the first time he's done so since we arrived here. "Tell me, Grace."

"I'll tell you, but only if you promise to let me go once I do." I lift my chin, crossing my arms tightly across my chest. My toes sting against the cold sidewalk, but I force myself to act unaffected.

"I promise," Sebastian says.

"His name was Walter Pruce," I say. My breath is ragged, unsteady. "I haven't seen him in years though, so whatever you're thinking—"

It happens again. The blur of motion, the sensation of running without moving my feet. As the world spins around me, I realize I'm being carried. It's longer this time. Long enough that I feel Sebastian's hands on my side and shoulder. Long enough that I kick my legs and flail my arms. My fist connects with flesh, but Sebastian doesn't react.

We just keep moving, moving, moving. Until suddenly, we slam to a halt.

This time, I collapse onto the ground when Sebastian

releases me. He stands several feet away, and I lean into the grass, digging my fingernails through the dirt. Beautiful, solid, unmoving dirt.

I try to look up at Sebastian, but my head's struggling to accept I'm no longer moving. One turn of my head, and I'm dizzy all over again. My stomach clenches, and before I can stop it, I puke across the grass.

"Oh hells," Sebastian says, putting more distance between us.

I wipe my mouth and grunt in response. I'm too disoriented to point out that this is *his* fault, not mine. He has no right to be grossed out.

Rather than saying anything, I lift my head slowly. We've somehow traveled *miles* in a matter of minutes. We're on the opposite side of town now, in the park across from Aberlena University. We're tucked against a thick patch of trees, but surely people can see us.

I'm still too dizzy to stand.

"Fuck," Sebastian says. He scrunches his entire face, even pinching his eyes. He looks like he wants to say more, but I don't give him the chance.

"What. Was. That?" I demand. "How did you do that?"

"It doesn't matter," he says.

I shift to sit on my butt, scooting as far as I can from my own puke. Sebastian blinks a few times, hard, as if forcing himself to be in the present. He looks unsettled, but despite running several miles just now, he doesn't look tired.

He should be exhausted.

No, he should be dead.

No amount of tiredness would make this logical. You can't run ten second miles. That's not how the world works.

"You are Grace Pruce," he says. His fists clench and release at his sides, but his attention bores into me. He sounds almost angry as he continues. "I need you to come with me."

"First of all, my name is Grace Renolds. Second of all, if you needed help, you should have just asked. I probably would have said yes. You didn't have to...do whatever that was. I'm a nice person. I *like* helping people."

"You are Grace Pruce," he repeats, and now, I'm positive he's angry. There's nothing to distract from the blazing fury in his eyes. "You are a filthy, sour-blooded witch, and I am not asking for your help. I am taking it, whether you permit it or not."

My heart beats in my throat.

Oh god.

Oh god. This man is crazy. He thinks I'm a witch. He's going to take me to his basement to sacrifice me in some sort of freaky ritual.

"You promised to let me go," I say. "You *promised* if I told you my dad's name, you'd let me go."

Sebastian's mouth twists into a brutal grin. He stalks forward, slow but intent. I shove to my feet, ignoring the way my head spins at the movement. I stumble back, making it only two steps before he lunges.

I scream. It's high-pitched and piercing, cutting through the darkness like a new blade. I didn't know I could scream like this, but I force every drop of air out of my lungs and into the universe.

Help me, I beg no one and everyone. *Don't let him hurt me.*

Sebastian's hand clamps over my mouth. His palm smashes my lips, and his nails dig into my cheek.

"I am not fae," he whispers. His chest presses against my back, his lips tickling my ear with each word. "I am a vampire, Grace, and I am a fucking liar."

With one hand still over my mouth, the other tightens across my chest, fingers clenching my shoulder. He's got me pinned, trapped, and the second he starts moving, this will be over. He'll take me somewhere out of sight, and nobody will ever know what happened to me.

How long before Tessa reports me missing? Before Libby wonders why I'm not answering her calls?

This man is crazy.

He thinks he's a vampire.

He's going to kill me.

My thoughts whirl faster and sharper, and in less than two seconds, a sharp panic shoots up my spine.

I need to get away. I have to get away.

Get away. Get away. Go!

I've never felt panic like this. Raw and sharp and all-consuming. It grows into a physical, biting pain, until it bursts out of me like an exploded grenade. It's an instant relief, like taking a breath after you dive too deep in the water.

I don't remember moving.

I don't remember doing anything at all.

But suddenly, Sebastian's hands fall away. His body hits the ground with a heavy thud, and by the time I turn, he's writhing in the grass. Despite the poor lighting, I can see it. A dark stain blossoms in the center of his chest, growing larger and brighter, until finally I realize...

Blood.

Something tore open his chest, and I feel inexplicably certain it was *me*.

"Wait," I say. I crouch to his side, hands fluttering over his chest, but not touching him. "Wait, no. Undo. Undo that! No, I did not mean that."

I'm talking nonsense and babbling, tears streaming down my cheeks. There's no way I just killed a man by wishing for it, right? I look over each shoulder. We're still alone. He's still dying.

There's no other explanation. Somehow, this *had* to be me.

I touch his chest, reeling back when my skin meets damp warmth. Blood. There's literal blood on my hands.

"I didn't…"

I should put pressure on this. Or call an ambulance or… something. I've got to do something.

But doesn't he deserve to die? something dark within me whispers. *Wasn't he going to hurt me?*

I shove the thoughts away and dig my phone out of his pants pocket. A piece of paper comes with it. My fingers stain the edges with blood, and I shine my phone light over it.

It's a folded copy of my drivers license. My name and South Carolina address, my weight from two years ago and a grainy picture from when I dyed my hair brown.

My hand shakes.

Sebastian stares blankly up at the night sky. Dead, I realize. He's dead, and whether or not it was my fault, there's no way to save him now.

I shove my phone and the scrap of paper into my purse. Sebastian's opposite pocket is empty.

I get to my feet. I don't let myself check my clothes for blood. I don't let myself hesitate a moment longer.

Instead, I do what I should have the moment I saw Sebastian at Barco's.

I run.

5

NOT IF YOU'RE INVOLVED

SEBASTIAN

Fucking witch. If I didn't need her, I'd kill her. I'd follow her hideously delicious scent to her apartment complex, drag her out by her ankles, and remove her head from her body. I'd drink every addictive drop of her blood, and I'd never have to think about her again.

I peel off my shirt.

No. I am not some infant vampire without an ounce of self-control. I am Sebastian Fucking Vulce, and I will not be destroyed by an inexperienced witch who doesn't know how to work her powers.

I clench the blood-stained shirt in my fist. Not bad for an inexperienced witch.

I use the clean side of the shirt to wipe the remaining blood from my chest. Some of it has already dried to my skin, but there's nothing to do about that. I walk through the park with only the earliest tinge of sunlight on the horizon. If I wasn't a sunwalker, I'd be dead.

Dead at the hands of an oblivious witch.

How embarrassing.

I storm through the entrance of Aberlena University. It's

probably six in the morning, but the campus is blissfully quiet. Aside from a student studying in the corner, no one notices my shirtless, bloody trek through the main building. I cross the lobby and take the farthest stairwell in the back. There's a heavy lock over the door.

If a human attempted to unlatch it, they would fail.

For me, the door swings wide with ease, granting me access to the tall, winding staircase. My shoes click against the stone steps, each one mocking my failure.

I can already imagine Cora's face when I tell her. She'll probably be impressed, as if Grace's attack on me was anything more than simple luck.

Unless, of course, Grace isn't innocent or inexperienced at all. Even if Walter Pruce died years ago, that doesn't mean she isn't trained. Maybe her mother is an estranged witch, or maybe someone else found her years ago and taught her exactly how to fend off the likes of me.

No, I decide. If Grace knew she was a witch, she wouldn't have come here. Not knowing who her father is.

I reach the top landing of the staircase. It's a tiny platform with a single wooden door. I shove through it, feeling pathetically satisfied at the cracking sound it makes when it hits the stone wall of the Paragon.

I may have been bested by a clumsy witch, but I'm still a fucking god here. I'm still strong enough to crack through femur bones with my bare hands. I'm still fast enough to cross the entire Night Realm in less than a day. I'm still powerful.

...So long as I'm in the shadows.

I curse and try to bury the thought. It doesn't work, especially not now that the sun has broken the skyline and my body is pathetically weak. I feel every slow, laborious step of my trek back to the manor, and by the time I've reached the entrance, I'm sweating.

I burst through the double ebony doors and stride across polished wooden floors. In the years since we were cursed, I have poured a disgusting amount of time into this place. There's new paint on the walls, a deep shade somewhere between maroon and black. The once empty pots have been filled with flourishing plants. Even the doorknobs have been replaced with shiny brass handles.

If my followers have to be trapped here for half of their days, the least I can do is make it hospitable.

Hospitable. Who the fuck have I become?

I cross the room, sharply nodding to a few vampires as they disappear into the feeding room. For a brief moment, the sounds and smells of fresh blood taunt me. I could feast, but I resist the urge, stalking to the western wing instead.

Few people live in this part of the manor, and that's the main reason it became home to our resident witch. It's safer here, and it helps to contain her odor.

Reaching Cora's door, I slam my fist against the wood. I've rarely visited her here, and yet, she doesn't look surprised to see me. She only smirks, a slow and taunting gesture. I can't decide if she's more amused at my blood-stained, naked chest or the fact Grace *still* isn't with me.

"I don't want to hear it," I snap before she says a single word. "I need a potion. Maybe two."

The smirk remains on Cora's face, but she abandons the doorway. She doesn't invite me in, and I don't ask.

Her quarters are a smaller version of mine, but still bigger than most of my followers. She has a living room, a kitchenette, a spacious bedroom, and an attached bathroom. A few years before she moved in—and before she cast spells to keep me out —I'd designed this room for Oskar. He'd wanted to share the place with his wife. Once she died, he lost all interest, and it became the perfect place to house Cora.

I peer to the left, then the right. As far as I can tell, she hasn't made many changes. The furniture is all the same, but now, black fabric covers most surfaces. There are black drapes over the windows, black blankets over the couch cushions, and a shaggy black rug lining the kitchen.

That's where Cora stands now. She opens one of her cabinets, revealing copious amounts of herbs, brightly-colored liquids, and small organs in jars.

"All right," she says, looking over her shoulder. "Pick your poison."

It's nightfall by the time I leave the manor. I changed into a black shirt (better to hide the blood) and added a long coat. They're not as popular as they once were in the human world, but I'm not going for subtlety anymore. Enough is enough. I have officially run out of patience for Grace Pruce. Tonight, I'm dragging her to the Echo if it kills me.

Or, more aptly, if *she* does.

I pat the oversized pocket of my coat as I cross into Aberlena. Cora created four potions for me, and they're all clanking together. A blue vial for memory loss. A red one for confusion. A pale yellow one for sleep. And a deep purple one for paralysis.

If all goes well, I won't need most of them. Ideally, I won't need any, but I'm not naive enough to expect that now.

Following Amelia's instructions, I borrow a man's electronic to make a call. Then, I continue to Grace's apartment. By the time I reach it, the moon is high in the sky, reflecting off dozens of windows. Most are lit, showing men playing a rudimentary game in one and a group of people watching a movie in another. Grace should be on the fourth floor, in the third apartment from the right. The light is on, but her drapes are shut, making it impossible to see her.

I wonder if she's hunkered down, unsettled and horrified at what she's done. It's either that or she and her dull roommate are celebrating my death. She must think I'm dead, after all.

Fucking ripped a hole in my chest, and I'm convinced she didn't mean to do it. She's scared and untrained—a dangerous combination.

I stand at the apartment building entrance. I could easily break the lock pad and rip the door off its hinges, but that wouldn't get me far. I'd still be stuck out here on the sidewalk, barred by an invisible barrier only my kind can feel. And I've learned my odds of being invited in are far higher if I *don't* destroy the building before asking.

I lean against the wall, waiting for the building owner to arrive. I'd found his phone number at the same time I'd found Grace's new address. A quick call, claiming I was a locked out tenant, and he was on his way.

A couple approaches from off the street. The man types the code to the door, earning a short buzz. The door unlatches, and he holds it open, tilting his chin toward it.

"You coming in?" he asks.

If only it was that simple, I think. I shake my head.

Minutes later, the owner arrives. He's a tall, beefy man with a hundred-fifty pounds of muscle and at least four inches of height on me. He grins with the confidence of someone used to being the strongest in the room. He doesn't pause to size me up —he already knows he could overpower me if needed.

At least, he *thinks* he could. If I were blood and flesh and human, he'd be right.

"Hey, man," I say. Humans speak differently than we do, and I do my best to flatten my voice. "Sorry about this."

"Not a problem," he says easily. He digs a set of keys from his pockets and enters the door code with his opposite hand. He doesn't look back at me as he swings open the door and steps into the building.

The door starts to close, but I don't grab it. Instead, I stand at the threshold, looking at the building's shabby interior.

The owner catches it just before it closes, shooting me a bemused expression.

"Well, come in," he says with a snorted laugh. "You need a special invitation or something?"

Come in will do perfectly, thanks.

"Sorry, I'm out of it today," I say. I do my best to mirror his carefree expression, but I'm already mapping out the building's interior. There's an elevator to the left, a set of stairs just beyond it.

"All right. Remind me your name," he says. He pulls up a chart on his phone that has a list of tenants and their respective apartments. I could easily pick a name off the chart and pretend it's me, but that only prolongs the inevitable.

"Tyler," I tell him.

While he's scanning the list, I consider my options: force feed him the confusion potion or...

I lunge forward, punching him in the temple. He collapses like he's made of paper, his stocky frame crashing against the cheap carpet. He's not bleeding, but I can already tell he'll have an impressive bruise. I watch him until I'm sure he's properly unconscious.

Then I heave his limp body over my shoulder and take the stairs two at a time. Once I reach the fourth floor, I count the doors, coming to a stop in front of 415. I shift the man on my shoulder and knock on Grace's door.

As I wait for her to answer, I make the mistake of breathing in through my nose. Fuck. This place smells dangerously delicious. It's a concoction of human blood, all congested and desperate to be devoured. I'm still feeling it, the heady over-whelm of bloodlust, when the door swings open.

It's Tessa, not Grace. Her dark eyes widen in surprise, and I capitalize on it. I'm through the door before she fully realizes it's me. I slam the door behind me and glance over the space. There's a collection of dark furniture and a fish tank in the corner. The whole place reeks of sage and looks like an elderly woman's library.

It's hard to believe pretty and poised Grace lives *here.*

"What..." Tessa trails off, her eyes snapping from me to the motionless man over my shoulder. Her mouth continues bobbing, but no sounds come out.

I unceremoniously dump the building owner onto the floor. His head smacks a kitchen chair as he falls. Two bruises and counting.

"You're from the bar," Tessa finally says. She's blinking rapidly, as if she's trying to make sense of my appearance.

I study her, the way she balks at me, the way she steps away, eyes flickering toward the owner's body. She's confused and scared, but it's clear...

"Little Gracie didn't tell you, did she?" I ask. I can't keep the smile from pulling over my teeth. Of all the possibilities I considered, this isn't one of them. "She came home last night and acted like everything was fine. Is that right? As if she hadn't torn a fucking hole through my chest."

Tessa's own chest heaves, but she remains silent, eyes wild.

"To be clear," I say, stepping over the building owner's body, crowding Tessa's space. "I don't mean a metaphorical hole, like she hurt my feelings. I mean a fucking hole. Right through the skin and bone. Left me to bleed out in a fucking park."

I don't realize I've raised my voice, that I'm screaming, until a closed door springs open. Grace stumbles into the living room. She's wearing a frilly pajama set, white and dotted with miniature hearts. Her blonde hair is piled on top of her head, and her face is clean of makeup.

Beautiful, terrible little witch. She doesn't have any right to look comfortable and content after what she did to me.

"No," she says. Her voice is barely more than a trembling breath. "You're...You should be...You were..."

"Dead?" I offer.

Keeping myself between the women and the door, I push forward until they're both standing in their cramped, hideous living room. From the corner of the room, a pair of guppies stare at me with blank black eyes.

"Unfortunately, little witch, I am more difficult to kill than that."

"Grace, what is he talking about?" Tessa demands. For the first time, she looks away from me and the owner lying prone behind me, to stare at Grace. "He's lying, right?"

"Call 911," is Grace's only response. She's trembling, near vibrating, but her blue eyes remain locked on mine. "He's *dangerous*, Tessa."

"Rich words from a murderer," I say. Before Tessa can move, I wrap a hand around her throat, keeping her in place. I'm squeezing hard enough that her breath catches.

"It was self-defense," Grace stutters. Her lip wobbles, and the tears start falling. She looks from me to her friend, to the unconscious man behind me. "Just let Tessa go. She has nothing to do with this. Neither does he."

I tsk at her, squeezing Tessa's throat again. Her hands clasp over my wrist, nails digging hard enough to draw blood.

"You don't even know who this man is," I say. "He could very well deserve it."

"Not if you're involved," Grace says. "Just...Please, Sebastian. Don't hurt them to punish me."

"Ahh, so you agree you deserve to be punished?" I ask.

I tug Tessa into me, flattening her back to my chest. She's fallen perfectly still, except for her pulse jumping against my palm.

"I'm sorry," Grace says. She's talking to Tessa, not me, tears dripping to her chin. "I didn't—it was self-defense. And I didn't know...I couldn't...I panicked, Tessa. I don't even know what happened—"

"Sure you do," I say, cutting her off. "You used your nasty little witch magic on me, tried to split me right in half. Then you waltzed home, acted like everything was fine, and pretended it never happened. Isn't that right?"

Grace doesn't respond. She won't even look at me, and it sends a stab of irritation through my gut. Even now, with her life at stake, with her friend in peril, she's not cowering like she should. I'm not sure she's listening to a single word I say, so I'm startled when her hard blue eyes flick to mine.

"Let my friend go, right now, or I'll finish what I started," she snaps. The first time I saw her eyes, I thought they made her look delicate. Like a flower, like an innocent. Now, they're the startling blue at the base of a flame, beautiful but dangerous.

"You so much as lift a finger, and I'll snap her neck," I say. My voice flows easy, like unraveled velvet. Despite the tears on Tessa's face and the terrified fury of Grace's expression, I feel calmer than I have in days. *This* is where I thrive, where my mind operates best. "I'll snap her neck, rip your landlord to shreds, and drag you to the Echo with those pesky hands tied behind your back."

Tessa lets out a quiet sob. Her body shudders against mine, and once the trembling starts, it radiates through her every breath. She's sobbing within seconds, and the unbreakable bad-ass persona she's created shatters in my hands.

Fucking humans. They're all the same once threatened.

They cower and crumble and fall to pieces at the first sign of a threat.

"You know my father," Grace says.

"I did."

"Is he dead?"

"Yes."

Grace doesn't flinch. She doesn't look to Tessa for help. She doesn't even glance at the unconscious man in her kitchen. She only glares at me, hands tightened into fists.

"What are you going to do to me?" she asks. "If I go with you, what's going to happen?"

Not *if*, but *when*, I want to correct. I don't let myself speak that out loud. Grace is coming with me, tonight, but it will undoubtedly be easier if she comes willingly.

"As I said, I need your help." I step closer, dragging Tessa with me, until I'm close enough to Grace, I could grab her. "You won't be harmed. And once you're done, you'll be set free."

"If only you were fae," she whispers. "I might believe you."

She throws both hands toward me, palms out, fingers bent. I clench, tightening my hand over Tessa's throat. There's a heavy beat, a pause, where none of us breathe.

And then...

"Oh come on!" Grace screams. She waves her hands again, thrusting them toward me with little rhyme or reason. "Do something!"

"Mmm, looks like you need practice, little witch," I say, grinning at her. "You've played all your cards, and now you're empty-handed."

She whirls away from me, sprinting for her bedroom. I let her go. She's probably going for her phone. Let her call. We'll be long gone before the police arrive.

"Don't kill me," Tessa whispers. "Look, my name is Tessa McDowell. I'm twenty-six. When I was little, I wanted to own a

Christmas tree farm. Now, I want to do something with animals, even though I'm allergic—"

"Save your don't-kill-me speech for someone else," I grunt. I dig through my coat pocket until I find the blue and yellow vials.

I spin around, pressing Tessa's back to her black bookshelf. Her eyes widen, and she opens her mouth, as if to scream. Before she gets the chance, I'm pouring both vials down her throat.

As much as I'd prefer to snap her neck and move on with it, Grace might be more amenable if she knows I didn't kill her new roommate. If nothing else, she'll make good bartering power in the future.

A strange gurgling sound bursts from Tessa's mouth as I force the liquid between her teeth. She's trying to reject it, to keep from swallowing, but I don't give her the choice. I pinch her nose, force her to swallow, just so she can take a breath.

Once she has, she gasps erratically and starts sobbing. She's gagging and spasming in my hands, and I briefly wonder if it was deadly to combine the potions. I should have asked Cora.

Something heavy smashes against the back of my head. If I were in sunlight, it would have undoubtedly taken me down. But here, in the darkness of night and in the protection of Grace's apartment, I barely feel it.

I release my hold on Tessa, satisfied when her body folds to the floor.

"What did you do?" Grace sobs. She pushes past me and crouches beside her roommate.

"She's fine," I drawl. "Check her pulse if you must. She'll wake tomorrow with a nasty headache and little memory of today."

"You killed her," Grace says. She's patting at Tessa's cheeks, shaking her shoulders as if to wake her.

"I didn't," I say. I roll my eyes, not at Grace, but at myself.

Why am I even bothering? I don't need Grace to like me, and from the fact she just tried to kill me *again,* I should know better than to try.

"Help is coming," Grace tells Tessa's unmoving body. "They'll be here any minute."

Grace is too busy fretting over Tessa. It's a massive flaw. Caring about people makes you vulnerable. She's an easy target now that I understand her weakness—and what a pathetic human weakness it is.

Grace doesn't see me move, and by the time the purple vial is at her lips, it's too late to fight me. She coughs and thrashes and gags, but ultimately, she goes down as easily as her roommate.

She collapses to the floor, eyes open, slowly blinking up at me. Every other part of her has gone limp.

"Sorry, little witch," I tell her. "Can't risk those powers coming out."

I swear, those blue irises turn to flame all over again.

I scoop her into my arms, stepping over Tessa as we go. I pause at the landlord. I should have given him a potion—the red confusion one would have been perfect.

Oh well. No changing it now.

I shift Grace to direct her eyes to the ceiling. She can't see when I step on the man's neck, but she might hear the way his throat collapses, the way his final breath chokes between his lips.

Once I'm sure he's dead, I push through the door. I run the entire stretch from Grace's apartment to my own manor, feeling the push of destiny—of *hope*—for the first time in years.

6

———

THE LAST DESCENDANT

GRACE

I can do this. Mom and I used to watch Dateline all the time. We'd get two bags of popcorn, bring all our blankets out to the couch, and binge several episodes in a row. We'd yell at the lady getting murdered, telling her how to escape, as if she wasn't already dead. By the time I was eighteen, I felt like I knew all the tricks.

Attempted kidnapping in public? Scream your lungs out. The odds of them hurting you with an audience is far less likely than if they get you alone.

Locked in a trunk? Kick the tail light and stick your hand out until another driver notices you.

Being kept in multiple places? Leave clues for the police. Strands of hair. Spit. Blood. Whatever.

Be observant. Gain your abductor's trust. Stay calm and find an opportunity to escape.

I'm pretty sure Mom and I watched most, if not all, of the Dateline episodes from the last ten years. None of them featured paralysis-by-potion, abduction to a new world, or a vampire assailant.

In other words, I'm screwed.

"Okay, focus," I whisper to myself. "Figure it out."

Avoiding or escaping a kidnapping seemed so much easier when I watched it on TV. Now that I'm here, kept in a barren room with one door and no windows...I have no idea what I'm supposed to do.

I don't even know how long I've been here. I've been pacing the room ever since the paralysis faded. My brain is too overloaded with the past twelve hours to make sense of anything. From being sped across Aberlena, to entering Aberlena University and somehow exiting in this unfamiliar world, my brain doesn't *want* to think. It doesn't want to stay calm. It wants to panic, to leave me huddled in a ball, scream crying until I wake up.

I wonder if Tessa has woken up, or if that's just another of Sebastian's lies. If she's dead, it's all my fault. A ragged sob leaves my throat before I can stop it. I should be out of tears by now, but they're still coming, steadily streaming down my face.

"No," I snap at myself. "*Focus*, Grace. You have to stay calm."

I know I'm in some sort of stone mansion. It was hard to make sense of anything while we were moving, but I think I'm several miles from the Aberlena University look-alike building. Even if I manage to break out of this room, I'll have to figure out how to get back to it. There's got to be a map somewhere in this place. Or maybe, I'll find an empathetic soul who will help me escape.

An empathetic vampire, Grace, really?

I pace the room again. It's about the size of my college dorm room. It's all grey stones, weathered wood floor, and a twin-size bed in the center. There isn't a dresser or a TV or anything that suggests I'm not an absolute prisoner.

There's no toilet either. So if Sebastian doesn't come back in the next couple of hours, I'm going to have to pee in the corner like an actual animal.

Pace.

The police will be at my and Tessa's apartment. They'll make sure she survives Sebastian's attack, and same with the landlord. They'll both be fine, and they'll make sure the police know what happened to me. There will be footage of Sebastian arriving at the building...

Unless vampires don't show up on film? Is that just mirrors? Is that even *true*?

Pace.

Realistically, I don't *actually* know Sebastian is a vampire. That's what he said, and he's proven to be far more dishonest than honest. He's probably just an insane cult leader, and that liquid he gave me was some sort of muscle relaxing drug. The wound I *thought* I gave him was actually just an illusion. A prank, a magic trick, *something* logical.

This is all fake. That's it. It has to be.

I stride to the wooden door. Iron stripes line it, but there's no handle on this side. I slam my fist against the wood.

"Hey!" I scream. "You can't just leave me in here!"

No one responds.

I press my ear to the door, straining for sound. It must be too thick, or maybe I've been left here to rot. That might be the best case scenario. Something tells me starvation will be better than whatever Sebastian is planning.

I wet my lips. My stomach curdles at the thought of torture. I've never claimed to be tough. I'm fragile, delicate, and I'm not too proud to admit I've got a low pain tolerance. If Sebastian is gearing up to torture me, I'm never going to last.

I don't knock again, too afraid of what will happen if he answers.

～

He comes hours later. At least, I think it's multiple hours. It's impossible to know without a clock or a window. All I do know is that I've been sitting on this bed, knees drawn to my chest, long enough that my butt hurts. I've been thinking about New York and what I *should* be doing with Libby. Depending on the time, she's probably out with friends for dinner, having bougie drinks and making weekend plans. Maybe they're celebrating her new job.

"Hello, little witch," Sebastian says. He stands in the doorway, studying me with a careful expression. "It's time to go."

"Back to Aberlena?" I ask, even though I know it's stupid.

"No. I have someone for you to meet," Sebastian says. He leans against the doorframe. "I think you'll like her."

"I highly doubt that," I say. I shove back on the bed, until I'm as far as I physically can be. If there was anything other than a sheet on this bed, I'd wrap it around myself like a pathetic shield.

"It's time to go," he says again. He beckons me with his hand but remains outside the door. "Come."

I grind my teeth together, not moving for a prolonged moment. I know it's useless to defy him. He can easily overpower me, and I'm sure he's got a whole slew of those vials somewhere on his person. He's shed the long coat from earlier and now wears black slacks and a buttoned shirt with the sleeves cuffed.

"Grace—"

"It's cold in here," I say as I shove to my feet. "Since you supposedly *need* me, you should turn up the heat. Otherwise I'm going to die of hypothermia."

I stop a foot short, lifting my chin to glare at him. He's only a couple inches taller than I am, but there's something undeniably frightening about his appearance. It's the curl of his lip, I decide. The subtle turn of his mouth that promises violence without care.

Sebastian steps back, into the dimly lit hallway. He sweeps his hand in a wide gesture, signaling for me to walk in front of him. I keep my chin tilted as I walk, striding past elaborate paintings, drape-covered windows, and the occasional stone bust. It feels like we're on a movie set, designed to look like an ancient European castle.

There are no lights. No signs of electricity. Small candles hang on the wall, spaced evenly and ineffectively dim. Does this place not have modern technology? Are they *really* relying on freaking wax candles to see?

The odds of getting heat in my room vanish the farther I walk.

Maybe the door we stepped through brought us, not to another place, but to another time.

I reach a split in the hallway and pause.

"Left," he says.

I glance back at him, surprised at his distance. It's unsettling in a way I can't explain. I certainly don't *want* him standing against me, hand on my neck to keep me obedient. And yet, it seems like he *should* be.

I glance down the right branch. It's lined with doors and as eerily empty as everywhere else in this place. I turn left. This hallway is empty too, but the doors are packed more tightly together. Some are blank, but most feature a metal sign, branded with one old-fashioned name or another. *Tomas. Cecilia. Adelaide. Rasmus.*

We continue on like this. Sebastian only speaks to give directions, and I remain silent. I keep mental tabs as we go, searching desperately for doors that lead outside. None ever appear, and eventually, we arrive at the end of a hallway identical to all the others. Only now, there's nowhere to go. I study the gold plate on the door.

"Cora?" I ask, turning toward Sebastian.

"Our resident witch."

I lift an eyebrow, but before I can ask any questions, Sebastian knocks. The door opens immediately. A woman with a tight black ponytail and large features stares at me. Her attention is different from Sebastian's. It's less hostile, less desperate. She's looking at me as if I am somehow both friend and foe.

"Grace Pruce," she says eventually.

"Renolds," I correct. Because after I turned eighteen, I changed my surname to match my mother's. I believed Walter Pruce had abandoned us, despite my mother's claims, and I didn't want a tie to the man who didn't want me. Now, I feel a flicker of guilt. Maybe, if I ever get out of this hellish place, I'll hyphenate.

"Pruce," she says again. She tilts her head, eyes sharpening. "Your father never spoke of you."

"How nice," I say flatly.

"For the best," she says. She has one hand on either side of the doorframe, as if barricading us from entering. "You would've been slaughtered years ago if the coven knew."

I don't know what that means, so I don't respond. I should point out that, despite my father's supposed protection, I've still ended up here. Held captive for a reason I don't understand. If I can't find a way out of here, I have no doubt they'll slaughter me eventually.

"She's weak," Cora says. For the first time, she looks at Sebastian. "I'm surprised."

"Half-human then?" Sebastian asks. He stands to my right, a step behind me.

"Most likely," she says, nodding. "Hopefully it's enough."

"It will have to be," Sebastian says. He steps closer, shoulder brushing mine. I instantly shift to the left, breaking contact. If he notices, he doesn't comment. He only stares at Cora. "It has to be enough, Cora. Understand?"

"Yes, Master," she says. Her throat bobs, the first indication she's unsettled by the man behind me.

Master?

Sebastian clearly has a god complex, and I'm not sure there's anything more terrifying than a man who assumes he's above all else.

"Let's get started," she says, returning her gaze to me. Her eyes are dark and wide-set, making her look far more innocent than she probably is. "Come in, Grace."

Despite myself, I glance back at Sebastian. I don't trust him by any meaning of the word, but he's yet to physically harm me. Even when I was paralyzed and completely defenseless, he didn't draw blood or violate me. He only carried me to my cell and left me face-up on the bed.

He's stated he needs me several times, but who's to say Cora feels the same way? Who's to say she won't kill me the second he leaves?

"Just you," he says to me. He nods at Cora. There's nothing reassuring about his gaze, nothing gentle or soft. His eyes are cold and hard, as if he's desperate to be rid of me.

I look away, embarrassed I turned to him in the first place. With a quiet breath, I step into Cora's room. This time, I don't look back.

～

"It's not working," Cora says.

We've been at it for two hours and sixteen minutes. I know, because unlike anywhere else I've seen in the Echo, her room has a clock. It hangs above her kitchenette, adjacent to a small window. Through the glass, I see glimpses of a barren landscape with jagged mountains in the distance. The town, the place with a look-a-like university building, must be the opposite direction.

"I don't even know what I'm supposed to be doing," I remind her. I drop my hands, turning to glare at her. She's stood behind me for the last hour while I hold my hands out like a zombie. Every now and then, she lets me lower them to get feeling back in my shoulders.

"You're supposed to be channeling your magic."

"And again, I have no idea what that means."

"Clearly," she bites. She rounds the couch and roughly takes my hands in hers. She doesn't look at me as she crouches, turning my palms toward the ceiling and then the floor.

"Maybe I'm too human," I say.

I study the houseplants that line the wall behind her. They're all in black pots and though they look dead—shriveled and limp—I'm weirdly confident they're not. I think she's somehow growing dead plants. They sprawl along her stone wall, filling the room with the overwhelming scent of death and decay.

I bet she and Tessa would get along.

"You should get a fish tank," I tell her absently. "My new roommate says—"

"No," Cora interrupts. Her voice is harsher than I expect, but her attention remains on my hands. "No fish."

No fish. Got it.

I sit in silence for as long as I can bear. Truthfully, it's not long.

"Maybe it's just not going to happen. Maybe Sebastian doesn't need me like he thought. Did you ever think of that? He probably needs some other witch. I might not be a witch at all, you know—"

"You are the last Pruce," she says.

I don't know what that means, and she must gauge that from my expression. Her dark eyes flicker over my face. She frowns as she rotates my hands again.

"What has Sebastian told you of the curse? Of *why* he needs you?"

"He's told me nothing," I say. I grit the words through my teeth. "He's only said that he needs me. And then he knocked out—or killed, I don't even know—my roommate and my landlord. He dragged me here and locked me—"

"Enough," she interrupts. Her eyes meet mine again, and rather than echoing my frustration, she looks bored. "You are ridiculously loud."

"So I've been told," I say, slumping against the couch. It's black velvet and comfier than it looked. Far better than the dingy bed in my cell. "But I'm not going to apologize. I'm completely in the dark here. Held against my will. Called horrible names. Threatened—"

"Too. Loud," Cora snaps. She drops my hands, but rather than going back behind the couch, she sits beside me. "If you promise to stop talking for five fucking minutes, I'll tell you everything you need to know."

I seal my lips, terrified she'll take it back if I so much as say *yes*.

"You are the last Pruce, the last descendant," she says. She holds her hand over the back of the couch and bends two fingers. Without so much as turning her head, she beckons to something unseen. I follow the movement, eyes widening as a steaming mug floats across the room.

It bobs through the air, never spilling a drop, and lands in Cora's palm. I stare, mouth gaping, as she takes a sip. It takes every ounce of my self-control to keep from blurting the thoughts in my head.

That teacup just floated!

You just moved a teacup with your mind!

That was magic! You just did real, actual magic. And I saw it!

Cora watches me as she places the mug on her short coffee table, as if expecting me to break. A test, I decide.

When I stay quiet, she settles against the couch.

"The Echo is a vast and wild place," she says. "There are many peoples here, not just witches and vampires. There are different realms and laws and species. Twenty years ago, Sebastian—King of the Vampires—ruled over it all. He'd grown reckless with power though. Eventually, he paid the price."

Cora grabs her mug from the coffee table, using her hands this time. She takes a long sip. The grassy tea permeates the air, almost strong enough to conceal the smell of rotting plants.

"Back then, your father led the witches," she says. "He was the last of the Pruce bloodline, a powerful and respectable family. Despite his refusal to have an heir, most people loved him. It was only the council, particularly Madam Lyrie, who couldn't stand him. She was the one who took over after his death. When she told the story of what had happened, she claimed your father sacrificed himself to protect the Echo. I always doubted that. The fact you're here, that you *exist*, proves I was right."

"How would my father dying—" I clap a hand over my mouth, stopping myself. "Oops. Sorry."

Cora studies me silently. Just when I'm sure she's going to revoke my story privileges, she continues.

"Madam Lyrie was desperate to punish Sebastian and his kind," she says. "She and the council cursed them to burn in the sun, and they used a blood seal to make it unbreakable. As the last of his line, your father was the obvious choice. Without Pruce blood, the sun curse could not be broken. And without a living Pruce..."

I swallow, staring at the dying plants, rather than Cora. I

barely remember my father, but tears still sting the corners of my eyes. I don't want to imagine it. I don't want to believe it's possible.

Is that what's going to happen to me?

"Sebastian's mighty empire fell in a matter of days," Cora continues. "All the power, the success he'd found, collapsed. And until you arrived in Aberlena, I thought he would never get it back."

I force myself to keep quiet, if only because I want more. I want to know every detail, every secret this place keeps about my father. About me.

"You can ask," she says.

I look at her, shaking my head softly. For once, I don't have anything to say. I'm not sure what to ask, where to start.

"You are the only one who can break the curse, Grace," Cora says. "Sebastian won't release you until it's done. Whether that's months or years, you won't be set free until the vampires are."

My mind whirls, each thought flashing too quickly to make sense of them. I'm straining for logic, for hope, for a plan and coming up empty. I'm only staring, realizing what a mistake I made by coming to Aberlena. Promising myself that if I can get back there, I'm taking the first flight to New York.

"You can't run," she says. I jerk my chin to look at her. Before I can ask if she's read my mind, she levels me with a look. "If you run, the witches might be the ones to find you next. They'll kill you faster than they killed your father. Understand?"

I force myself to nod, even as the words refuse to take meaning in my brain.

It's too much, this is all—

"I'll call for Sebastian," she says. "We'll try again tomorrow."

7

I SUGGEST YOU COOPERATE

SEBASTIAN

"Sorry, Master," the servant says. He's a human, and though he's only been with me for five or so years, he's one of my favorites. He's desperate to be one of us, and maybe after the curse is broken, I'll grant that wish.

For now, I need him exactly as harmless and submissive as he is.

"Still?" I ask. It's more a growl than a word, and he slinks away from me, cowering against the wall.

I'm in the library, flipping through pages of a long-forgotten text. It's one of many we've stolen from the witch covens over the centuries. I've been going through them ever since delivering Grace to Cora's doorway, but I've yet to find anything more than passing mention of the Pruce bloodline.

I'm hoping there's something, a hidden clue to unlock Grace's potential and transform her into what I need: a witch who can actually access her magic. Without it, she's useless.

She's *also* useless if she's dead.

"That's, what, three days now?" I ask, as though I don't already know. As if I haven't been counting each of her rejected meals.

I haven't mentioned it in the small amount of time I've spent with her. I only see her twice a day. Every morning, I walk her to Cora's quarters. And every evening, I return her to her own. We don't speak, and I don't mention the fact she's starving herself.

I assumed if I did, she'd dig her heels in harder.

"Yes, Master," the servant says. "I can try—"

"I'll handle it," I say. I shove to my feet, crossing the outdated library. This room is one of the more neglected places in the manor. A well-worn rug covers the hardwoods, and none of the bookshelves have been dusted in years. Still, it's a favorite of mine. The other vampires don't visit, so it's quiet. Peaceful. Easy to hide within, getting lost in the smell of worn parchment and ancient texts.

"Sorry, Master," the servant says again.

I don't respond, brushing past him and taking off down the corridor. Grace spent the day with Cora, and according to our resident witch, today was *as terrible as the others.*

Every day Grace doesn't access her magic is another day the witches might realize she exists. The last thing we need is a coven army showing up to slaughter my only chance.

As I walk through the manor, the sun falls outside. Just as it disappears beneath the horizon, countless bedroom doors open, vampires crowding the hallways. There are nearly five hundred here in residence, with thousands more spread throughout the Night Realm.

I ignore their exaggerated bows as I pass them, only stopping once I've reached Grace's quarters. A lone vampire stands against the wall opposite her room. Beatrice lifts an eyebrow.

"Hello," she says. She dips her head, eyes flitting back to Grace's door. "I wasn't expecting you tonight."

I don't reply.

I unlatch Grace's door, shoving it open to reveal her curled on the twin bed. Her room is disgustingly warm. Vampires don't get cold, but witches do. They're too much like humans. Cold and hungry and needy.

"Your room is warm," I announce from the doorway.

The lump on Grace's bed startles, and she springs upright. Wide blue eyes lock on mine, growing larger, then narrowing at my presence.

"There's no way it's morning," she says. Her hair is a tangled mess around her face, and I'm realizing I haven't allowed her to bathe since she arrived. She looks greasy, unkempt.

She smells fucking delicious though. This entire room radiates her mouthwatering scent, and I'm sure she doesn't even realize it. Does she know what a temptation she is? That I can't have anyone but Oskar or Beatrice guard her room? I'm not sure even some of my most practiced followers could resist her. Sprawled out, sleepy, smelling of blood and lavender.

"Well?" she snaps. "Is it morning or not?"

My lip ticks into a smirk without permission. She grows less cautious, less terrified by the day, whether she realizes it or not.

"I warmed your room," I say, rather than answering her.

She regards me for a long moment. Something in her face softens, and she brushes the hair from her eyes.

"Thank you," she says finally. A faint blush colors her cheeks, and the smell of her blood punches my chest. She swallows, face tense as if she has to force herself to continue. "And for the blanket. It's helped."

"Good," I say. My voice feels hollow, tinged with bitterness. "Tell me why you're repaying my kindness by starving yourself."

The softness of her expression instantly hardens.

"Kindness?" she repeats with a scoff. She lets the blanket fall to her lap. I might be imagining it, but I swear she's lost weight in a matter of three days. Her shoulders look bony beneath her T-shirt. My attention snags on her chest, where I can just make out her pebbled nipples.

Fuck me.

"You are not kind, Sebastian," she says. If she notices my leering, she doesn't comment. She only leans toward me, jabbing an accusatory finger my way. "You are a selfish monster. You've warmed my room to keep me from dying. Don't pretend otherwise."

She's dramatic. Her room might have been cold for her taste, but she certainly wasn't going to die. Cora went nearly a year before telling me she needed extra heat in her quarters.

"Careful," I warn her. My voice is low, menacing, and for a brief moment, Grace looks as scared as she should. She shrinks against the wall, eyes flickering over me, waiting for my attack, I assume.

When it doesn't come, she narrows her eyes, leaning forward again.

"You're not going to kill me," she says. "You *need* me, remember?"

"I do," I agree. I'm speaking through my teeth, letting the frustration and irritation boil too close to the surface. "But that doesn't mean you're untouchable, little witch. So unless you want me to go back to your little apartment and leave your friend in a hundred pieces, I suggest you cooperate."

"For all I know, she's already dead," Grace says. In a sharp motion, she tucks back beneath the covers and rolls onto her side. "Do what you will, Sebastian. I'm going to sleep."

"When I send breakfast in the morning, you will eat," I tell her. "Understand?"

Her only response is to pull the blanket tighter around herself. I mutter a curse and start to close the door, only to pause when she snaps back upright. She lifts her chin, glaring at me as she speaks.

"I don't like eggs," she says. "And I don't like meat."

"What?" I ask. My voice dips dangerously low, but Grace only glares harder.

"I don't like eggs," she repeats through her teeth. "And I don't like meat. If you want me to eat, send something edible. Like a salad. Or soup with grilled cheese."

"Do you think this is some sort of restaurant?" I growl. "You think I'm here to cater to your every whim?"

"Yes, clearly that's what I think," she deadpans. "Am I not at a five-star hotel with a Michelin chef?"

"I don't know what you're saying," I snap. Another burst of heat flares through my chest, not from the witches' magic, but from Grace's irritating scowl. She's talking gibberish and she knows it.

"Bring me tomato soup and grilled cheese," she says. "Treat me halfway decent, and I'll do whatever you want. Give me some entertainment, like a TV or some movies. I like rom-coms and psychological thrillers, but only if it's a crime of passion. Oh, and *Legally Blonde*. Also, I'm starting to stink. I need a shower. And new clothes. And shoes would be—"

"You are a needy little thing," I bite out. "You will eat whatever the fuck I send you."

Before she can reply, I storm out of her room, slamming the door behind me. Beatrice grins at me, and I can guess all the taunts she's not saying.

"Save it," I tell her.

"Yes, Master." The amusement is barely concealed in her voice.

I stride down the hall, ready to ignore every one of Grace's ridiculous demands.

∾

"Sorry, Master," the servant says. He stands at the library's entrance, holding a plate of six eggs and four strips of bacon. All untouched.

A deep growl radiates from my chest. Fucking needy little bitch. Demanding things to make a point. Screwing with my head as some sort of payback.

"Tell Oskar to accompany Grace to Cora's," I tell him. I turn back to the book opened before me. "I am in no mood to deal with her today."

"Yes, Master," he says.

Only once he's left the room do I allow myself to react. I throw the adjacent chair against the bookshelves, feeling a flicker of satisfaction when it explodes against the wall.

The relief is fleeting.

I slump back at the table and do my best to ignore thoughts of Grace. I've been working on this season's budget. For the manor, for the vampires. Oskar will have to meet with the were-wolves soon to discuss numbers, and my ego already hurts thinking about it. The Night Realm was once wealthy, second below only the Day Realm. Now, we're in fucking poverty. We're surviving on dwindling levies and our few exports: stone, salt, minerals. It's barely enough to afford us bloodletters, and now, Grace is wasting food for her own entertainment.

"Fuck," I mutter. I'm not going to get anything done until I take care of this.

I shove away from the table and head for Beatrice's room. She answers on the second knock, eyes sultry as she looks over me.

"Need to fuck out some of that frustration?" she asks coyly. She presses her palm to my chest, long fingernails digging through my shirt.

I hadn't come here for that, but now...I let my attention roam over her body. She's wearing a short, tight dress that shows off her tits *and* her spectacular legs. Her hair is wild and tangled, begging for my fist. If nothing else, I could have her on her knees before me, blowing me until I forget the worst of my problems.

Needy little fucking witch.

"Probably," I admit. "But first, I need to go to the human realm. Care to join?"

"Fine," she says, huffing out a sigh. She snags a leather jacket from behind her door. "But we're hooking up later. I've got some frustration to work out too, you know."

I don't respond, and I ignore Beatrice's attempts at conversation as we cross the Night Realm into neutral territory. By the time we arrive at the Paragon, she's fallen silent. She walks with her arms crossed and her eyebrows slanted, shooting me occasional pissed-off glances.

"Why did you ask me to come if you're going to ignore me?" she asks. She leads the way up the stairwell, shoving through the final door and striding out of the Echo without a moment's hesitation.

I'm a second behind her, blinking away the headrush that comes with jumping worlds. I let my eyes adjust to the brighter lights of Aberlena University before hurrying to match Beatrice's brisk pace.

"I don't know," I say.

"What exactly are we doing here, anyway?" she asks. Arms still crossed, scowl still in place.

Beatrice was supposed to get Grace off my mind. Instead, I've got *two* pissed women now.

"The witch has needs," I say finally.

"Like...?" Beatrice trails off before her eyes finally widen. "Oh, like her menstruation! I forgot witches do that."

"Hells, no," I say, though that *does* raise a good point. I'll need to see what Cora can do about stopping that. The last thing I need is her bleeding and a young vampire losing his head. Glancing at Beatrice, I admit, "She wants tomato soup."

Beatrice stops so abruptly I nearly crash into her. She glares at me, mouth open in horror, but I don't stop. I swivel around her and jog down the main steps of Aberlena. The sun is high overhead, and it instantly drains me of...*everything*. I feel weak and slow and vulnerable.

Beside me, Beatrice pulls on her coat. I didn't think to bring one.

"You did *not* bring me to come grocery shopping with you," she says. She holds my pace, craning her neck to look at me. She's much shorter than Grace, even with her heeled boots.

"I did not," I affirm. "I brought you to go grocery shopping alone. I have other agenda items while we're here."

"Then let *me* do the cool shit," Beatrice snaps. "Just because I'm a woman, doesn't mean I want to go grocery shopping for your new sex toy."

"Watch yourself," I say. I grab her arm, pulling her to a stop. We're near the park where Grace attempted to kill me. "Do *not* forget your place."

"Yes, Master," she says. Her chest is heaving, lips twitching, holding back a snarl.

We walk in silence until we reach a grocery store. There, I dig a folded piece of paper from my pocket. It's a list of ingredients for fucking soup. Tomatoes. Heavy cream. Three types of cheese.

I hand it to Beatrice, along with a few human monies, holding my breath as she takes it. Thankfully, she doesn't say another word. She clenches the notes in her fist, gives me a stiff nod, and marches into the store. I go into the neighboring building, some shop that's supposedly having a *BIG SALE!* on televisions and computers. I grumble under my breath, remind myself of the big picture, and head inside.

When we get back to the Echo, Beatrice leaves me with her grocery bags and another nod. Apparently, somewhere between expecting shopping and discussing Grace, sex fell off the agenda. Part of me wants to push it—I really *could* use a quick fuck—but I don't.

I take the bags to the servant kitchens and hope this makes the difference between Grace being useless and the key to our salvation.

WHEN I ARRIVE at Cora's room, she opens the door before I can knock. She and Grace share bleak expressions, and neither one looks at the other.

"She's hopeless," Cora informs me. She crosses her arms over her chest, lips twisting. "I've never met such a useless caster."

Grace doesn't say anything, but she releases a heavy sigh. Blush swims over her cheeks, sending a rush of blood-scented perfume through the air. I clench my breath in my lungs.

"You should do something about her blood," I tell Cora, ignoring her statement. "She's fucking dangerous like that."

Grace raises her eyebrow.

"Witches smell rancid to vampires," Cora elaborates. She glances briefly at Grace before returning her glower to me. "And I can't change her blood now. She's too old. It has to be done to infants or embryos."

"Fine," I say, even though there *must* be a way. For now, I'll deal with it. "What about her menstrual cycle? Have you found a solution?"

"My *what*?" Grace snaps. She shifts until she's blocking Cora, forcing me to look at her. "You've been talking about my period?"

"In case you've forgotten," I say. "You're surrounded by vampires. We drink blood. You spilling it every month doesn't exactly bode well for your survival here, now does it?"

"I thought witches are rancid?" she asks, eyebrow lifting.

"Most," I say. Without permission, my gaze flickers to her throat. Her jugular twitches with her pulse, begging to be tasted. "You smell fucking divine, Grace. Like nothing I can describe. We've yet to have a single conversation where I haven't dreamt of draining every drop of blood from your body."

The blush leeches from her face, leaving her pale and wide-eyed. Good. Let her be reminded of reality.

"Let's go," I tell her. Once she's stepped into the hallway, I regard Cora again. "Tomorrow must be better."

When I head down the hallway, Grace sticks closer to my side. Her eyes dart around us as we walk. I could tell her not to worry—none of my followers are stupid enough to attack her if she's with me—but I keep that to myself. Fear is good for people like her.

"Where are we going?" she asks.

We passed her quarters a few hallways ago. I figured she hadn't noticed. All the doors look the same in this part of the manor. Unmarked, heavy wood, accented with iron rungs.

"Sebastian?" she presses.

"Patience, little witch," I say.

She makes it two more turns before she clears her throat.

"If you're taking me somewhere to kill me, you should at least let me know. I'd like to request—"

"Of course you would," I cut her off. I stop in front of the library door, leaning against the wall to glare at her. "You *would* have a request regarding your murder. If only you put as much attention into your casting as you do your neediness, we'd likely be done with this by now."

She presses her lips together, eyes flickering away from me.

She swallows, and I follow the subtle movement in her throat. I take a breath even though I know I shouldn't. Her smell fills my nostrils, invades every thought, until I'm only thinking of her blood and how sweet she would taste on my tongue.

"I'm trying, okay?" she says. Her voice breaks, forcing my attention from her jugular to her eyes. Her dark blues water with unshed tears, and I watch, waiting for them to fall. Instead, she blinks them away, swallowing again. "I know you and Cora don't believe me, but I *am* trying. I just...I don't know what I'm doing. I'm in this strange place with crazy people, and they're asking me to do something that shouldn't exist. Okay? It's just—"

"Here," I interrupt. I can't take it anymore, the shaking lip, the welling eyes. I lean around Grace, my breath held, and open the door to the library.

She turns, stepping hesitantly inside the room. It's as dark, dank, and dusty as ever. Floor-to-ceiling bookshelves, all filled with ancient and weathered texts. A long dark wood table, cluttered with papers on one end and Grace's set-up on the other. Across from the table, there's a small fireplace and two over-stuffed armchairs. The fire is lit for the first time in over a century.

"What is this?"

"Your requests," I say. I don't mean to snap the words, but I do. "Your tomato soup. Your *Legally Blonde*, whatever the hells that is. And once you've eaten every fucking drop, you'll get your shower and change of clothes."

She looks over her shoulder at me, and that softness I glimpsed yesterday returns. Fuck me, she's pretty like this. I can't explain why, but I despise her for it. For that smile, for the gentle blush on her cheeks. I despise the way it makes me picture her naked, sudsy, head tilted back in the shower, water streaming between her breasts. Too easily, I imagine myself pressed against her back, fingers tracing—

"Thank you, Sebastian," she says. She reaches for my hand, and I jerk back as if her touch burns.

"Go eat," I tell her. Distance. I need distance. "I'll be here when you're done."

The hard stare is back. The heavy grimace. She hates me again, and I suddenly realize how vital that hatred is.

8

ALL OF YOU, MONSTERS
GRACE

Two days later, I decide Cora is right. I am hopeless. I've been staring at two bowls—one filled with clear liquid, the other with black stones—for half the day now. Cora won't tell me what I'm supposed to do, only that somehow, I need to combine the stone and water with my mind.

I glare at the bowls. Wait for something, *anything* to happen. Nothing does.

"This is pointless," I tell her. I slump back against the couch. The movement reminds me I'm wearing a stranger's clothes. All black, hideous, and one size too small. The shirt pinches at my armpits, and the skirt is barely covering my butt.

I add wardrobe options to my list of complaints for Sebastian. His right-hand man, a gray-haired vampire named Oskar, has been delivering me to and from my Cora sessions. I haven't seen Sebastian since the night he gave me *Legally Blonde* and tomato soup.

Apparently, he's tired of me, and I can't exactly blame him.

No. Screw that. I can one hundred percent blame him. It's his fault I'm here, and it's his stupid witch's fault I'm not making progress. She's asking me to defy gravity and logic, and she won't even tell me the secret to do it.

"I agree," Cora says. She sits on her coffee table, taking a deep chug of tea. She's almost always drinking it, and though the flavor occasionally changes, it almost always stinks. She hums to herself as she lowers the mug, then sighs. "I suppose we should get your menstrual cycle taken care of. You're nearing it, aren't you?"

"God," I say, dropping my head against the back of the couch. "If you could just smite me from the heavens, that would be great."

"What, you're embarrassed of your period?" Cora asks. She arches an eyebrow. "You've spent over a week with a horde of vampires, and the thing making you beg for death is *your period*?"

"No," I say. "It's the fact you and Sebastian and every single person I've encountered here treats me like a problem to be solved. If it's not my inability to cast, it's the fact I bleed. If it's not the fact I bleed, it's the fact I'm not eating well. If it's not—"

"Yeah, yeah, forget I asked," Cora says. She flaps her wrist at me as she rises, taking both her mug and my two bowls with her. "I get it. You're feeling sorry for yourself."

"Of course I am," I shriek. "I was abducted! I'm being held against my will. Crazy people are threatening to drain my blood."

"I think we'll call it a day," Cora says. She rings an old-fash-ioned bell beside her door. It's not very loud, but my babysitter always shows up within a matter of minutes.

Fine by me. I'm ready to go back to my room, eat whatever version of tomato soup the servants make, and sleep for twelve hours straight.

I shove off the couch, straightening my skirt as well as I can, and stand at the door. While I wait, Cora flits in the background.

She washes the dishes by hand, even though she obviously could do it with her fancy mind magic. If I could move things without touching them, dishes would be the first chore to go.

A slow knock comes at the door, and I straighten my posture without consciously deciding to. It's Sebastian. Oskar knocks like an FBI agent about to kick down the door. Beatrice knocks like an impatient twelve-year-old. Sebastian's knock is heavy and slow, like he has nowhere to be but you best answer quickly anyway.

Cora opens the door and I stand between her and Sebastian like a child of divorce. His eyes flick briefly to mine before settling on my teacher.

"Well?" he asks.

"Nothing," Cora says, and she says it as if it should be obvious. As if he shouldn't expect anything else, no matter how many more days they let me try.

She's not wrong.

"That's unacceptable," Sebastian says. His eyes are on me again, but his expression is impossible to read.

"I'm trying," I say. I hate how scared and pathetic I sound. It's inescapable at this point. I'm not naive enough to believe they'll keep me around forever. At some point, they're going to tire of this, and once they do, I'm done.

They'll kill me to try to break their curse, or maybe just out of pure spite.

"You've done it before," Sebastian says. His voice is low, addicting. For a moment, I am transported back to the bar, when I thought he was just a random guy hitting on me.

I don't argue with Sebastian. I know I used magic that night he attacked me. I saw it on his chest, felt his blood on my hands.

"That was different," I say. I'm glaring at him now, hands tight at my sides. "I panicked. I didn't even mean to do it. I swear, I'm trying everything. Cora isn't exactly the best teacher."

I expect Cora to argue, but when she doesn't, I only feel more stupid. We all know she isn't the one having issues. I tighten my fists again, and Sebastian tracks the movement. His gaze wanders to my skirt, lingering there for a noticeable moment.

"If you're done ogling my legs," I snap, satisfied when his attention snaps back to my face. "I'd like to go to my room."

"I'm sure you would," is his growled response. "Unfortunately for you, my patience is waning. You're not exactly a house pet I'd like to keep."

"May I recommend you release me then?" I ask sweetly. I can only hope he doesn't notice the way my knees tremble, the way my heart leaps in my throat. I'm treading dangerous waters, but I won't be treated like an unwelcome guest when he's literally holding me hostage.

"Actually, I have a better idea," he says. His smile is slow, leering, as he looks from me to Cora. His grin is almost demonic. "I'll be back in one hour. See if you can't find her some pants."

"She's twice my height," Cora says.

Sebastian doesn't respond. He's already through the door, and I'm left with a sinking feeling I won't like his idea one bit.

I don't know where exactly we are in Sebastian's manor. He's taken so many twists and turns, I have no idea where we've ended up. We stand in the middle of a gaping room, devoid of furniture. It looks like a ballroom, only without the elaborate decor and fancy chandeliers. The only light here comes from the windows. They stretch along the left wall, filtering in the final rays of an orange sunset.

Outside, Cora stands with a collection of Sebastian's henchmen. The pretty brunette and the old man who guard my cell.

Two men I've never seen. A short black woman with blood-red lipstick. They all stare at me through the elongated windows, whispering amongst themselves. Despite everything Cora's told me, they're standing outside in direct sunlight.

"Shouldn't they be on fire?" I ask, casting an accusatory glower at Sebastian.

He looks at Cora and his followers, frowning, before addressing me.

"I see Cora has been educating you on the sun curse," he says.

"Hard to break something if I don't know it exists."

I expect him to point out I've *still* yet to break it, even knowing it exists. He only nods toward the vampires watching me.

"Cora fixed us sunwalker spells," he says. "Sorry to disappoint you, love, but I won't be catching fire anytime soon."

"That *is* disappointing," I agree.

I cross my arms over my chest and do a slow rotation, taking in the room's details. The floors are wooden and scratched. The walls white and void of decoration. The only color comes from the window drapes, but they're all pulled to the side for my outside viewers.

"Does everyone have one?" I ask.

"No," Sebastian says. "It's a difficult spell."

He looks toward the door, as if expecting someone to appear. My stomach twists, hard as I try to ignore it. I already know something bad is going to happen. I know he's arranged something horrible to spur my magic, but I can only hope he's not about to risk my life.

That'd be a complete waste, right? I won't be breaking any curses if I'm dead.

"Sebastian—"

"They've returned," he says, straightening.

I follow his gaze to the doorway. It's the only exit out of this gaping room, and though Sebastian seems to have heard something, I can't. Even as I strain my ears, I hear only the sound of my racing heart.

"Remember, you are a Pruce," Sebastian says.

Without another word, he strides for the door, gesturing for me to remain in the center of the room.

"At least tell me what's about to happen," I say. My hands fidget at my sides, and I glance over my shoulder, at my outside audience. They're all wide eyed and motionless now.

By the time I look back to Sebastian, he's already disappeared from the room.

HE MAKES me wait for hours. The sun has fallen, casting the room in horrible darkness. Only three of the wall lanterns are lit, and their pathetic fire isn't enough to fully light the room. I'm surrounded by shadows and my own frantic thoughts. The outside spectators are my only company, and they've barely looked away since Sebastian left.

They know something is coming for me, and they're determined not to miss the show.

I use the time to practice magic, or at least, to *try* to practice. I end up with my hands dangling in front of me, useless and powerless as ever, until finally, the sole door opens. I'm unexpectedly hit with a wave of relief. What's coming must be terrible, but at least this is almost over.

"Sebastian?" I call. I try to sound brave. Annoyed, rather than terrified. "I want another day. Give me another day with Cora—"

Something moves in the doorway. It's too dark to make out its features, but I know it's not Sebastian. It's not a vampire or a witch or anything human at all. It's too tall, too thin, to be a person.

I suck in a startled breath at the way it moves. Spindly legs, bent at sharp angles, jolting it through the shadows. I stumble backward, keeping my eyes locked on the creature. I don't stop until I hit the far back corner.

A flicker of candlelight highlights the creature's face, just for a second. It has a bald, vaguely humanoid head and wholly black eyes. Shiny and reflective, like a dead TV screen. Pallid skin covers its entire body, stretched so tight it looks translucent. And while the upper body is similar to a human's naked torso, with arms and a heaving ribcage, its lower half is monstrous. Eight gaunt legs, longer than I am tall, lurch toward me, the sharp ends stabbing into the hardwoods with each step.

"What are you?" I ask. My voice comes as a horrified whisper, and I blink again, hoping the monster disappears.

It doesn't. It only emits a strange choking sound, tilting its head as it watches me. Its mouth splits into a wide grin, showcasing two rows of jagged teeth.

"No," I say through a broken sob. "No, Sebastian. Please. One more day. Give me just one more day—"

Sebastian doesn't respond. He's not outside with the others, but he's clearly not here either.

The creature screams, the sound something between a human wail and an animalistic roar. It's loud enough I barely hear my own cries as I sprint across the room. I try for the door, but the creature spins, charging. The windows are my only other option, my only other chance.

I make it there in four strides, slamming against the glass. With both fists, I strike the window again and again, until the glass shakes and my bones tremble.

"Help me!" I beg. "Please—I can't. Please!"

The pretty brunette grins at me, eyes wild with satisfaction.

"Monsters!" I scream. "All of you! Monsters!"

Something—one of the creature's legs, I think—catches my side. I'm airborne before I can comprehend what's happened. For five horrible seconds, my stomach drops and my breath leaves my lungs. Then I strike the far wall, landing on the ground in a heap.

I blink at the floor, at my hands trembling against the wood, at the collection of massive spider legs standing too close. I follow that pale skin up and up and up, over the misshapen rib cage and across broad shoulders and finally to those hideous, vacant eyes. They reflect me, cowered here on the floor. Something cut my cheek, and my blood drips down my face, dotting my knuckles.

The creature smiles at me, revealing dozens of small, pointed teeth. It's the mouth of a piranha, and unless I do *something*, it's going to devour me whole.

"Don't," I say. I lunge to my feet, legs shaking as I flatten against the wall. The spider-creature watches, tilting its head, smile growing wider by the second. "You stay there. You've got nothing to do with me. Whatever Sebastian did to you—"

At his name, the creature roars. Its jaws open inhumanly wide, as if the bones came disconnected. I shrink against the wall, but keep my eyes steady

"I have nothing to do with him," I say firmly. "I'm a prisoner, just like you. If we work together, we can both—"

It surges for me, moving exactly like spiders in the real world. Fast and erratic, sharp legs blurring against the floor. I'm screaming, running, even though I know it's useless. I sprint for the door. Ten feet, and I'll break through. If it's locked...*No*. It won't be locked. It'll be open. I'll reach it in eight feet.

Seven.

Six.

One of the creature's legs catches my hip. I'm thrown again, farther this time, crashing against the window. I don't know if it's the one where Cora and the others are watching. There's no time to look. By the time I've hit the floor, I'm moving again. The creature shoves me to the center of the room, as if I'm weightless.

I come to a stop on my stomach. Everything hurts, and I'm pretty sure my ankle is broken. I've never broken a bone. I've never even had a bruise that lasted longer than a few days. Now, I feel like I've shattered. There's nothing left in me to stand up.

The most I can manage is to crawl for the door, nails scraping against the floor as I drag myself.

It's useless. The creature is too fast, too powerful. Its leg shoves my hip, forcing me to my back as it towers over me. I'm facing its soft underbelly. If I had a sword—or any fight in me at all—that's where I'd attack.

Instead, I only lay there, tears streaming to my ears.

"Stop!" I scream. It's more of a sob than anything else. My mouth tastes of blood, but I have no idea whether it's from a swollen lip or something internal.

The creature stabs, a sharp, punching motion, aimed for my gut. I roll onto my side, moving just far enough to dodge the strike. It's going to kill me, I realize. There's no way...

Focus, Cora had told me. *You have to focus.*

So I try. I hold my hands toward the creature's underbelly and dig for whatever magic supposedly lives within me. I scream, fingers extended, arms trembling.

"Come on!" I shout. "Do something!"

I ignore the creature as it shifts, focusing only on my hands, only on my buried magic. Sure that if I can just find it, I'll be able to—

Its leg stabs through my stomach. It's as quick as a bee sting. One moment, its leg is lodged in my body. The next, the creature has vanished entirely. I'm left alone, staring up at the dusty, arched ceiling.

A strange groan fills the air, and it takes me a moment to realize it's *me.* I grasp my stomach with both hands, but it does nothing to stop the bleeding. There's too much blood, pooling across my waist and onto the floor. If the creature doesn't come back for me, a vampire undoubtedly will.

I blink against a haze of darkness. I'm going to pass out, I think, and maybe that's for the best. If I'm going to die a horrible death, it'd be better not to feel it.

I loll my head to the side, scanning the room for the creature. My magic must have worked. Somehow, I must have killed it.

I finally find it in a lump of discolored flesh near the windows. I stare for a long moment, before realizing it's the creature's shriveled legs and nothing else. A trail of blood leads from the lower body to its upper half across the room. The torso is almost to the wall, strewn across the floor with organs exposed and those blank black eyes frozen in death.

The creature isn't just dead. It's been brutally ripped in two.

"Did I do that?" I whisper. I'm not sure who I'm asking, and I'm not sure *why.* It's obvious—

"Afraid not, little witch," Sebastian says.

I twist toward his voice, grunting at the sharp spike of pain. Sebastian strolls toward me, coming from the direction of the door. He pockets a key, staring down at me with an unreadable expression. He's covered in blood. It's the same inky black that spills from the creature's body, and I realize *he* killed it, not me.

"It seems you were going to let that thing kill you," he says. The blood stains his chin and chest, coating both hands. Despite his taunting words, Sebastian doesn't look relaxed. His face is strained, jaw tight as he looks over me.

"Don't worry, I'm sure someone will finish the job," I say. I look down at my stomach, at the blood pooling between my shaking fingers. I'm surprised there isn't already a horde of vampires eating me alive.

"The door is locked. No one can get in."

"Why? So you can eat me yourself?"

"Hells, Grace. You should be thanking me," he says, voice clipped. "If I hadn't—"

I don't plan to move. I don't consciously decide to do anything. All I know is I want him gone. I want him so far from me, I never have to look at his stupid face again.

He flies across the room, and my hand moves, powered by magic I don't understand. I bend my fingers, slamming Sebastian against the wall, holding him there. Though I'm not physically touching him, I swear, I can feel his breaths against my palm. I can almost feel his cold, dead heart beating.

"Fuck you," I say.

My words are barely a whisper, so quiet I'm not sure he hears me. Still, they're the last I hear as I lose consciousness, and I close my eyes with a smile.

9

NOD IF YOU UNDERSTAND

GRACE

He's back. That's the fourth time today and the ninth time since I woke yesterday morning. I don't know how long I laid unconscious before waking in my bed. All I know is that, while I slept, someone healed my body. I assume Cora. I haven't asked. I haven't spoken a single word to Sebastian or to the servant who brings my meals. I haven't spoken to anyone at all, and I'm not planning for that to change.

If they need me to break their curse, they'll have to figure it out without my cooperation. Until the moment that creature stabbed through me, I'd been willing to help. I'd even told Sebastian that, and how did he repay me?

He fed me to a literal beast and expected a *thank you* for not letting it kill me.

Now, Sebastian stands in my doorway. He wears a crisp white shirt, black slacks, and the same long coat he wore to abduct me from the human realm. He's regarding me with a hesitant expression, and it's somehow more unsettling than his usual arrogant one.

It's as though he can't decide whether I'm worth dealing

with. Like maybe he should just kill me and use my corpse to break the curse.

Let him try, I think. *Maybe, when my magic comes the next time, I'll use it to kill him.*

If only I knew how to make death stick on him.

"You haven't eaten," is the first thing he says. He crosses his arms over his wide chest, frowning at me.

I don't reply. I roll onto my side, turning to face the stone wall instead of him. Truthfully, my body is sore from laying in bed for two days straight. I've only gotten up a handful of times to go to the bathroom. Other than that, I've laid right here, staring and sulking.

"I brought your electronic," he says next.

He means the laptop he gave me a week ago. It has *Legally Blonde* downloaded on it, along with a few rom-coms. That has tempted me far more than the regular delivery of tomato soup. Time would pass faster if I could rot my brain with some classic movies. But watching a movie feels as good as admitting defeat, as *complying*.

I'd rather starve and die of boredom than let Sebastian think he's won.

"Grace," he says.

I close my eyes, squeezing them until they hurt.

"Come," he says. "I'll walk you to the washroom."

Usually, Beatrice is the one who babysits my bathroom breaks.

"I'd rather pee the bed," I tell him. I've still got my eyes closed and my back to him, and yet, I feel when he moves from the doorway.

In all the time I've been here, Sebastian has rarely entered my cell. It's unsettling, feeling him lurk over me, his legs bumping my mattress. My entire body clenches without permission.

"Come," he says again. "You can't lay here forever. Let's skip the theatrics, shall we? There's too much work to be—"

"Go to hell, Sebastian," I say. I lurch into a seated position, satisfied when he startles. "I'm done trying to help you. You're a terrible person, and you know what? The witches were right. You all *deserve* to burn."

His jaw ticks, but for once, the man doesn't respond. He only watches me, face carefully still, eyes recklessly wild. He opens his mouth. Closes it. And finally, leaves, slamming the door behind him.

I stare for over a minute before believing he's left for good. Then, I roll onto my side and drift back to sleep.

I DON'T KNOW what day it is. I have no idea how much time I've lost while in the Echo, only that the world must be looking for me by now. Even if Tessa didn't report me missing, Libby would have. There are probably pictures of my face on telephone poles and on news segments. I bet Libby has a whole mob of people sharing my story on social media.

They could spend the rest of their lives hunting for me, but they'll never find me here. I'm not sure they could, even if they knew about the doorway Sebastian used in Aberlena University.

I stare at myself in the mirror. My occasional trips to the bathroom are the only time I leave my room. Sebastian hasn't returned since I snapped at him, and though I'm relieved, I'm also going insane.

I touch my cheeks, studying the sharp angles of my face. I've lost too much weight, and yet, I no longer feel the pangs of hunger. The black clothes Beatrice brought today are baggy and boyish, but I don't care to complain. Who cares if the fabric swallows me alive? I feel dead anyway.

"Is your plan to sleep for the rest of your life?"

I startle at the sound of Beatrice's voice. In the past, she's never entered the bathroom while I'm in it. I meet her expectant gaze in the mirror. While I look like a skinny wet rat, my skin flushed from the hot shower, Beatrice is beautiful and put together. I'm not sure if they have clubs in this hellish world, but she always looks ready for a night out.

"I'm not sleeping now," I say. I trail a finger from my cheekbone, over my jaw and down my throat. My skin looks like crap. It hasn't seen moisturizer in weeks, and my diet of tomato soup and bread isn't helping. Not that I've eaten in days anyway.

"Yeah, because you had to pee," she says.

"And shower."

"He's going to lose his patience with you eventually," she says. I've gone back to studying myself, but I can still see her in my peripheral vision.

She's a vampire. I can see her in the mirror.

Yet another myth, broken.

"I'm surprised he hasn't already," she adds. She's less than a foot from me now, her breath tickling my neck. She smells like iron, like *blood*. "I've been nothing but supportive of his decisions, but truly, Grace, I wish he'd let me kill you."

I clamp my teeth together, meeting her eyes in the mirror again. Part of me wishes he would too. At least it would put me out of my misery. I'd never have to eat tomato soup. I'd never have to feel like an idiot while Cora heaves and sighs in the background. And I'd definitely never have to see Sebastian again.

Unfortunately, there's a stubborn part of me that won't allow it. It still feels self-preservation, an inexplicable urge to stay alive, despite it all.

I turn, facing her until our noses almost touch. Her eyes sharpen, lip curling until I can see her canines. Her teeth, like

Sebastian's, like Oskar's, are perfectly straight. I haven't seen a single fang since I've arrived.

Another myth, apparently.

"Sebastian wouldn't let you kill me if your life depended on it," I tell her. My heart races as she glowers at me, eyes turning lethal. Predatory. I force my shoulders back, pretending she can't hear the terror radiating from me. "He may be your *master*, but you are nothing more than a convenient fuck for him."

I don't see her move. Her hand latches around my throat, and we're moving before the choked gag leaves my mouth. The manor blurs around us as she runs, one hand on my throat. My head spins, even after I've squeezed my eyes shut. I hang onto her wrist with both hands, legs kicking, trying to find traction against her body or the floor.

We jolt to a stop, and I tumble across the ground. I let out a pathetic gasp as I land on my back, the wind and sense knocked out of me. I blink up at the ceiling, only to realize there isn't one. We're outside.

Jesus. This is the first time I've been outside since Sebastian dragged me here.

Despite everything, I devour the sight before me. A mostly-darkened sky, touched with streaks of light from the setting sun. I blink, then close my eyes. There's a cold wind blowing, tickling my wet hair against my shoulders.

"For fuck's sake, Beatrice!"

It takes me a moment to place the garbled voice. Oskar. I blink again, tilting my chin toward the sound. I'm lying on a slab of stone bricks, and behind me, there's a massive grey statue. Tilting my head, I realize it's an enormous replica of Sebastian. He *would* have a statue of himself.

"Where's Sebastian?" Beatrice demands. Her voice echoes through the space, bouncing back at her.

I push onto my elbows, struggling to breathe. Luckily, I'm not bleeding.

"Where is he?" she repeats.

I follow her gaze to the corner, where a massive stone table stands against an ivy-covered wall. Oskar sits with another man. I don't know his name, but I recognize him. He's one of Sebastian's men, one of the watchers.

"Not here yet," the man says. "And you should be thanking your stars for that, Beatrice. He'd skin you alive for that move alone!"

"I've had enough," Beatrice says, but her voice wobbles and so does her bravado. "She's useless, and I'm done wasting time with her. I don't know how long he's planning to coddle her, to let her live in that room, doing nothing. If she's not going to break the curse, what are we letting her live for?"

"Beatrice."

We all startle, turning to look at the courtyard's entrance. Sebastian stands in the open doorway, jaw set as his attention flickers briefly over each of us. He looks to me last before returning to Beatrice.

"Is there a problem?" he asks.

"No, Master," she says. Gone is the fearsome, untouchable bitch she was seconds ago. Now, she looks small and pathetic, childish in her tantrum. Good. Let them all see *exactly* who she is.

"I disagree," he says. He strides forward, hands tucked in his pockets. His approach is smooth, but slow, like a predator closing in on prey. "I gave you simple instructions, didn't I?"

"You did," she says. She presses her lips together, as if trying to keep from saying more, only to immediately break. "Why do you let her live? Why is she *here*, Master, if not to do as you've instructed?"

An unexpected flicker of pity stings through my chest. Beatrice may not be locked in a cell, but she's stuck in a worse prison than I am. She truly believes everything she's saying, as if the world exists only for Sebastian's purposes.

"He is not god!" I shriek. I'm looking at Beatrice, but my words are for everyone in this courtyard. "None of you are. You're nothing but monsters."

Beatrice bares her teeth at me, a violent hiss radiating from her throat. She lunges for me, her movements surprisingly slow. She doesn't make it halfway to me before Sebastian catches her throat. He holds her in place, squeezing hard enough to draw a sharp breath.

"Let me make one thing clear, Beatrice," he says. His voice drops, a rumble so deep it sounds more like a growl. "She is irreplaceable. *You* are not. You touch her again, and I will ensure it's the last thing you do."

Her lips part, but there's no sound. Tears trail down her cheeks as she stands, perfectly still in his chokehold.

"Leave this courtyard immediately, and do not return until I give explicit permission. Nod if you understand."

It seems to take all of her effort to do just that.

Sebastian releases her, and she goes without another word.

When Sebastian returns me to my room, he doesn't leave as I expect. He lingers at the door, hand on the knob, back to me. And then, he steps into my room, closing the door behind him. He leans against the heavy wood, studying me from where he stands.

"She isn't wrong," he says. "I should not let you live as you do. Openly defying me. Refusing even the simplest of tasks. Wasting every meal we deliver. I should kill you, Grace Pruce. I should hand you over to Cora and let her dissect you for parts, until we can make something useful of your father's blood."

Tears roll down my cheeks, but I don't break eye contact. I will not allow him to make me small, to make me as pathetic as Beatrice just looked.

"You are not wrong either," he says. "We are not gods. We are vampires. And perhaps we *do* deserve to burn."

I try to act unaffected by his words, but by the way his mouth quirks, I know he can read my surprise.

"I am a monster, Grace," he continues. "That means I don't care what I deserve. There is nothing I will not do to get what I want. I will lie, steal, torture, slaughter. I will do *anything* to break this curse, even if that means killing you. Do you understand?"

"Yes," I say through gritted teeth. "I am *well* aware of who you are, Sebastian. You don't—"

"I will do anything," he says again, cutting me off. He strides across the room, forcing me to retreat until my back hits the stone wall. He only stops once our chests are inches apart. "But *only* if I must. If you are willing to try again, I am willing to adjust my method."

"Adjust?" I echo. I can barely breathe with him this close, his green eyes intense on me.

"I will stop treating you as a prisoner," he says. "I will not throw you into battle unknowingly. I will not kill you without due notice."

"How kind of you," I mock.

"I will *help* you," he says, ignoring me. "Kindness is *not* my nature, but I will try."

"Why?" I ask. My voice shakes as I speak, and my heart begs me not to listen, not to fall for his false words. I know better, especially from evil-hearted creatures like him.

"If I kill you, there's no going back," he says. He steps away, giving me space to breathe, to think.

I don't respond. I remain against the wall, chest heaving, eyes burning. Sebastian crosses the room. He pauses as he reaches the door, looking back at me.

"Let me know what you decide."

"I don't forgive you," I tell him. "I will *never* forgive you."

"Good," he says, surprising me. He looks away, voice lowering again. "After you attacked me in the park, I assumed *fear* triggered your magic. But it wasn't fear, Grace, was it? It was *hate*."

He waits for me to respond, but I don't. I don't tell him his explanation is one I've considered for nights on end. The same one I've feared. Because if he's right...perhaps I belong with these monsters more than I thought.

10

GIVE ME SOMETHING
SEBASTIAN

"Where did you get this?" I ask.

Grace stands before me, dressed in a pair of grey pants and a shirt that must belong to Cora. It's too small on her, showing off a strip of her thin stomach. It's almost as bad as that damned skirt she'd worn. It switches something in my brain, until I'm barely paying attention to the paper in her hand.

I need to focus, but instead, I'm studying her body like it's a work of art. Maybe it is. Smooth skin, long legs, full lips.

Not for the first time, I wish she wasn't a witch, wasn't human, wasn't essential to my plans. She'd look absolutely divine in my bed. Blonde hair loose over my pillows, knees bent, cunt exposed. She'd probably touch herself while I watched, instruct me to wait before touching her. As if I could resist—

"Sebastian." Her sharp voice jolts me out of the fantasy, and thank heavens for that. I was getting carried away, and I'm not sure I was going to stop anytime soon.

I meet her narrowed eyes.

"Were you..." she trails off, mouth curling in disgust, then horror. "Don't you even think about touching me."

She looks repulsed, but her pulse quickens. Most likely in fear...and yet, some carnal part of me hopes it's arousal. Maybe, once all is said and done—

"Don't," she says again. The word shakes, and I huff out a breath. Fear. That's definitely fear.

"I am not *that* kind of monster," I tell her. I look back to the paper in her hand. She's lowered it since my gawking, but she raises it again now, extending it toward me. This time, I take it.

I stare for a prolonged moment, trying to recognize the paper. Worn, wrinkled, cheap. The human must have given it to her. Oskar wouldn't be stupid enough to give her anything without permission. No one else has access to her, now that Beatrice proved untrustworthy.

"Are you literate?" she asks, scoffing irritably. "Apparently I should have—"

"I am not," I say. Her eyes pop wide, and I see the regret instantly cross her face. "You're going to mock me for it?"

"No. I didn't—" Her lower lip bobs, as if she's holding back tears. Worse, a flush of blood heats her cheeks, sending her scent into the air. It's too much, too tempting...I squeeze my eyes shut.

In my head, I could kill her so easily. I could have her body drained of blood before Oskar realized it. He's mere steps away, blocked only by a single door.

I could do it though. I could sink my teeth into her and—

I tighten my hands into fists and hold my breath. After a long moment, I open my eyes, taking a step to put distance between us.

"I can read, Grace," I say finally. I force my lips into a teasing smirk, as if I haven't just fantasized murdering her. "You shouldn't be so judgmental."

I don't allow myself to look at her as I finally read it. It's better that I don't see the blood rushing through her cheeks, just beneath her soft skin. With my breath held, I can't smell her, can't imagine the way she'd taste.

I read the list. Once. Twice. Slowly, my fake smile evaporates. Needy. Little. Witch.

"A list of demands?" I say, looking up at her. She stares right back, those blue eyes hardening, sharpening like jagged glass. I toss the list at her feet. "You seem to have forgotten—"

"I have not forgotten anything," she interrupts. She snatches the paper from the floor and shoves it against my chest, holding it there. "You said you would adjust your ways, so long as I tried again. This is me, saying I'll try again. If—and only if—you keep your end of the bargain."

"I agreed to not treat you as a prisoner," I say. "I never promised royal privileges. My own team doesn't get this stuff."

"Well, you said it yourself, they're replaceable," she shoves the paper against my chest again, her nails scraping through my shirt. It shouldn't be arousing. It's *not* arousing. Grace pulls away, letting the note fall between us. "I am not replaceable, Sebastian. So if you want me to try again, this needs to happen first."

My entire body turns hot. I am a caged animal, and she's threatening me with fire. The heat boils deeper, until it's all I can feel, until the rage bubbles through my veins and into my lungs.

"Perhaps I should visit your little friend. Tessa, right?" I snap. Despite the way Grace steps back, I move forward, raising my voice with each word. I'm yelling by the end, charging forward until we reach the wall. "Let's see if that gets you to try again!"

Grace stares at me in shock, but just when I expect her magic to explode, to tear through me as it has twice already, she closes her eyes. Her eyelashes are wet, tinged with unfallen tears. The sight sends an ache through my jaw, and I realize I'm clenching it tight enough to crack teeth.

I force myself to relax, to step back. Grace is nothing but a pawn, a necessary means to an end. There's no reason to lose my mind. Once she breaks the curse, I'll send her back to the human world, or hells, even to the coven, if that's what she wants. For now, it doesn't matter if I hurt her feelings, if I make her despise me.

"I've already warned you," I say, lowering my voice. "If you think—"

Grace's eyes open, wild and violent, and she cuts me off before I can manage another word.

"You so much as hurt Tessa," she says, "And I'll kill myself while you think I'm sleeping. You and your fucking *team* will be left to break the curse with my cold, curdled blood."

My chest heaves with each breath, lips stretching over my teeth. I don't realize I've extended my fangs, that I've leaned closer to Grace, until her breath hitches.

"Scare me all you want, Sebastian," she says, words trembling. "It doesn't change the truth. You need me, and I think we both know...you need me *alive*."

I press my hands against the stone, caging her between my arms. It takes every ounce of strength not to buckle right here. To give up everything for one moment of weakness. It's only the fact I can't decide *what* I want most—to kill her, to taste her, to fuck her senseless—that keeps me from acting.

"It's time for you to leave," she says. Her breath is hot on my ear, and my cock twitches.

It's that, far more than her request, that makes me flee her room like a coward.

Only once the door is closed do I take a breath. The stale air of the manor fills my lungs, but I can still smell *her*. It's as though her scent has taken residence inside me, and now I'm not sure how to get it out.

"You all right, Master?" Oskar asks.

I blink. He's standing at his usual post, stationed directly across the hall from Grace's room. Unlike Beatrice, he hasn't once complained over watching her. Truthfully, I think she might remind him of his late wife.

"Fine," I grit out. Behind me, Grace bangs on the door.

"You're in trouble with that one," he says. He gives me a knowing smile.

I storm down the hall, wishing he was wrong.

GRACE'S LIST *of Demands*

1. *New clothes: No offense to whoever is loaning me these clothes, but I need a new wardrobe. These outfits are hideous and don't even fit. And no, don't just bring me more random hand-me-downs. Let me order some online or go shopping.*
2. *Better food: The tomato soup was definitely an upgrade, but it's not exactly a balanced diet. I need some variety. Let's add: pasta, Chinese noodles, salad (Caesar or Cobb are my favorites), stir fried veggies, and French fries, if that's a thing you have here.*
3. *On that note, how about something to drink other than water? Surely you guys have Coke or Sprite or even freaking lemonade. I'd kill for a vodka-cran, if I'm being honest. I might even drink milk...I'm THAT desperate.*
4. *More entertainment: I looked through the movie options on the laptop last night. Not super impressed. Can you add some more 80s/90s rom-coms to the rotation? I'm not too picky, so any will do. Oh, actually, you should add* Ten Things I Hate About You. *That's a great one.*
5. *Increased freedom: I don't like being locked up like a dog. You said you won't treat me like a prisoner, so I want free*

reign of the manor. I'm going Yellow-Wallpaper insane in here.

6. *Basic respect: You've already said you'll stop being horrible, but I want basic respect on top of that. Stop yelling. Stop attacking. Stop being such a freaking asshole all the time.*

Hopefully, this all sounds simple enough. Because it is <u>simple</u>, Sebastian. Treat me well, and we'll give this another shot. Keep being a jerk, and I'll go back to my sulking.

"You called, Master?" the human asks. He stands in the doorway to the library, one hand on the latch, the other fidgeting at his side. He's blissfully transparent, so nervous his pulse is unsteady.

I look up from the table. I have a spread of texts in front of me, and after an hour of searching, I still haven't found anything useful. Not even a passing mention of the Pruce line.

"Was it you?" I ask. I arch an eyebrow, watching the way he shifts from one foot to the other. "Did you give Grace paper? A pen?"

The minute twitch of his lip gives me all the answer I need. And still, I remain quiet, waiting for the confirmation to fall from his own lips.

"Yes," he says. He's trembling as he leans against the door, hiding behind it as though it's a shield. "Was I...should I not have?"

I rise from the table, tearing a page from my notebook. As I cross the room, I study the human. He's small, fragile.

"You do not give Grace *anything,*" I say. "Not a piece of paper. Not a kind word. Not a lingering glance. Do you understand?"

"Yes, Master," he says. He hasn't stopped trembling. "I'm sorry. I didn't know—"

"Grace is more dangerous than she lets on," I say. "The moment you let your guard down, she'll tear you to shreds. Understand?"

"Yes, Master. Sorry, Master."

"If it happens again, I'll tear your head from your neck," I say. I flick the piece of paper toward him, and he barely manages to catch it before it hits the ground. I wait until he's righted himself to continue. "Grocery list. Find what you can here in the Echo. The rest, have Amelia take you to the human world."

The human straightens, chest puffing out with determined confidence. I'm sending him to the market, not into fucking battle, but I suppose he's just relieved to be breathing.

Once he's gone, I journey from the library to Grace's room. Oskar stands at his usual post, and he smiles as I approach.

"Training?" he asks. He raises an eyebrow. "I thought you gave Cora the day off?"

"I did," I say. I can't keep the bitterness from edging my voice. Grace *should* be training today, but instead...

I knock on her cell door, only pausing for three seconds before opening it. She's in bed—*shocking*—but at least she's awake. The electronic sits beside her, and a movie plays on the screen.

"Get up," I tell her.

To my surprise, she does. She closes the laptop and crawls out from the covers, wearing a black frock. It's one of Cora's, but it's too short on Grace. She looks downright seductive, her long legs on full-display, her arms crossed, pressing her cleavage together.

Maybe new clothes won't be so terrible after all.

"Well?" she asks.

Her word is a sharp blade, grating against my last fucking

nerve. Despite our last encounter, she doesn't look afraid of me. No, she looks pissed yet confident, as if she holds some unseen power over me.

Maybe she does, a voice taunts. *Maybe it's* her *game, and you're the pawn.*

I shake my head roughly, banishing the thought like an unwanted pest.

"Show me magic," I say roughly. "Give me *something*, Grace, and you can have something off the list. New clothes. Better food. More entertainment."

"Freedom?" she asks. She arches a defiant eyebrow, and I have to restrain the growl from escaping my throat.

"Your so-called freedom would last ten seconds," I say. "You wouldn't make it to the end of the hallway before someone had you spread out and bleeding."

Her jaw clenches, and I can hear her teeth grinding.

"That sounds like a convenient excuse for keeping me locked away," she says.

I'm in front of her before she can blink, and she gasps, falling back against the stone wall. I have her exactly where I did last night, only now, I keep myself from touching her, from encroaching her space.

"I would've had you," I whisper. Goosebumps dance across her shoulders, and I watch them, rather than her face. "You'd be dead."

"You forget I've taken you down twice," she says. "Maybe *you'd* be dead."

"I haven't forgotten," I say. I finally look into her eyes. Dark blue. Violent flame. It tempts a smile from my lips, but I resist the urge. "Magic is nothing if you can't control it, Grace. Ask the Nectoa."

"The what?"

"The beast," I say. "The spider that attacked you."

"That *you* attacked me with," she corrects. She holds my gaze, nose scrunched in disgust.

"I'll tell you what," I say, choosing to ignore that statement. "If you can prove you can handle yourself, I'll grant you free reign of the manor."

"Really?" she asks. Her eyes light, and a brilliant smile breaks her heavy scowl.

Fuck. I haven't seen her smile like that since the bar. Back then, she didn't know to fear me. To *hate* me.

"Yes," I say. I keep my voice, my face, carefully blank. "If you can consistently bring me to my knees, you can explore all the dusty crevices of this place."

"Okay," she says. She's still beaming at me, and it's taking all my focus not to look at her mouth. "Okay, yeah. I can do that."

"Five times minimum."

"Can I try now?" she asks. She's literally bouncing on her toes, as if she's momentarily forgotten I'm the one trapping her here at all.

I take a step away, giving her space to move from the wall. She levels her feet shoulder-width apart and closes her eyes. Palms toward me, she scrunches her entire face as she concentrates.

Nothing happens.

We stand like this for a long time. Long enough, I finally allow myself a glance at her mouth. Her lips look soft, full, so fucking delicious I'm desperate to bite them. I'd happily bite any part of her. Her neck, her tits, her stomach, her thighs.

Fuck.

I fed this morning, but I'm clearly overdue. I need to eat more when she's here. I make a mental note to do just that, and then I spend the next several minutes studying the ceiling of Grace's bedroom.

I'm surprised nicer quarters weren't on her damned list.

Clothes. Entertainment. Food. But apparently this dingy closet-sized room is adequate for her. I glance at her twin-sized bed. I don't recognize the blankets—I have no idea where Beatrice found them. They look old though, as if she dragged them out of a dusty attic.

She probably did.

I make another mental note, and then, I feel it. The softest pinch in my stomach that radiates down to my knees. It's not enough to make me fall, but I have to shift my weight to keep from losing my balance.

Grace's eyes are still closed. Her mouth is moving silently, and I can't decide if she's muttering a spell or if she's giving herself a pep talk. I doubt Cora has taught her a spell though. That's too advanced, and the reminder pangs my stomach far harder than Grace's attempt at magic.

We have so much work cut out for us, and if the witches realize she exists, we might not have the time to accomplish it.

"C'mon, Grace," I bark. Her magic fades from my skin, but I push harder. "Do it. Think of how much you hate me."

Her eyes flash open. Gone is the excitement, the twinkle of determination. The blue flames are back, framed by her slanted blonde eyebrows.

"Trust me, I'm *always* thinking how much I hate you," she says. She closes her eyes again, but her face remains strained. "That's not the problem."

"Then what?" I goad. "You're too weak? Too soft?"

"Maybe," she mutters.

I suck in a deep breath, even though I shouldn't. Her scent fills the entire room, and this close, I can hear each pulse of her heart. Warm, decadent blood. So close, so devastatingly delicious.

"Fuck that," I say. "You're not. You tore a hole through my

chest. You threw me across the room. So do it. Enough with the excuses. Make me—"

Her magic rams against me like a drunkard, clumsy but effective. I don't fall to my knees. It's not a strong enough wave to fully take me down. It *is* enough to send me staggering across the room. My legs feel unsteady, like they're not entirely my own. I don't stop moving until I've crashed against the opposite wall.

Almost immediately, Grace releases her hold on me. She leans forward, dropping her hands to her knees. Through heavy breaths, she stares at me, eyes bright with triumph.

"That's one," she says. She's grinning, even as she gasps for air. "Only four more."

"The challenge is to bring me to my knees," I say. I make a grand gesture toward my legs. "Clearly, I'm *not* on my knees."

"Oh come on," she says. Her voice pitches. She rises to her full height, only to slump back against the stone wall. "I still took you down! I moved you across a room—and on command!"

"I know," I say. My lips quirk into a lopsided smile. "And it's good. It's progress."

She rolls her eyes and starts for the bed, face already morphing into a scowl.

"What, no clothes then?" I ask.

Once again, her eyes spark, and for the moment, her demand of freedom is forgotten.

11

ONE OF EVERYTHING

GRACE

"This isn't the way we came in," I say. We walk down a cobblestone road, leading away from the manor and in the opposite direction of the lookalike university. We're alone, surrounded by rocky earth on either side and a massive mountain in the distance before us. It's hard to see from here, but I think there's a town at its base.

"I didn't realize you were paying attention," he says.

"It might have been blurry, but there was nothing else to do," I say. "Seeing how you *paralyzed* me."

"Hells," he says, scoffing under his breath. "Can we not fight already? We've barely left the manor. I thought you'd be *happy*."

"I'm never happy when I'm with you," I say.

It's not entirely true. This *is* the closest I've felt to happiness since arriving in the Echo. I've spent far too long within the walls of the manor, especially in my own cell. The glimpse of the courtyard had been nice, but it was too chaotic to enjoy it.

"So why aren't we going back that way?" I ask.

There had been food stands and little shops. They were far closer to county fair booths than stores, but still.

"Too dangerous," Sebastian says. He frowns at me, as if gauging whether I'm truly curious or snooping.

He should know by now...the answer is *both*.

"The witches might sense you," he says after a pause. "It's unlikely, but not worth the risk."

I don't know how to respond to that, so I don't. We walk in silence for several minutes, and I breathe in the air. It's fresh, but still not quite right.

"The air here is weird," I tell him. "It's different than in the real world."

"The real world?" he asks. He has a possessive hand on my lower back, pressed against the thick fabric of my borrowed clothes. We're matching now, wearing long black coats made of heavy wool. If we were in Aberlena, where people I knew might see me, I'd be mortified.

For now, I'm just happy to be warm. The sun is still out, but we probably only have ten minutes left of daylight. Soon, the sun will fall behind the horizon, leaving us in darkness and frigid wind.

"Yeah," I say. "That nice, pleasant place you stole me from? Have you already forgotten it?"

"This is *also* the real world," he states. He keeps a careful watch on our surroundings, looking behind us every few steps. "And the air is no different from yours."

"It is different," I insist. "It smells funky...like burnt hair."

He glances down at me, arching an eyebrow.

"I'm surprised you can smell that," he says. He nods toward the mountains. "It's the dragons. I didn't figure you'd scent it. Most mortals can't."

My steps falter, and I lurch to a stop.

"I'm sorry, *dragons*?" I stare at him in disbelief. "You're kidding, right?"

"Come," he says. He forces me forward with the press of his

hand. "We need to put as much distance between us and that manor before nightfall. My men have instructions to stay put for the night, but someone might decide to test it. I'd rather not have to slaughter anyone in front of you."

"Because they'd try to kill me?" I ask. Now I'm the one who looks behind us.

The manor stands in bleak magnificence, more like a castle than a mansion. Its dark stones are framed by the dying light of the sunset, and farther, by rows of houses.

"Yes, they'd try to kill you," Sebastian confirms. "And I figure you'd be in a sour mood if you had to pick clothes while covered in blood."

He's not wrong, but I don't tell him that. We walk for another five minutes in silence. The sun dips lower behind the mountains, staining the sky orange and purple. It'd be pretty, if I weren't so busy scanning the clouds for freaking dragons.

"So, there are vampires," I say. I tuck Sebastian's coat tighter around myself, shivering against the wind. "There are witches. Spider-people things called Nectoa. There are, supposedly, dragons. What else should I fear in this place?"

"Everything," Sebastian says. He releases a long breath as the sun finally loses its battle in the sky. The world darkens, and Sebastian shrugs off his coat. He wordlessly drapes it over my shoulders. "We've got one of everything in this damned place. If you ever find yourself alone, don't trust anyone or anything. There are few creatures that wouldn't like to devour you, in one way or another."

I swallow. I look back to the manor, but it's disappeared from view.

"We'll run the rest of the way," he says. He holds his arms toward me, as if he honestly expects me to leap into them.

"I don't want to be carried." I scowl, stepping out of his

touch. "This is the first time I've been outside in, like, a year. Let me enjoy it."

"It'll take us two days at this speed," he says. He closes the distance, hand finding my back again. "Trust me, there will be plenty for you to explore in the Flight Realm."

"Flight Realm," I repeat. I eye the mountains. "How many realms are there?"

"Four or five, depending on who you ask," he says. He tilts his head at me, once again holding out his arms.

"I'm asking you," I say. Not because I care what he specifically thinks, but because I can tell all this talk is irritating him.

I smile, watching his fingers twitch as they fall back to his sides.

"Four realms, one neutral territory," he says. "We're in the Night Realm now. Flight Realm is by the mountains. Day Realm is to the southeast. Float Realm is in the southwest. It's mostly the ocean, but part of the shore, too. Neutral territory is at the center. That's where we came in. The humans live there."

"Humans?" I ask, unable to hide my surprise. "There are humans here?"

"Of course," he says. This time, he scoops me up without waiting for permission. I gasp, and he grins down at me. "What do you think we eat?"

Before I can reply, we're moving, and the world blurs around us in streaks of darkness.

ONCE SEBASTIAN STOPS, he returns me to my feet. I shove a foot of distance between us and hunch forward, hands braced on my knees. Even though I'm standing still, the world spins for another thirty seconds. I suck deep, steady breaths into my lungs, until finally, I'm centered again.

I'm still bent over when Sebastian moves to my side. His hand is back, centered just above my waist. When I look at him, his eyes aren't on me. Instead, he's scanning our surroundings.

The nearest mountain peak, which was miles away only a few minutes ago, now blots the sky to the east. It rises over us and the quaint town at its base. *Village* might be a more accurate term. Whatever you'd call it, this place is vastly different from Sebastian's Night Realm.

There, the buildings are dark stone, covered in gnarled ivy and looking older than time itself. Here, the architecture is simple. The buildings are made of stucco and pale clay, each one topped with a flat yellow roof. They're impossible to distinguish, even up close, and they look flimsy enough to be taken out by strong wind. There's little landscaping in the surrounding area, and I'm convinced this place is long-abandoned.

"Stay at my side," Sebastian says. It's a command, rough and low, spoken directly against my ear. "Speak to no one. If we are separated, find your way back to the manor. Tell no one who—or what—you are."

"Hard to tell someone who I am when I'm forbidden from speaking," I say. My words are more snarled than spoken, but Sebastian doesn't react.

"Let's go," he says. He guides me into the village, and we walk in silence.

I don't know where, exactly, the Night Realm became the Flight Realm. The cobblestone road has long faded though, leaving us to walk along a path of flattened dirt. The nearby mountains are lively. I can see sparse trees and hear the distant caw of birds. Here, at its base, we're standing in a lifeless desert.

"This is Hava," Sebastian says.

There are no numbers on the buildings. No street signs. Nothing at all to indicate where we are or what we're looking at.

Despite this, Sebastian strides forward with his typical, unflinching confidence.

I suppose that comes with being immortal.

"Hava is one of very few places within the Echo that tolerates my kind," he says. He leads us down an unmarked street, sticking close to the nearest buildings. With one hand still on my back, the other glides along the stucco walls to his right. "Most have no qualms with killing us. Here, we're safe, so long as we arrive with full stomachs and heavy pockets."

"It looks...quiet," I say. I scan the empty street in front of us. I haven't seen anyone—or even a sign of life—since we arrived. For all the wagons, there are no horses. There are no people. There aren't even lights in the endless stretches of buildings.

"It's freshly nightfall," Sebastian explains. "Ever since the curse, this whole world closes its doors once the vampires come out to play. Hundreds, thousands of us, all coming out to feed with the dipping sun. It's too dangerous for Hava to be alive yet. They won't open their doors until near daylight. By then, my men should be sated, and the Flight Realm should be safe."

"You're saying people are in all these houses," I say. I sweep our surroundings again. I'm relying mostly on moonlight to see. The nearest lit windows seem miles away, pressed high into the mountainside, rather than here.

"Yes," Sebastian says.

"I'm surprised the vampires don't just break into their houses," I say. "Rip their throats out and feed."

I'm fishing, and I'm sure Sebastian can tell. If he can, he doesn't seem bothered.

"Some of your human myths are based in fact," he says. His mouth slants into an easy smile. "Vampires must be invited by the property owner. No invitation, no entry. It's why I needed your landlord."

I swallow. My steps slow as we near the end of this street. It meets the foot of the mountain, sloping upward and gradually growing thick with trees. I glance between the final few buildings. They look the same: dull, unassuming, unlit.

"Is he alive?" I ask. I don't look at Sebastian as I do, even as I feel his gaze on my face. "Is Tessa?"

"The landlord is dead," he says. "Tessa probably woke the next morning with little memory of the days before, but otherwise, she's fine."

He's so cavalier as he speaks, as if he doesn't feel an ounce of guilt. And why should he? It's clear these vampires don't see humans as anything more than their personal playthings. I sense it for myself too. I may be a half-witch, but I am as soft, as breakable as any human. They judge me for it, look down on me as if it's a personal failure, rather than basic reality.

"Come," Sebastian says. He leads me across the street and stands before the final door. He raps his knuckles against it, and it opens immediately.

My eyes widen as I stare at a creature almost as startling as the Nectoa. It's a man, his broad frame filling the doorway. He wears form-fitting leather, criss-crossed with thick belts. There's at least one knife in each, I realize, sheathed but no less intimidating. The blades are different lengths and widths, probably made for gutting unsuspecting witches like me.

I stumble backward without making the conscious decision. It's not the man's muscular frame or even the weapons that have me moving. It's his *wings*. Massive and black, tinged with dark red at the edges. They're tucked behind his back, but they're large enough I can still see them.

Sebastian steps, angling his body in front of mine. I move farther behind him. I'm not against using him as a shield if this guy tries to attack.

"Nicasi," Sebastian says.

"Sebastian Vulce," the man returns. His dark gaze flickers toward me, then back to Sebastian. "You've brought a human?"

"May we come in?"

"Always." Nicasi steps to the side, waving for us to enter.

Sebastian shifts, urging me forward. I keep my eyes on the strange bird-man until we're fully inside and he's shut the door. Only once he's crossed the room do I let myself study the building's interior.

Wood paneling covers the walls, sand-colored tiles line the floors, and strange furniture fills what appears to be a living room, combined with a dining room. Through one doorway, I can make out a cramped and cluttered kitchen. Through another, a bedroom with an unmade bed and a pile of clothes in the corner.

"This is *not* a shop," I accuse. I drop my voice to a hushed whisper, glaring at Sebastian. "You said we were getting clothes. And unless this man-bird-creature wears a size four, I don't think we're going to find what I need here."

Despite my lowered voice, the bird-man laughs. It's a loud guffaw that makes his entire gigantic body shake. He must be close to seven feet tall with enough muscles to be three hundred pounds.

"Where'd you find this one?" Nicasi asks. He leans against the wooden table. It only comes to mid-thigh, where it'd probably be at my belly button. "She's not your usual type. In fact..."

He trails off, sniffing the air like he's a dog.

"She's not of the Night Realm at all."

Nicasi steps closer until I'm forced to cower behind Sebastian again. If this man makes my abductor nervous, it's impossible to tell. Sebastian stands at ease, both hands in his pockets. He lets me shrink behind him without so much as a glance.

Another deep inhale, but this time, Nicasi frowns.

"Not human," he says. "Can't place her smell though. What did you say she is?"

"I didn't. Now, enough with the questions," Sebastian drawls. "Get your wares or we'll look elsewhere."

A broad smile stretches Nicasi's mouth.

"Is that right?" he asks, punctuating the question with another booming laugh. "Go ahead. Tell me how many harpies invite you into their home."

Harpy. I add it to the ever-growing catalogue of Echo creatures. Sebastian wasn't kidding. They really do have one of everything.

"The wares," Sebastian repeats.

"What's your name, sweetheart?" Nicasi asks. His dark eyes settle on me, that goofy grin still in place.

I don't answer. I've always hated condescending nicknames. *Sweetheart. Love. Baby.*

"Damn, tight leash, Sebastian?" Nicasi asks. He's clearly teasing, eyes bouncing from me to Sebastian. And still, I find myself seething.

What an asshole.

"I'm not a dog," I snap. "Or do you even have those here?"

Sebastian curls his arm around my shoulders, tugging me sharply against his side. There's a warning pinch in his grasp. A reminder that my leash *is*, in fact, tight.

Nicasi's smile drops.

"Not human...and yet, not of the Echo," he says. He tilts his head, eyes narrowing. "Is she—"

"Nicasi," Sebastian says, tone shifting. "Some questions are better left unasked."

A heavy silence hangs in the air as I finally realize my slip-up. I roll my lips together, frozen as Nicasi studies us for a strained moment. Then, he turns, disappearing briefly into the attached bedroom. I hold my breath and look at Sebastian. He doesn't return my gaze. His eyes are steady on the bedroom door.

He relaxes, only slightly, once Nicasi joins us again. The giant man drapes a collection of clothes along a short table and the adjacent couch.

"Look quickly," he says. Any teasing from before has evaporated. "Be gone by the hour."

With that Nicasi goes back to his bedroom. He starts to close the door, stopping when only a crack remains.

"You were never here, Sebastian," he says, a note of warning in his voice that wasn't there before.

"Understood."

Sebastian keeps his arm around me until Nicasi disappears behind his closed door.

"What was that—"

"Look quickly," Sebastian says, cutting me off. "You've only got a few minutes."

"He's not worried we'll steal anything?" I ask. I try to make my voice teasing, but it only sounds shaky.

"Quickly, Grace."

I swallow, forcing myself not to say another word as I flip through the clothes. They're not exactly my taste: they're too bland, too beige, but they're still better than the ill-fitting black options I had at the manor.

Once I'm done, I drape the clothes over my arm. Sebastian tosses a few strange metal coins onto the table, and we silently depart. We're no more than a couple steps out the door before Sebastian holds his arms toward me.

This time, I let him carry me without asking twice.

12

DON'T YOU DARE

SEBASTIAN

"Don't ask," Grace snaps as she opens the door.

I've barely knocked, and she's already there, glowering at me from the doorway. She typically sulks in the background, pouting while Cora details the progress she's made—or more often, *hasn't* made.

Still, the last few sessions had been good. Grace moved a book from one shelf to another. She lifted a teacup and accidentally broke it against the ceiling. Today is different. Even if she hadn't spoken, I would have known. It's unsettling, the number of things I notice about her now.

I've been spending too much time with her. I blame the season. It's almost spring, and work has fallen to a lull. I've already finished our budget, our military enrollment, and the schedule of building repairs, ordered by their greatest need. Now, I'm bored with too much time on my hands and the urge to give every minute to *her*.

I can't explain it. Grace is pure, bubbling sunshine, and I should hate it. Instead, I'm growing a never-ending list of her preferences, cataloging them like I might one day need them. Her favorite movies. Meals. Clothes.

Worse, I've memorized her insecurities too. Her demands. Her wants. Her endless fucking needs.

In the week since she got new clothes, she's added multiple items to her list. A pair of shoes like the ones she saw Beatrice wearing (granted). A mirror in her bedroom (denied—potential weapon). Makeup and face wash from the human world (granted, though according to Grace, Amelia got *all* the wrong stuff).

Still, I've realized there is nothing Grace demands more of than herself.

Cora stands in the kitchen, leaned against the counter. She holds a mug of tea, watching me through the rising steam. Whatever she's drinking today smells of mint and dirt. I raise my eyebrow in a silent question.

"That counts as asking," Grace says. She presses closer, glaring at me. She's tall for a woman, only an inch or two shorter than I am. "If you *must* know, Sebastian, today was terrible. I didn't move a pillow or change the color of Cora's mug or even freaking feel a single thing. I *failed*, okay?"

She's breathing hard now, chest heaving as her face flushes with blood. I've been engorging myself for the past week, feeding twice daily until I feel sick with it. I've brought two new bloodletters from the neutral territory, keeping them on site for twice what I'd normally pay.

It doesn't matter. It's not enough, and I'm starting to doubt there ever will be enough.

Her scent fills my every breath, until all I can smell is delicate lavender and hot blood and *Grace.* Despite the fullness in my gut, I hold my breath in my throat.

Fuck.

"Can we go now?" she asks. Her blue eyes are wild, darkened with whatever makeup Amelia brought back from the human realm. She might think it was the wrong stuff, but hells, she looks stunning.

"No," I say. My voice is steady, even as my thoughts spiral away from me. "We need to get past this, Grace. You should be farther than—"

"I know," she snaps. "Trust me, I know, Sebastian. I know. Unfortunately for you, I'm an incompetent *idiot*. I can't do anything right. Not even a basic kid's spell. So you can forget about me breaking the curse. I'm too stupid—"

I capture her chin between my thumb and index finger. She startles, falling silent. I'm frozen too. I hadn't planned to touch her, and now, I can feel the heat of her skin, her blood, beneath my fingers.

She's so soft, so fragile. I could crush her bones with my bare hand, and it would be nauseatingly easy. It makes me want to push her away, out of sight, out of harm's way.

It makes me want to pull her closer.

That choice feels easier. A tiny tug, and she steps into me. I tilt her chin, forcing her eyes to mine.

"You are not stupid," I say. I glance at Cora, then back to Grace. Her eyes are blue, but not like flames. Like shallow water. "Who told you that?"

"I don't need to be told," Grace says. Her eyes remain firm on mine, but her mouth bobs as she searches for something to say. Finally, she wets her lips, and I can't help tracking the movement. Her lower lip glistens as she speaks. "I know who I am, Sebastian, or at least who I used to be. I was fun. I was happy. I was kind. I liked who I was, but I also knew who I wasn't. I wasn't smart. Or strong. Or interesting. Coming here might have changed my life, but it hasn't changed me."

I stare into her eyes, letting a brief silence fall over us. I'm grasping for something to say, for a way to give her confidence.

To make her understand she's more than she realizes. Far, far more.

But I'm not like Grace. I don't know how to be fun or happy or kind. I only know violence and anger and pain, and none of those are particularly useful right now.

"Oh this place will change you," Cora says. She's still in the kitchen, her voice high and mocking. "Just wait…"

I don't acknowledge the resident witch, and Grace doesn't either. She's staring at me as intensely as I am her. It's only the reminder of our audience that makes me move. I release Grace's chin and guide her into the hallway. Without telling Cora goodbye, I close the door between us.

Grace doesn't speak as we walk through the manor. She keeps her arms tight at her sides, and if she's bothered by my hand on her back, she doesn't show it. Her eyes have shifted into the color of ice.

We're several turns in the wrong direction before Grace glances at me.

"My cell is the other way. Where are we going?"

"The ballroom."

She instantly stiffens beneath my touch, and my stomach tightens in response. It's not that I regret the incident with the Nectoa, and yet, a part of me wants to erase it. For me. For her.

She's quiet as we walk, and though I grasp for something to say, I am too. Before long, the heavy oak doors come into view. Grace stops, turning to face me.

"So that's it then?" she asks. Her voice cracks. Her eyes water, making them bluer. Brighter. Prettier.

"I am not going to hurt you," I say.

Grace flinches, and the uneasiness in my gut flares through my entire body. Her expression says everything she doesn't voice out loud.

You've already hurt me.

Everything you do hurts me.

I hate you.

"I want to try something," I tell her. "I think it might help. I'll stay with you. I'll tell you exactly what we're doing, and if you want to stop, we will."

She stares at me, until I feel those bottomless blue eyes threaten to swallow me whole.

"I want to stop," she says. She's trembling from her body to her voice. "God, Sebastian. I want to *stop*."

I stare at her, waiting for my insides to settle. They don't. It only feels like they're growing, twisting out of control. I swallow, careful to keep my expression blank.

"We can't," I say. My voice is hoarse, unrecognizable. I can't remember the last time I've felt so...unsure. "If we don't find a way—"

"Then don't lie," she says, cutting me off. I wish she'd yell, but her words are nothing more than a whisper. Tears streak down her face. She wipes them away, almost aggressively, and smears makeup down her cheeks. "If you're going to force me, then do it. But don't you dare act like I have a choice."

I am being flayed alive. My nerves are being cut, rearranged, twisted into something I don't recognize.

For the first time since we've arrived here, I lower my hand from Grace's back. Something within me demands I touch her again, and it takes active concentration to defy it.

"Come," I say finally.

Grace watches as I turn, not for the ballroom, but back in the way of her quarters. She remains frozen, only for a moment, before trailing after me. We don't speak for the rest of our walk, and when she goes into her room, she shuts the door without looking at me.

THE NEXT MORNING, I lay alone on the stone table in the courtyard. The sun is a gentle touch of heat against my bare chest, nowhere near warm enough to keep me from shivering. My sweater and coat lie discarded in the grass, but I make no move to pull on either. Instead, I lie against the cold stone, embracing its unpleasant chill.

It's late winter or early spring, depending who you ask. Cora would say winter. Grace would undoubtedly say spring.

I close my eyes.

Over the years, I've tried to embrace this: the indescribable sensation of being both vampire and not. Cora's spell allows me to lie here in the sun without catching fire, but it changes me, too. Right now, my skin feels as soft, as vulnerable as Grace's always is. It's hard to imagine. Walking around with this paper-thin skin, breakable bones, demanding lungs.

How strange to need air all the time.

I open my eyes. From here, I can see a row of windows. Though I can't see through them, thanks to the sun's glare, I know I'm being watched. Within each sun-protected window, there is a room full of vampires. Hundreds of my followers, trapped and desperate to feel what I am now.

I only had to live four years without sunlight. Some from my inner circle went six, eight, or more. And all those fuckers locked in their rooms haven't felt it since the witches cursed us. Cora cast spells over the windows, protecting us from the sun's rays while allowing a bit of light. But still, many of my followers have lived their entire vampiric existences in darkness.

Grace doesn't understand.

If she did, I have to believe she'd be less difficult. She wouldn't be crying, pouting, complaining. She'd be fighting right alongside me to break this damned curse, once and for all.

I look away from the windows, choosing instead to glare at the sun. This violent light steals everything from my kind, and she's my only shot at stealing it back. Our power. Our invincibility. Our freedom.

Hundreds, thousands of vampires' fates, all held in the palms of one woman. One stubborn half-human, half-witch who can't be bothered to figure out her own magic.

"Master."

I jolt upright. The air catches in my throat, and I choke out a cough until I can breathe again. Oskar stands in the courtyard, leaned against my statue. I have no idea how long he's been standing there, watching me.

"Hells," I say. I press a palm to my chest, feeling the erratic beats of my pathetic, mortal heart.

"Apologies," Oskar says. His lips twitch though, in a way that suggests he isn't sorry at all.

"Did she go?" I ask. I study the stone building's architecture rather than meeting the watchful gaze of my oldest friend.

"Reluctantly, but yes," he says.

I'd tasked him with leaving Grace at Cora's this morning. I should have done it myself, and yet...I'd asked Oskar. I'd come here instead to lay out like a drying cloth.

"A bit cold for sunbathing, isn't it?" he asks.

I don't respond. I pull my sweater over my head, following it with my coat. It's the one Grace borrowed when I took her to buy clothes from Nicasi. It smells of her, and only her. In the sun, I can't scent her blood.

I brush past Oskar and head for the manor doors. Just when I think he's letting me off the hook, he clears his throat. And though I know better, I slow my steps. When I turn, he's already looking at me expectantly.

I give him nothing, leveling him with my flattest expression.

"Would you like to tell me?" he asks.

"No," I say, but I don't move. I watch him for several long seconds, waiting for him to press. When he doesn't, I swallow my pride like a vial of poison. "The Pruce witch isn't making progress."

"I know her name," Oskar says. His flat grey eyes spark with amusement. "As do you."

"She should have made progress by now," I say between my teeth. For whatever reason, my tongue feels thick in my mouth. It's difficult to speak, to explain the unpleasant sensation that's lingered since yesterday's interaction with Grace.

"Yes," he says. He tilts his head, studying me.

"She'll make the progress," I say. I sound defensive, even though it's the truth. "She just...it's taking longer than expected."

"What's plaguing you, Master?" Oskar asks. He steps closer, and I hate the look on his face. Almost paternal, as if he's going to comfort me.

"Nothing," I snap. "It's only a matter of time before she figures this out. And if she doesn't..."

My words trail. I'm not sure what I plan to say.

I'll threaten her.

I'll kill her.

I'll break the curse with her decaying blood.

I don't say anything at all. I turn on my heel, making it several steps before Oskar speaks again.

"If I may, sir," he says. His voice is firm, yet cautious. "Perhaps Grace's problem is not with her magic, but with her fear."

I look back, even though I don't want to. I'd much rather storm to my quarters to shower this sunlight off my skin.

"She doesn't trust us, and she's smart not to," he says. "She doesn't know what will become of her once she breaks the curse. I wouldn't be eager to help either, if I suspected I'd be killed in the end."

Oskar's words hang in the air, prickling against my skin worse than the sun's heat.

"Perhaps if she trusted you, she would be more willing to

help," he says. He bows his head as he speaks, as if he knows he's treading treacherous waters. "It is only a thought, Master."

"A good thought," I admit, even if the words sound painful. "I will consider it."

I turn to leave again, and this time, he doesn't stop me.

13

———

A RED BILLBOARD

SEBASTIAN

I can't remember the last time I've felt nervous. Anxious, sure. Irritable. Impatient. Even uncertain.

But nervous?

It's been decades.

I shove the strange sensation to the far reaches of my mind and knock on Grace's door. After leaving Oskar in the courtyard, I'd spent the day pacing this manor until there wasn't a square of flooring my boots hadn't touched. Eventually, I'd returned to the stone table, and I'd laid atop it, glaring at my statue and then the sun itself.

I hadn't meant to fall asleep. Even when my body was weak and mortal, sleep didn't come easily to me. I rarely did it, and when I did, it was never on accident. When I woke, dazed and confused and feeling inexplicably drowsy, I made a decision.

I knock again.

The door opens a crack, and Grace peeks out, eyeing me with suspicion.

"Can I come in?" I ask.

"What?"

"Can I come in?" I repeat. She only stares blankly. "To your quarters?"

"You mean my cell?" she asks. Despite the bite of her words, her voice remains a whisper.

"Whatever you wish to call it," I say. I clench my breath tight in my lungs, refusing to crack already.

I can be patient and kind and whatever else is required to make her trust me, to help her break the curse.

"Since when do you ask for permission?" She releases the door, letting it fall open. She stands in place, however, crossing her arms over her chest. It's meant to be an intimidating stance, but she's pushed her breasts together. Her cleavage teases me from her low-cut shirt.

"Grace," I say. It comes out more as an irritable huff than her name.

"If I say no?" she asks. She arches an eyebrow, dangling her question from yesterday in front of me.

It's a reminder that I've never given her a choice.

Hopefully, it's a way to prove I do not have to be her enemy.

"I will leave," I say. I tighten my fists. I don't point out that I'd let her say no yesterday too, that I'd walked her back to her quarters, even when I'd wanted to train.

I don't say anything as she considers it. I make myself wait, digging my nails into my palms, until she steps sharply to the side.

Behind me, Oskar lets out a quiet laugh. I'd almost forgotten he was there, standing guard outside her room.

"You're dismissed," I tell him without looking back. I walk past Grace into her room, shutting the door behind me.

With the hallway closed off, I study Grace's small room. The more I look at it, the more it does seem like a cell. A single bed. No other furniture. Not even the mirror she'd requested. The clothes we purchased from Nicasi are folded neatly on the floor, lining the far wall.

"I can get you a dresser," I say. I nod to the clothes. "Or hooks, if you'd prefer."

"You're being nice," she says, and it's a blatant accusation.

Though I've moved to the center of the room, my knees touching the foot of her twin-sized bed, Grace remains at the door. She has a hand against the stone wall, and she's watching me with narrowed eyes.

"It's a new manipulation tactic," I drawl. Rather than holding her gaze, I look over the room again. "I'll send new bedding, too."

"I think manipulation works better if you don't announce it," she says.

I ignore her. I carefully step between her clothes and the bed, moving the blankets until I find what I'm looking for. Beneath her pillow, the electronic I purchased for her sits, folded shut. Technically, it's one of many. Amelia goes to the human world once a week, charging multiple of these at once, so Grace never has to go without.

I drag it into the center of her bed and carefully open it.

It's flimsy with a black screen and dozens of buttons, each labeled with a letter. A computer, it's called. I've seen them while visiting the human world, but it's still difficult to understand. They write on these machines. They write and they read and they watch. Everything a person can do in life, humans prefer to do it here.

I push a button, and the screen lights. I blink at it. I'd had the human servant download her requested entertainment, and it looks like one of the films is onscreen now.

An image of a dark-haired woman and a blond man takes up the screen. Neither of them are moving.

"What are you doing?" Grace demands. She's still at the

door, arms still crossed, cleavage still teasing me. Despite her harsh tone, she's shifting, fingers digging into her elbows.

"What is this?" I return. I twist the computer until it's facing her. "What are you watching?"

"It's called *She's All That*." Grace steps toward me, still glaring but seemingly unable to resist. "Have you seen it?"

"I've never seen a movie, Grace," I say. "No one in the Echo has seen it. We don't have time to sit around, watching stupid shows."

I realize a moment too late that I've snapped at her. Apparently, I'm not only out of practice with kindness, I'm also bad at it. I open my mouth to apologize, but nothing comes out.

Luckily, Grace doesn't break down. She glares a little harder, but steps closer. She's on the opposite side of her bed now, separated from me by this flimsy mattress.

"You've never seen a movie," she repeats. "Well, no wonder you're all in such terrible moods all the time. Movies are *healing*."

I work my jaw. I want to say something kind, but everything coming to mind is either rude or fucking mean.

I click a random letter on the computer, hoping to start the movie. Instead, it makes a loud pinging noise at me.

"Here," she says. She swats my hand out of the way, clicking a button I hadn't noticed.

Before I can feel annoyed, the movie starts. I blink at the screen. The brunette woman and blond man are moving now, as if by magic. The colors and sounds are human-like, and yet, slightly different. Distorted, if only slightly. I squint at the moving picture, feeling an unexpected pinch of nausea.

"And this is a romantic comedy," I say. I barely register what the characters are doing. "These two are going to fuck?"

A startled laugh bursts from Grace's mouth. Despite everything else, it's a pleasant sound. I lean closer without deciding to.

"Well, these two aren't," she says. "Actually, nothing like that happens at all. It's not pornography. It's a 90s movie. A rom-com. You know, boy meets girl. Girl is unexpectedly charming. Boy falls head over heels. Boy inevitably messes everything up, but the girl loves him anyway."

I glance from her to the screen.

I'm trying to understand the nonsense that just came from her mouth when she pauses it again. Now, the screen is on a dark-haired guy, his features blurred, frozen in time.

"Why are you here, Sebastian?" she asks.

I'd had a simple plan when I knocked on Grace's door. I was going to offer a new agreement, something that benefited both of us, something that made her trust me and believe I wasn't going to decapitate her once I got what I wanted.

Now, I'm stuck staring at the screen, words caught in my throat.

"Sebastian," she says. Her voice is clipped, demanding.

"Who's this guy?" I ask, nodding to the dark-haired man on the screen. "He looks pissed. Is he about to break up the other two?"

Even with my eyes on the screen, I can feel Grace watching me. She lets out an irritated huff before dropping onto her bed. Folding her long legs beneath her, she rests the computer on her lap.

"*This* is Zach," she says. "He's the heart throb. The one we're rooting for. The dumb boy who loves Laney, and who Laney loves, even though she's obviously too good for him."

I swallow.

"Laney," Grace says, only to pause. She taps a few buttons, and the screen again changes. We're back to moments earlier, with the brunette girl standing with the blond man. She taps a finger to the screen. "Laney is the main girl. She's far too good for Zach, but we let it slide 'cause he's good-looking and it *was* the nineties."

"And that guy?" I ask, gesturing to the blond.

Grace studies me again, as if checking to see if I'm fucking with her. Then she's locked back on the screen.

"That's Dean," she says. "And honestly, he's just an asshole."

"Not the lover," I say stupidly, because I have no idea what else to add.

"Definitely not," Grace says. "I mean, he has *blond* hair. That's a red flag by itself."

"Red flag?"

"Yeah, a red flag. Like: *stop here! This guy is obviously a tool! Just look at his hair!*" Grace pitches her voice as she talks, and my lips twitch into a smile. "If a guy has blond hair, that basically means he's either going to be the bad guy or in the friendzone. Sometimes both."

"I have blond hair," I say.

Grace laughs so hard she snorts.

"Exactly," she says.

"So I'm a red flag?"

"Sebastian, you are a red billboard."

I frown, studying the blond man on the screen. He looks like any other human. Soft, slow, weak.

"Anyway," Grace says, dragging out the word. "Now that we've covered *She's All That*, are you going to tell me why you're here?"

I stare at the screen. Once again, words elude me. I know why I'm here, but it feels stupid. Grace doesn't hate me. It's clear from the way she's sitting that she trusts me well enough. If she didn't, she'd be cowering at the door. She'd be begging me not to kill her.

She knows I won't kill her.

Yet, a voice adds silently in my mind. *She knows you won't kill her yet.*

I swallow.

"Play it," I say. I nod to the screen.

"The movie?" she asks. Her blonde eyebrows stretch toward her hairline. "You want to watch it?"

"I want to understand," I say, and I guess that's partially true. I do want to understand. Only I want to understand Grace, not her movie. I want to know her, to understand how she thinks and feels.

If I can find a way into her mind, maybe I can speed up her progress. Maybe we can break the curse long before word gets out that she's here, that she exists.

"All right," she says slowly. She drags her finger across the computer, and the images flash across the screen, too fast to make them out.

"Slower," I command.

"Relax," Grace says with a laugh. "I'm just starting it over. It won't make sense otherwise."

Another click of a button, and the movie starts. Grace shifts, as if making room for me on her bed. I stare at the empty space, long enough that she realizes what she's done.

"Actually, you can stand," she says.

"Yes," I agree. My voice is strained, but I doubt she can tell. I doubt she knows I'm imagining crawling into that bed, biting into her flesh and consuming her every last drop.

She shifts back into the center, and we watch the entire movie like this. With her lying on the bed, making occasional comments—not to me, but to the characters on the screen, as if they can hear her. And me, standing to the side, perfectly still.

I'm watching her more than I am the screen.

By the time it's over, she's yawning and I realize I held my breath for the duration of the entire movie. Now that it's over, I steal a tiny breath. Her lavender and blood perfume burns my throat.

Hells, I want to fuck her. Forget drinking her blood. She's too beautiful like this, laid back in bed, beaded nipples visible through her shirt. It's a temptation I'm not sure why I'm fighting. If there's even a chance she'd let me...

Blonds are the bad guys or in the friendzone.

"Is that guy going to bring me dinner?" she asks, jolting me from my thoughts. "I'm getting hungry."

So am I, I realize. Not hungry, exactly, but less than over-stuffed. It's dangerous, considering we're confined together.

"I'll call for him," I say. I cross the room, only pausing once I've reached the door.

I rattle my brain, desperate for some meaningful parting words. Instead, my mind remains blank, and I eventually leave her, lying on her bed and wishing she'd ask me to stay.

14

———

DON'T EVEN THINK ABOUT IT

GRACE

Sebastian looks good on his knees.

It's not the most practical thought when I'm supposed to be concentrating. Cora has us stationed in the middle of the auditorium, a large room, but still a fraction the size of the ballroom. Sebastian is on his knees, and I stand before him, palms aimed at his shoulders.

He looks stunning. Dark blond hair tousled, mussed from where he's run his hand through it too many times. Sharp jawline highlighted by the sunlight pooling through the window. Green eyes turned up at me, gazing like he's at my mercy.

He's not.

It's only an illusion.

I stretch my fingers, flaying my hands as wide as they'll go. Cora said it can help distribute the magic. I'm not convinced, and not only because I've failed every single exercise we've attempted today.

"All right, center yourself," Cora coaches from the wall. She's standing far enough away that when I look down, it's only Sebastian I see, as if we are alone.

My thoughts try to run from me. They've been doing that often, especially in the days since he watched a movie with me. He's been different since that day, and my mind keeps forgetting it's not reality.

I might be stupid, but I'm not a fool. I know when I'm being played, and Sebastian the Vampire King is playing me. He's trying to be buddy-buddy so I let my guard down and erupt with magical powers—or whatever the hell is supposed to happen. He, like Cora and Oskar and everyone else, thinks my magic comes down to mental energy.

I haven't admitted this out loud yet, but I'm still questioning whether I'm the person they think I am. What if Walter Pruce wasn't actually my father? What if I'm just a half-witch he happened to discover on the East coast during his travels? And what if—

"Focus, Grace!"

I try. I really do. It's just hard when Sebastian is gazing up at me, looking far more man than he does vampire. He's unjustly good-looking. He might be faking being a decent person, but there's nothing fake about how good he looks right now.

I can imagine this scene unraveling in a completely different way. Instead of keeping him on his knees with magic, I do it with charm alone. I rest my foot on his shoulder, let him kiss my inner thigh, all the way up to my center. My core clenches just at the thought of his tongue meeting my clit.

I wonder if he's good at it.

He *must* be. He's a vampire, damn it. He's probably had a hundred years of practice.

Then again, vampires tend to move in hyperspeed, and maybe sex is no different. He'd come before I realized we'd even started.

"On the count of three," Cora says. Her voice breaks through my spiraling thoughts, but it's far too late.

The goal of this exercise is to keep Sebastian on his knees. It's supposedly easier than knocking him down, but so far, I've yet to restrain him. And now that my mind has drifted, I'm royally screwed. I'm definitely not centered, but I can't let them know that. I glare at my hands, like I'm deep in concentration, furrowing my brows for full effect.

"One," she says. Her voice echoes to the high-arched ceilings. "Two. Three!"

My magic is nothing but a buzz in my fingertips. It's the most pathetic attempt I've had out of the ten we've done this hour. Sebastian rises to his feet as if I haven't touched him, and I'm honestly not sure I have.

I drop my hands, gasping for breath. My magic barely made an appearance, and yet, I'm exhausted. My clothes are damp with sweat, and there are droplets—actual *droplets*—of moisture on my forehead. Thank god I opted not to wear makeup, otherwise it'd be all over my face.

"Pathetic!" Cora screams. "That was the worst one yet."

"I know," I say. It comes out as a groan. "It's not working."

"That's because you're not trying," she snaps. She pushes from the wall and starts toward us, only to stop when Sebastian lifts a hand.

He closes the distance between us, studying my face.

"You were distracted," he says.

"I'm *exhausted*," I correct.

"Distracted," he repeats. Then, his mouth slants in a devious smirk. He lifts an eyebrow in challenge. "What were you thinking about Grace?"

"The same thing I've been thinking about since we got here," I say adamantly, but my heart races all the same. I don't think vampires can read minds. No, they can't. I would have realized by now. I swallow, clenching my teeth. "I'm trying to keep your ass on the floor, but it's not working."

"Careful, Gracie," Cora calls out. "Master will rip your pretty little head off if you talk like that."

"I won't. And you won't speak another word of it," Sebastian says. He turns toward Cora, posture stiff. I wait for him to threaten *her* head, just as he did to Beatrice, but he only says, "You're dismissed, Cora. We'll meet again tomorrow."

Her large dark eyes bounce from Sebastian, to me, then back to Sebastian. Her lips part, as if to say something, only for her to decide better. She bows her head and exits the room without another word.

"It doesn't bother me," I tell him once she's gone. When Sebastian's eyes meet mine, I elaborate. "The threats. I know you guys can't kill me yet."

"We are not going to kill you. Ever."

The intensity of his voice flips my stomach, and I try desperately to stay in reality. He's playing me. I'm being played. It's not true.

"And it does bother you. Your heart raced when she said it," he says. He smiles again, giving me an almost coy look. "I'm quite observant, you see. I notice when things change. Sights. Sounds. *Smells*."

"What are you saying?" I ask. It's the most I can say, because if he's implying what I think he is, I'm going to throw myself off the nearest cliff.

Another grin.

"Your heart is racing again," he says. He steps closer, hands tucked into his pockets. He's the picture of nonchalance. With a teasing wink, he adds, "I wonder why."

"Sebastian," I say, unable to keep the horror from my voice.

"You smell fucking perfect," he says. The amusement drains from his face, replaced with something unreadable. "Truly, Grace. You have no idea how much I'd like to spread you across this floor and taste where you're yearning for me."

Anguish, I decide. That's a look of anguish on his face, as if he's disgusted by me, the fact I'm wet for him, the fact he'd like to taste it.

"Who says it's for you?" I snap.

"Fair enough." His jaw muscle ticks, eyes hardening as he looks at me. "I like to imagine it anyway."

"I'm sure you do," I say. My face must be bright red, and I blink to keep the tears from falling.

I'm pathetic. The fact I can even get turned on by someone like him is humiliating enough, but now he's bringing it up? Shoving it in my face, ensuring I know he sees right through me?"

"Grace," he says, just as I choke through a sob. "Hells, I wasn't—"

"Of course you were," I snap. "This must be so entertaining for you! Such a good ego boost, as if you need one. You're holding me prisoner, locked up and kept while I'm useful. I know you're going to kill me, Sebastian. I should hate you. I *do* hate you, and yet, here I am, getting wet just looking at you. Makes you feel good, doesn't it? Doesn't it!"

I'm screaming by the end. I don't realize it until I've stopped and a deafening silence surrounds us. My throat burns as tears stream down my face.

Oh god, as if my nonexistent magic wasn't enough reason for him to kill me.

Sebastian's jaw is still clenched, the muscle there twitching as he steps closer. Both hands find my face, thumbs resting on my cheekbones. I might be imagining it, but it almost feels like his hands are shaking.

"No," he whispers finally. "No, it doesn't make me feel good."

I don't say anything. I'm still heaving, struggling to get my breath under control.

"I don't like this, Grace," he says. "I don't like that I *need* you to break this curse. I don't like needing anyone, and I hate that it's you. I hate that you're nice and sweet and pretty, and that I'm crumbling you bit by bit, day by day. I *hate* it.

"But I do need you," he whispers. "I need you, and I want you, and it fucks with my head. I wasn't mocking you for getting turned on. I *liked* it. I wanted you to invite me to do exactly as I offered."

I try to swallow. It doesn't work. My throat is too dry. I try to remember the last time I had water, if only to keep myself from looking at his lips.

Wasn't I wondering what it would be like? Would it be so terrible to know?

"But I can't touch you," he whispers. He releases my face and steps back. "Because I need you, and you...you need to focus."

He walks to the far wall, only pausing once he's nearly reached the door. He holds an open palm toward me in invitation.

"Let's call it a day," he says finally. Then, almost as an afterthought, he adds, "For the record, I am not going to kill you, Grace. If we work together, we'll break the curse. After that, I'll help you go wherever you want. Back to the human world. Over to the witches. Whatever you want."

I stand frozen, and he gestures again.

"Come," he says, clearing his throat. He runs a hand through his hair, looking at the exit instead of me. "We'll pretend it never happened."

Maybe he will, but something tells me I won't be able to. Every time we do this stupid exercise, I'll be thinking about it. About him.

It's going better. Three days after getting turned on by Sebastian and him freaking *smelling* it, our training is going better. I don't know if I believe his vow not to kill me. Actually, scratch that, I *definitely* don't believe his vow. I think he'll let me live as long as it's convenient. If it's anything more than a slight nuisance, I assume the promise won't stand.

With these people, all it takes is a split second of anger, of impulse, and someone is dead.

"One more time?" Cora asks.

She's back at her place against the wall, scrutinizing my every move. We've done this for over an hour, and though I'm covered in sweat and beyond exhausted, I'm not doing a terrible job. I can only keep Sebastian down for two seconds. Five seconds on the good rounds. It's probably nothing worth bragging about, but I'm grinning anyway.

It's not only progress, but consistent progress. Any other time I've showcased magic, it's been erratic, impossible to control. Those times didn't feel earned, as if I hadn't been involved at all. This is different. I feel the magic zipping beneath my skin, like tiny electrodes shocking my muscles.

"Hello?" Cora calls. She shoves from the wall, face already twisted in annoyance. "Should we do one more, Master?"

I look at Sebastian, surprised to find him watching me. He raises an expectant eyebrow, as if to say, *what do you think*?

My vision blurs and I have to blink to keep from doing something mortifying like cry. I manage a nod.

"One more," Sebastian confirms. He doesn't look back at Cora as he lowers to his knees. "We'll make it a good one."

"Easy for you to say." I don't fight the teasing smile as I get back into position. Arms raised, breath steady. "I'm doing all the work."

"Just think about how much you hate me," he whispers.

"I always am," I say. It's ridiculous how my heart pulses, how my entire body warms at the inside joke.

Do not get turned on, Grace. Don't even think about it.

I breathe deeply and close my eyes. It's easier to focus when I'm not looking at him. With my eyes closed, this moment is mine alone. Mine and the magic sparking beneath my skin.

"One," Cora counts. It's what she does every time, and part of me feels like this would be easier if she'd just stop talking. Or better yet, leave. "Two. Three!"

I cast. At least, that's what Cora would call it. I'm not entirely sure how I know I'm doing it. Even once I open my eyes, it doesn't *look* like anything is happening. It's not nearly as epic as it is in movies. There's no colorful mist in the air, and there's definitely nothing like what I saw in *Harry Potter*. Nothing has changed at all, except Sebastian.

I can see the bewilderment on his face, the way his eyebrows tighten as he attempts to stand. Even the muscles beneath his shirt shift as he tries to move. I don't know how long I hold him, only that I feel ready to pass out by the time I lose my grasp.

The buzz of magic evaporates from my fingers, popping like an overfilled balloon. The moment it disappears, I collapse forward, catching my hands on my knees. I take deep, ugly breaths, blinking hard to keep the room from spinning. It takes longer than usual for my body to stabilize.

"Sorry," I finally gasp. I feel like I'm going to puke. My stomach roils as I force myself to stand. "I think I'm tired."

When I look up, both Sebastian and Cora stand before me. She's whispering something in his ear, and he's grinning at me.

"I have a few ideas," Cora says. She plants her hands on her hips, stepping closer. She's short enough she has to tip her chin to look at me. "You do much better with your eyes closed. As soon as they're open, you fall apart. You get distracted too easily, like a fucking rabbit. It's fine though. I'll come up with some exercises to strengthen your concentration."

I'm nodding along, doing my best to absorb everything Cora says. I'm still not convinced she's the best teacher, but seeing as she's my only option, I need to figure out how to learn from her. If I want to survive this place, I'm going to need magic to get out. Maybe by breaking the curse. Maybe by breaking through my cell wall and running for my life.

"I'm going to see about an eggroot tea," Cora continues. "It might be just what we need—"

"You're dismissed," Sebastian interrupts.

I shift my attention from Cora to the man behind her. His mouth is a flat line, but his eyes crinkle, as if it's taking effort not to smile. He's pleased, I realize. I've known him long enough to recognize his approval, and I want to clutch the feeling to my chest.

He's pleased.

Grace Renolds lives to see another day in the vampire house.

"You're welcome," Cora says, rolling her eyes. She doesn't address me as she leaves. Her clicking footsteps sound across the room, eventually disappearing through the doorway and into the hall.

"That was over a minute," he says as soon as she's gone. His voice is low, almost seductive—or maybe that's my body's wishful thinking. "Sixty seconds, Grace."

"I'm sweating," is my only response. As much as I've craved improvement, and approval, I don't know what to do now that I have it.

"Me too," he says. His smile finally breaks through. "Which is saying something, since you did all the work."

"Hating you really *does* help," I say.

"Come." He jerks his chin toward the exit and I fall into step beside him.

It feels less threatening than it should, the two of us walking together. We pass more than one set of vampires, and I instinctively shift closer to Sebastian. He does the same, his large hand a constant presence on my lower back.

When we reach my room, I find myself desperate for him to stay. I can feel it, the question begging to be asked, hanging dangerously in my chest. I *want* him to stay, and that's exactly why I don't invite him in.

15

GIVE ME A LITTLE CREDIT

SEBASTIAN

"It's about time you took me on a field trip," Grace declares as we near the courtyard entrance. Her blonde hair is loose at her shoulders, and despite her simple outfit of a white tank top and brown shorts, she looks stunning. She's too good looking. Too tempting. Too enticing, even when she's not making sense.

"A field *what*?" I ask.

"Oh right, I forgot," she says, voice falling flat. "I'm in the land of un-fun, where people kill each other and no one goes on fun school adventures."

I don't fight the smile that tugs my lips.

"A field trip, *Sebastian*, is something normal people do to make learning fun," she says. "Like, in fifth grade, my class went to the state capitol to learn about politics. Then, in ninth grade, we did an overnight camp to learn about the environment or biology or something like that."

"Sounds like you retained a lot."

"Oh shush. It was *fun*," Grace says, grinning. "You know you're just jealous of the human experience."

I am most certainly not, but I can't bring myself to say it. I'm too busy enjoying her. The way she rolls her eyes. The lightness of her steps. Things are getting better, I decide. After months of tension, we're *finally* getting past her unwavering hatred of me.

I pause as we reach the courtyard entrance. Stepping in front of Grace, I peer into the quiet yard. My followers sit around the stone table, and even from here, I can tell they're sated. I'd instructed they over-feed before this meeting, and it's clear they listened. Theo looks full to the point of nausea. Better than even the smallest amount of hunger.

"They've all fed," I inform Grace, turning toward her. "If you feel threatened though, tell me."

"Okay," she says, voice soft. Her relaxed expression from moments ago is gone. Now, there is only uncertainty and terror as she looks over the inner circle. "You haven't told me what we're doing. Is this...are we breaking the curse *now*?"

"No," I say, startled. "Of course not. It's not time yet."

"Okay," she says again. Her lip trembles as she speaks. "When the time *does* come, can you just...will you—"

"I will tell you," I say. "I promise."

I touch her chin without thinking, without considering. It's meant to be a comforting gesture, but I should know better. Grace recoils, as if my touch physically hurts. I drop my hand, forcing my eyes back to the courtyard. After an uncomfortable beat of silence, I clear my throat.

"Come," I say.

I lead her across the cobblestone, and past my statue, thankful when she doesn't comment on it. As we approach the table, my inner circle finishes their conversations. Oskar and Theo abandon a piece of parchment between them. Amelia brushes off Milas's final attempt at flirting. Beatrice stares at me, eyes flitting to my hand on Grace's back. Luckily, she doesn't glower like I expect.

"We will make this brief," I say.

I stop at the head of the table, opposite Oskar. Milas, Amelia, Theo, and Beatrice fill the seats on either side.

"Glad to see you're all fed," I continue. "Keep your movements slow and steady. Anyone makes a move for her, I'll kill you. Understood?"

"Yes, Master," they echo.

"It won't be a problem," Beatrice says. She sits near Oskar, her eyes flitting between me and Grace. Her expression is carefully blank as she nods at me. "I vow it, Master."

"Good," I say. I sit and gesture for Grace to do the same. Her leg bounces hard enough to shake her chair, and though my fingers itch to comfort her, I resist. "Everyone, this is Grace. Last descendant. Curse breaker."

Whether she realizes it or not, Grace lifts her chin and straightens her posture. It takes all my effort not to smile.

"Grace, this is my innermost circle," I continue. Pointing at each, I quickly run through their roles. "Oskar manages everything within the manor. Milas scouts throughout the Echo for resources and contacts. Amelia works as our vampiric representative in the Night Realm and the Echo at large. Beatrice trains the military. Theo, our newest member, helps where needed. Once we break the curse, he'll eventually hold a military position, as well."

Grace nods along, body stiff, but eyes alert. I force myself not to focus on her and instead address my followers.

"We're a long way from breaking the curse," I say. "Many uncertainties remain, particularly where Grace is concerned. For now, it's important we ensure we are ready, the moment the curse falls."

I rummage a scrap of parchment from my coat pocket. Cora's swirled handwriting covers both sides, and I pass it to Milas.

"Cora has finished her list of needed ingredients," I say as he reviews it. "Have it all collected by the end of next week."

"Yes, Master," he says, dipping his head.

I return the nod and continue the meeting, touching on only the most pressing of matters. Grace watches with intense curiosity, eyebrows scrunching as we switch from topic to topic. I can almost imagine the questions she's stacking within her mind. I'm sure I'll hear every one of them before the day is through.

When Grace stiffens beside me, it takes me a moment to figure out why. Oskar's partway through his list of projects, but he's moved on from simply housekeeping needs.

"At least three," he's saying. "Five would be better though. We could open an additional feeding in the early morning. As it is, we're too crowded during the seven o'clock..."

I'm barely listening to Oskar. I'm too focused on the way Grace breathes, the way her heart thrums erratically in her chest. I keep my eyes focused on my oldest follower, but my attention belongs wholly to her.

Her soft hand brushes against mine. At first, I assume it's a mistake. Then, her fingers touch mine again, and this time, she closes her hand over my knuckles. She squeezes, hard enough it would hurt me, were I human. When I look over, I can't decide if she's trying not to cry or scream.

I twist my wrist, trying to take her palm in mine. I'm not sure why. I've never held hands with a woman, not even for basic comfort.

It doesn't matter. The moment our palms touch, Grace's slips away. She moves both hands to the table and refuses to meet my gaze for the rest of the meeting.

ONCE THE MEETING is over and we're alone in the sunlit courtyard, I turn to Grace. She's purposefully avoiding my gaze. She studies my statue, mouth curving downward, disgusted by the stone version of me. I'm disgusted by him too. It's his fault we ended up here, cursed by the witches, damned to eternal darkness.

"Grace," I say softly.

"I grabbed your hand," she says. She speaks each word like a curse, like she's committed an unthinkable, unforgivable crime.

"Yes," I say. I don't fight my smile. None of the others are around to see it anyway. "You did."

"I shouldn't have," she says. She's still looking at the damn statue.

"I didn't mind." It's more honest than I should be, but Grace only scoffs.

"*I* minded," she snaps. "I'm here because of you. You stole me from my life. You're keeping me here, and no matter what you say, I already know...You're going to use me just like you use those bloodletters. Strip me naked and cut my flesh, drink from me until there's nothing left."

"No one is going to touch you, Grace," I say. My voice is a rough growl. "I know I can't give you what you want. I can't let you go. But I *swear*, I am not going to kill you. All right? Once this is over, you're free. I promise."

A lone tear streaks down her cheek. We came here immediately after she showered. She's not wearing makeup, and her exhaustion shines without it.

"What do you want me to do?" I ask. There's an unpleasant burning sensation in my chest. I can't explain it. It's not because I feel *bad*. I don't feel bad. I'm not sure I have in my centuries of existence.

"I don't know," she says. She sounds as tired as I feel. She's still avoiding my gaze as she rises, but I catch a glimpse of her eyes. Pale blue, like ice, like the frigid depths of winter.

She wordlessly crosses the courtyard. I'm a step behind her, hands in my pockets. It's still early, so most of the house is tucked away in their rooms. Vampires don't need sleep, but ever since the curse, many of them do. They live their lives during the night hours, only to sleep once the sun rises.

We easily maneuver through the hallways, and I let Grace lead most of the way. It is only when we near Cora's wing that I press a hand to her lower back. She stops, looking over her shoulder at me.

Through the window, the sun shines on her blonde hair, making it almost white. Stunningly, stupidly beautiful.

"What?" she asks. Molten, fire-dipped blue stares at me, daring me to pick a fight. Inexplicably, I'm tempted. I prefer this, this *anger*, over the withdrawn, absent hue.

"Do you want to see?" I ask.

She raises an eyebrow.

"The bloodletters," I clarify. I work my jaw, questioning my own sanity, but pressing forward anyway. "If you want, I'll show you them. They're not stripped naked. They're not devoured alive. It's a transaction. Controlled. Safe. Efficient. They're all paid, all here by their own volition."

She swallows, and her gaze drifts toward the nearest windows. I want to ask what she's thinking. Is she pretending she's somewhere far from this horrible place, far from *me*?

"We have to feed," I tell her, as if she doesn't know this. I'm sure she can hear the desperate, almost frantic tone in my voice, so I squash it. Guilt, shame, is for the weak. I am many things, but I am not weak. "We need blood or we'll die. But we're not monsters."

Not anymore, I add silently. *Not since the witches stole that option.*

"Okay," she says.

I let out a sharp breath. This is good—it's what I wanted, after all. And still, the stupidity of it catches up to me, only moments behind the relief.

"You stay by my side," I say once we start moving.

We're headed for the southeastern wing. A good number of followers reside on the second and third floor, but the main level is reserved for feeding. At this hour, it should be quiet. Bellies should be full, bloodletters should be packing up for the day.

"If it's too much, you tell me," I say. My hand finds the small of her back, even as my eyes study our surroundings. "If the sight of blood makes you pass out, tell me now."

"Give me a little credit," she says, scoffing. She falls quiet after that though, fingers fussing with her shorts as we arrive at a single wooden door. It's small, unassuming to anyone who doesn't reside here. Any vampire would know what's on the other side though, regardless of whether they've visited.

I take a final breath, holding the air in my chest. I've been drinking far too much blood for the smell to trigger me, but I'm not taking chances with Grace at my side. I tighten my hand, clenching the loose fabric of her shirt in my fist. A sliver of her skin brushes my finger, and a jolt of electricity zips through me.

Focus.

"Only a glimpse," I tell her. "It's too dangerous to linger. Understood?"

She nods, face solemn, terrified.

"I won't let anyone touch you," I say.

I don't wait for her response. I push the door, letting it fall open on its own accord. Though Grace attempts to walk inside, I keep us in the doorway, my hand a tight fist against her back.

"From here," I whisper.

She looks at me. I wait for an eye roll or a glare, but only get another nod. She leans forward, craning her neck to study the room.

It's one of the largest spaces in the manor, second only to the ballroom, and it's nearly as bare. The walls are covered in dull red paneling, and the windows are painted black, blocking even reminders of the sun. Despite the grand space, there are only two lights, casting an eerie glow through the entire room. It's difficult to see much more than the rows of identical tables and the people filling their seats.

To a passerby, it might look like dozens of couples on dates, facing each other, lips pressed to wrist or throat or chest, as if stealing kisses. Few mouths are smeared with blood.

Unlike a hunt in the natural world, feeding here is subdued. Boring.

"Bloodletters are paid a standard wage for each feeding," I tell Grace. I don't know when I stepped closer, but her back is now against my chest. The hand that once gripped her shirt rests on her hip. Surprisingly, she doesn't pull away. Instead, she leans against me as I speak. "Most come weekly, some monthly, few daily. They allow us to feed, and in exchange, we don't shred their veins or take more than they can handle."

My lips brush against Grace's ear, and I force myself to pull back. Thirty seconds against her, and I'm already pushing my limits. I slide my hand to its usual place on her back.

"Do you hate it?" she asks.

I still at the question, replaying it in my mind as if I might have misheard her.

"Do you hate feeding like this?" she asks. She turns, glossy eyes looking up at me. "Do you wish you could devour them? Rip them—"

"We are vampires," I interrupt. "Of course, we prefer to devour them. We crave the hunt. We're beasts, Grace."

She whips around, striding away from the room. I swing the

door shut, and blissfully, the sound of feeding fades. Grace doesn't slow her steps, even once I've caught up to her.

"You can't outpace me. You realize that, right?" I ask.

"I don't want to look at you," she says, almost groaning the words. "You make me *sick*, Sebastian."

I grip her shirt, forcing her to stop. To look at me.

"I *know*," I say through my teeth. "I understand, Grace, but I am not going to apologize for what I am. We are all beasts here. We love the hunt, the kill, the torture. I didn't show you that to prove we weren't monsters."

"There was a reason you showed me that?" she asks. Her eyes are glistening, so blue they barely look real. She's going to cry, I realize.

"Yes," I say. I can't keep the exasperation from my voice. I step closer, forcing myself not to flinch when she steps away in response. "I wanted to show you that, while we may be beasts, we can control ourselves. We can suppress our urges. I've been doing it with you for months, Grace."

"I'm supposed to be impressed that you haven't drank my blood?" she asks. Her voice hitches, and blood rushes to her face. "You're asking me to *thank* you?"

"Hells, Grace!" I shout. "I'm not asking you to do a damned thing, and you know it. I'm trying to explain—"

"You don't need to explain," she hisses. She shoves out of my hold, harder than necessary.

She stumbles, crashing against the wall. As she turns to glare at me, she steadies herself with a hanging portrait. It's a painting of a long-dead vampire, whose name I don't even know. The frame is simple and black—and apparently—*sharp*.

Grace grabs the painting, her soft palm meeting that hard edge of the frame. And that's all it takes.

I smell blood before it even bursts through her skin.

For a fraction of a second, I stare at her palm, at the rush of scarlet spreading beneath her fingers. I've stopped breathing, but I swear, it's already in my nose, my lungs, my soul.

"Sebas—"

I don't give her the chance to finish. I slam against her, harder than I mean to. There's no time to explain. I don't try to stop the bleeding, or even to cover it. Instead, I throw Grace over my shoulder and run as if my life depends on it.

Because it does—*all* our lives do.

16

DON'T LET THEM MOVE
GRACE

Sebastian is moving faster than he ever has with me in his arms. It's nauseating, the way the world spins, colors blurred and noises distorted. I'd expected him to wrap my hand, to say something irritable. Instead, he'd thrown me over his shoulder and run without uttering a single word.

I press my face against Sebastian's back, bloodied hand gripping the crisp white of his long-sleeved shirt. It's too disorienting to watch the space around us, and I study the way my blood spreads over his clothes. I can't remember a time I've bled like this.

"No!" Sebastian screams, slamming to a stop. If it weren't for his grip over my legs, I would've flown right off his shoulder. His voice is unrecognizable, more of a roar than anything else. "Don't you fucking—"

He doesn't get the chance to finish his command. Something slams against his chest—and my legs. Sebastian doesn't move, but I do. I fling to the hardwood floor, landing hard on my hands and knees.

By the time I rotate onto my butt, too much has happened for me to comprehend. All I know is a vampire lies across from me, his head separated from his body. The vampire's eyes are bloodshot, the skin around his mouth and eyes pale, almost translucent. Even in death, they're staring at me, as if desperate for a taste.

Sebastian stands over the man, his mouth and throat coated in dark blood.

Dead. Sebastian just killed that guy, and it was undoubtedly my fault.

"I'm sorry—" I start, but Sebastian doesn't let me finish the thought.

I'm already back in his arms, and we're moving again. This time, he holds me bridal style, between his arms, as we sprint once more. I realize I still don't know where we are. I should have looked, should have paid better attention.

"I'll kill you!" Sebastian screams, pausing again. "Another fucking step, and you're all dead."

I tense, curling myself tighter against his shoulder. *All*?

"Master," a voice says. Feminine, light, but unfamiliar. "Please—"

"Go!" he roars.

I bury my face into his shirt and cover my face with my hand. The blood smears over my cheek, warming my skin, taunting me.

Do something, I beg myself. *Don't just sit here, waiting to die.*

I don't know how many vampires we were originally up against, only that we are far outnumbered now. Three in front of us, blocking the way toward my cell. Behind us, there are at least two more. Sebastian shifts his stance, keeping both within our frame of sight.

"Don't make me," is Sebastian's final warning.

Somehow, even before a single one has moved, I know his words are in vain.

I focus on the three in front of us. A pale woman with

brunette hair, twisted in ringlets. A dark-skinned woman with braids. A man with a buzz cut and a dramatically broken nose. As I study them, I channel my magic to my palms.

The brunette woman moves first. I twist in her direction, throwing my hands, palms out. I even close my eyes, channeling Cora's advice.

It doesn't stop her.

That's Sebastian, who somehow holds me with one hand and catches her neck with the other. I open my eyes just in time to see his teeth sink into her throat. Her blood splatters across my face, mixing with my own.

"Put me down," I tell him. "I can help!"

I expect him to resist, to pull me closer.

Instead, he drops me immediately. I'm shaking hard enough my knees fail, and I stumble onto all fours. Sebastian stands in front of me, putting me between him and the wall.

The woman's lifeless body would be enough to keep any sane person from attacking, but the remaining vampires don't hesitate. They charge forward, all at once now, eyes wild and locked on me.

My heart beats painfully against my ribs. It feels as though I'm being punched from the inside out. I don't let myself dwell on the fear or the pain or anything beyond keeping myself alive.

To their knees, I tell myself. *Drop them to their knees, and don't let them move.*

Sebastian is overtaken. I don't look at him, only at the ferocious vampires clinging to his arms and body. The dark-skinned woman is clawing his chest and throat. Her eyes are on me, so distant I'm not sure she's fully aware of what she's doing.

I start with her. I focus on those dead, distant eyes before closing my own. Magic pulses beneath my skin. I can feel it—not just its presence, but its shape, as if my adrenaline has sharpened it into something tangible.

My arms shake as I push the magic toward the woman. She releases Sebastian, letting out an animalistic grunt as she slams to her knees. Her brow scrunches, and a pathetic wail pulls at her lips.

It takes everything, every ounce of concentration, every strained breath, to keep her on her knees. She's bowed before Sebastian's feet, as if praying to his altar. And with one hand still aimed at her, I do the same to the man with a buzzcut. He's harder to contain, especially one-handed.

He is a rabid dog, ripping against my magic like it's his chain.

Blood splatters.

Another man's head hits the floor, and seconds later, it's joined by yet another. They must be the two from behind us. I don't recognize their faces, but their eyes are as haunted, as empty as the two still alive.

"Fuck," Sebastian growls. "Good job, Grace."

"What are you going to do with them?"

The man is dead before I finish the question.

"Master—"

The woman is dead before she finishes hers.

We're surrounded by mangled, decapitated corpses. Five of them. Six if you count the one from minutes ago.

Six lives, vampire or not, are gone because of *me*.

"I'm sorry," I say again. Back to trembling, cowering, even though I know it wasn't my fault, not really.

"Come, little witch," he says.

I'm back in his arms, eyes closed, only opening them when I hear Oskar's voice.

"Hells!" he shouts. "What happened?"

"Get Cora!" is Sebastian's only response.

He hauls us into my cell. Slams the door. Falls back against it. I'm still in his arms, but I don't try to get down at first, and he doesn't loosen his hold.

"Sebastian," I whisper finally.

My feet hit the floor, but his hand lingers around my side, fingers brushing the sliver of skin between my shirt and shorts.

Maybe it's the adrenaline.

Maybe it's the near-death experience.

Maybe it's the stricken look on Sebastian's face, like he was terrified for *me*.

It's stupid, to believe it had anything to do with me. I know what I am to him: a device. A weapon. A curse breaker.

None of that keeps me from grabbing his collar. From pressing my bloodied hand to his hair, pulling his mouth against mine.

There's a momentary pause, when Sebastian's lips are motionless, hard. Just as I'm about to pull away, he breaks.

He surges forward, slamming me against the wall. It is only his hand that keeps my head from hitting stone. He shifts, cupping my face with both hands, tipping my chin the way he wants. He kisses me like he's been waiting his whole life for this one moment.

I may have started this kiss, but there's no doubt who's in control now.

Sebastian growls—literally, freaking growls—into my mouth. His tongue dominates mine. Exploring. Tasting. Claiming. All the while, he's pressing closer, one hand wandering down my side, skimming over my breast, until it reaches my hip. His hand lingers there, tracing the exposed skin.

A pathetic moan vibrates my lips, and I'm too desperate to feel embarrassed. Sebastian grunts in response and shoves his thigh roughly between my legs. It's instinctual, unavoidable, the way my hips seek his. I'm shamelessly grinding against his leg, moaning and trembling, like I've never been touched before.

I let out another breathy moan, and Sebastian's mouth trails from mine to my cheek, to my jaw.

I lean into him, only for him to slam me back against the wall. This time he doesn't catch my head. I open my eyes, stunned, expecting to see a mocking grin, for him to taunt me and my pathetic desperation.

Instead, I am alone. He's gone, and I am alone, trapped with my racing thoughts and a bleeding palm. I stare at the place he stood only moments ago, and finally, the realization of what I've done crashes into me. Embarrassment and shame flood through me, chilling every inch of my body and settling into the deepest corners of my heart.

17

WE'VE BOTH DONE THINGS

SEBASTIAN

uck. Stupid. So stupid.

I pace my quarters and force myself to wait. It's an hour, or close to it, before Cora finally arrives. Her eyes widen as she takes in my appearance. I haven't changed, so I'm still filthy. My damp clothes stick to me, and my face itches with dried blood. John's. Luther's. Quincy's. Clyde's. Ruth's. Nat's. All people I had sworn to protect, to guide, to lead. Dead, by my hand, their bodies likely burned and buried by now.

I slide my tongue over my lower lip, where I can still taste blood. Not theirs, *hers.*

I straighten my fingers before clenching them into fists. Witches don't have supernatural smell, not like vampires, and yet, I swear she knows. She knows that while six blood types came from murder, one came from passion. From recklessness. From the most addicting, dangerous of kisses.

"Well?" I bark.

It's been close to an hour, and my body still feels like it's malfunctioning. I'm too jittery to stand still, to do anything but pace and shift and worry.

"She's fine," Cora says after a prolonged pause. "I stitched her up."

"Showered?" I ask. Because while I'd been specific for Oskar to get Cora—and to let no one else in Grace's room—I'd immediately left after that. It was too dangerous for me to linger. After saving her from my ravenous followers, I'd suddenly needed to protect her from *me*.

What a crazy, needy little witch. What was she thinking? Was she trying to commit suicide? Tempting me with her warmth, her taste, her literal blood?

I shouldn't have kissed her at all. It should be a testament to those lips, to the little gasps from that sweet mouth. Her blood should have hazed my thoughts too much for me to kiss her. To do anything but sink my teeth into her palm and drink until there was nothing left.

"Yes," Cora says. She's staring at me with a skeptical expression. "I see you haven't."

"I was afraid she'd bleed out," I say.

It's not true. Her palm was bleeding, but not enough to die. She'd be uncomfortable though. Scared. Worried. Sticky and covered in as much blood as I am.

"She's fine," Cora repeats. "I'm surprised you weren't with her. Lingering like Oskar."

She's testing me, but she's working hard to hide it. She steps deeper into my room, eyes cautiously scanning her environment. She rarely comes to this part of the manor, let alone to my personal quarters. She studies my four poster bed and the wardrobe in the corner, the simple black rug over the scratched hardwoods. There's a short dresser, secretly filled with weapons rather than clothes, and a rectangular mirror hanging above it.

Despite the additional furniture and the large space, it's not much nicer than Grace's quarters. It's basic, stripped. It does have an attached bathroom though, complete with a claw-foot tub and an oversized shower. The second Cora leaves, I'm going to use both until I'm completely scrubbed of Grace's scent.

"I heard she held down two vampires," Cora says, finally returning her gaze to me. "That's good progress."

I don't respond. I'm not thinking of Grace's progress right now. I'm thinking of her soft lips and her wicked tongue. I'm imagining how her mouth would feel on my cock and what her cunt would taste like.

"What else?" I ask gruffly. "What else did she say?"

Did she tell you she kissed me? Did she tell you I kissed her back? Does she know how close I came to killing her? Does she know I wanted to?

I almost lost control—and I don't lose control. I've been a vampire far too long. I'm not a newborn. I'm not overcome with insatiable bloodlust like the six vampires we met in the halls. I am experienced, calculating, purposeful.

One taste of her sweet blood, and I almost lost all sense of myself. If I'd allowed myself even another second, I think I might have...

"Was there something else she *should* have said?" Cora asks.

"You're dismissed."

It takes all my effort not to roll my eyes. I shuck out of my shirt, and Cora immediately spins, facing the door, rather than me. She's almost thirty, but she's a witch living in a house of vampires. I doubt she's so much as seen a naked man.

"She requested you," Cora says. "And something called Pad Thai. She said you'd know what that means."

"I'll take care of it," I say. My words are close to a growl, but Cora doesn't seem to take the hint.

"If she's causing too many problems," she says. "Perhaps she can stay in my room. You'll know she's safe, and my smell alone will keep vampires from breaking down her door."

She's fishing still. I can hear it. Saying one thing, hoping to reveal another. Grace must have said something. She probably told Cora that we're an item now, that we're having Pad Thai for date night or whatever the fuck it is humans do in the mortal world.

"You're dismissed," I say again, harder this time. When Cora starts speaking, I cut her off immediately. "I've already murdered six people today. I would rather not add you to the list."

It's cruel, but effective. Cora doesn't look back as she strides from the room, chin proudly lifted, as if she's not bothered by me. And maybe she's not, maybe she knows she has this embarrassing truth over my head.

I flex my hands again. I should storm straight to Grace's room and set the record straight.

She kissed me.

I kissed her back, but only because I'm a man. A simple man with simple urges.

She's lucky I didn't kill her, and if she so much as thinks about trying it again, I will.

I stare at the empty doorway for a prolonged moment before finally striding to the bathroom. I'll do all of those things, but first, I'm going to shower.

I strip out of my pants and socks, leaving them strewn across the tiled bathroom floor. A quick glance in the mirror confirms what I already know: I'm soaked in blood. Even with my clothes discarded, dark red stains my skin. I stare for another moment before cranking the shower water as hot as it will go.

Aside from the clawfoot tub, which is white and gold, everything else in the bathroom is black. The interior of the shower is black tiles and a collection of soap containers on the wall. I dump an excess of soap in my right palm and use it to wash my hair and body.

I don't realize I've avoided my left hand entirely until it's the only place blood remains. Water thunders against my chest as I hold my bloodied hand in front of me. Even without smelling it, I know it's hers. I'd held this hand against her face, right where she'd smeared her own blood.

Despite knowing better, I press the hand to my lips, trailing my tongue over my palm. Sharp electricity spears through me. My cock is already hard. My brain is already fuzzy, desperate, needy.

Fucking needy little witch.

It's her fault. Kissing me, touching me, when she has no right fucking with my head.

It's her fault I'm licking her blood off my finger.

It's her fault I'm gripping my shaft, fucking my bloodied hand, pretending it's her warm cunt instead.

I let the thoughts consume me, until I'm thinking only of her soft skin and her sunshine hair and those blue eyes. Until I'm coming so hard I lose my balance and have to steady my opposite hand against the wall. My cum spurts across the black tile, and I gasp as I get control of myself.

I stare at the mess, feeling relief and irritation flare through me all at once. I feel better, and yet, I already know, it's not enough. One kiss, and she's turned me as needy as she is.

I curse. Wash the rest of her blood off me and pretend I can't still smell her. Shut off the steaming water and throw on a fresh pair of clothes.

Grace has started a dangerous game, and now it's time for me to end it.

WHEN I KNOCK, she ignores me. I know she's in her quarters—Oskar told me as much after I dismissed him. He lingers behind me, undoubtedly grinning. I shouldn't have knocked. It seemed like the thing to do, given the day's events, but I already regret it.

I've set a precedent, an expectation that, just because we kissed, I'll now be a gentleman and not walk in unannounced whenever I please.

I lift my hand, pausing with it on the doorknob.

"Hells," I mutter.

I ignore Oskar's snickering behind me and shove into Grace's room. Surprisingly, she's not in bed. She's just reaching the door, and she stumbles back to avoid getting struck.

Her blonde eyebrows slant, and her mouth mirrors them.

I know what that mouth tastes like.

It's a stupid, unnecessary thought, especially right now. I grit my teeth, banishing it and all similar ideas from my head.

"You're supposed to wait for someone to open the door. That's *literally* the point of knocking," Grace says. Blood rushes across her face, staining her cheeks with pretty blush. Still, she works hard to look annoyed. She juts her chin, as if I can't hear her heart racing.

"You took too long," I say. I shut the door behind me and lean against it. "I may be immortal, Grace, but even I have my limits."

"Please," she says, rolling her eyes. "You have the patience of a child."

My mouth ticks into a smirk without permission. I scowl, hardening my features.

"You kissed me," I say. *Accuse* might be the better word.

"And you murdered six people," she deadpans. "Guess we've both done things we're not proud of today."

"I did what needed to be done," I say. I level her with a stare. "I'd do it again. Every single time."

I brush past her and sit on her narrow bed. Her computer sits open on the floor, another movie filling the screen. It's not the one we watched together, and though I'm oddly tempted to ask about it, I don't. I sit on the edge of her bed, elbows on my knees.

"Why did you kiss me, little witch?"

I expect her to fold instantly, but she doesn't. She crosses her arms over her chest and leans against the door, glaring at me. She must know I can see through her. That I can *sense* her true feelings. The way her heart races. The distinct smell of her arousal.

"How's your hand?" I ask, if only to distract from *that*.

"Good as new." She faces her palm toward me, revealing a jagged suture line from her index finger to the center of her hand. Cora stitched her up, but it'll leave a nasty scar. She lowers her hand, eyes narrowing. "I had a lot of adrenaline after watching you murder a million people, okay? I wasn't thinking clearly. Obviously, if I had been, I wouldn't have kissed you. So if you can just drop it—"

"No."

"No?" she repeats. She finally moves from the door, shoulders tightening toward her ears. "Really, Sebastian? You're going to lock me up, make insane demands, and control my every waking moment. Don't you think you could cut me some slack, just this once?"

"No."

"Sebastian," she says. Her voice wavers enough that I almost feel bad.

Almost.

"It was stupid," I spit. "You were bleeding, Grace. You realize how close I came to fucking killing you?"

"But you didn't," she says. "I'm still here, at your disposal. You can still use me to break your curse and whatever else you feel like doing to me. You're still in control, so just...don't punish me for this. I assure you, I already hate myself enough for the both of us."

"Doesn't matter," I say, rising to my feet. I'm in front of Grace, grabbing her elbows. Her eyes widen with surprise, and she attempts to step backward. I hold her in place, leaning in until my lips brush against her ear. "You made me taste you, and now, I want to *devour* you."

Grace shudders, leaning closer. Our chests touch, and I can feel the hard peaks of her nipples against me. I place one hand on her hip and wrap her hair around the other. With a sharp tug, I tilt her head back, until she's looking up at me.

Soft. Pretty. Forbidden.

"You want that too, don't you?" I ask. Her blue eyes blink up at me, dazed and sated. I haven't even fucking touched her, and she looks ready to come. I breathe her in, letting her blood and arousal cloud my every thought.

"Sebastian," she whispers. Her voice is as breathy, as delirious as mine. "If you touch me, I swear to god, I'll never help break your curse."

With that, she slams her knee into my crotch. I choke out a gasp, releasing her hair as I stumble back.

"Hells, Grace," I cough. With one hand protecting my balls, I use the other to balance against the wall. The last thing I need is to fall on my knees in front of her. "I wasn't going to fucking force you."

"Get out," she says. She's crying. Actual fucking tears, running in thick streams down her cheeks and into her mouth. The smell of salt is stronger than her lingering arousal.

"Hells," I say again. I throw my hands up, moving for the door. "All right, I'm going."

I don't look at her as I pass. Still, I can see her surprise in my peripheral. As if she honestly expected me to hold her down and have my way with her.

"I'll never mention it again," I bark over my shoulder.

I wrench open the door, slamming it behind me. Then, I tear through the manor until I find the man I'm looking for.

"Master—" Oskar starts, but I wave him off.

"I need you back outside Grace's quarters. Have one of the humans bring her Pad Thai."

"Pad...what?"

I don't let myself explain. The servants will know what she likes. Right now, I need to get back to my quarters. Lick my wounds and pretend I didn't just get rejected *and* still call for her preferred dinner.

18

———

YOU KISSED ME FIRST

GRACE

I am back in the auditorium, practicing magic with Cora. It's the same exercise: keep a vampire on his knees for as long as possible. Only this time, it's not Sebastian knelt before me. It's Theo. He's the youngest vampire in Sebastian's inner circle, and I'm surprised I can feel the difference.

In my mind, a vampire is a vampire is a vampire.

With Theo knelt before me, I realize that's not the case. It makes sense, then, why I was able to hold two of my attackers down in that hallway. Sebastian is extraordinarily difficult to contain. Other vampires? Not so much.

"All right," Theo moans. He's trembling, face clenched with pain. He's managed to get one foot beneath him, but the other knee remains on the floor.

It's oddly satisfying, watching him struggle. I've spent too much time in this manor, I decide. Too much time around death and pain and grotesque rules. It's moments like this where I wonder if I realistically *could* return to the human world. I don't know what I'd do in Aberlena.

After this long fearing for my life, the thought of getting an internship at a newspaper seems ridiculous.

I might be too damaged, too broken to return now.

"C'mon," he groans.

I don't let up. It's not my rule. It's Cora's. I'm waiting for her to call it. Until she does, I keep Theo in place, smirking when his escaped knee smashes back to the hardwood. He glares at me, eyes thick with hatred.

"Stupid, fucking, foul witch," he says. He's still vibrating, and a flicker of guilt punctures my chest.

I'm not just keeping him on his knees. I think I'm hurting him.

For the first time since we started, I glance at Cora. She's at her usual place beside the wall, leaned back, arms loose, eyes watchful. It's only a momentary distraction, but that's all it takes.

By the time I look back at Theo, he's already on his feet. He lunges, hands clenching my shoulders. He hits me hard enough that we both fly backwards, him landing on top of me. His mouth splits into a grin, and a set of fangs pierce through his gums.

I blink, sure I've imagined it.

He forces my hands above my head, but there's no time to feel fear. Just as his lips touch my throat, his weight disappears. I watch as he's ripped away, up into the air, landing in a heap at Cora's side. I prop onto my elbows, eyes wide.

"Can't give them that in," she says.

"That had to be a record," is my response. "What was it, six minutes?"

"More like four," she says with a scoff. "Doesn't matter if you get yourself killed at the end."

"I imagine we can break your stupid curse *without* me needing to fight a vampire army," I say, rolling my eyes. "Isn't this just to 'awaken my magic' or whatever? I feel like this is proof we've done it."

Theo groans, moving to his haunches. He glances at me before glaring at Cora.

"Hells, woman," he says. "Was that necessary?"

"You should be thanking me," Cora says, not looking at him. "If you drew blood, Sebastian would have slaughtered you as fast as he did the others."

Theo opens his mouth, as if to argue, only to clench his jaw. He shifts his irritable gaze on me.

"I'm not the one who threw you," I point out.

He snarls. Honest-to-god snarls.

"You're making good progress," Cora says. She strides away from the wall, not stopping until she's reached me. She holds a hand down, and I take it, barely able to keep the surprise from my face.

"Is it enough?" I ask once I'm to my feet.

"I don't know," she says. "But we will soon."

Footsteps sound on the opposite side of the room, and we all turn to look at the doorway. Theo is back on his feet now, brushing off his clothes, as Sebastian enters. The vampire king isn't looking at him though. He's looking at *me*, an intensity so visceral, I swear it feels like he's touching me.

"What will we know?" he asks.

"If Grace's magic is strong enough," Cora says. "Milas found the last of my ingredients, and Grace here held Theo down for six minutes."

I glare at her. I *knew* it was six minutes.

Sebastian is still looking at me, but I'm doing everything to avoid meeting his eyes. It's been two days since I kicked him out of my cell. Two days since he listened without complaint. It was more than I expected, especially after I kneed him in the balls.

A flicker of guilt, so much worse than what I'd felt toward Theo moments ago, settles beneath my ribs. Logically, I know Sebastian has done far worse to me. He's kidnapped me, imprisoned me, fed me to a fucking spider-creature. He's ruined my life. He deserves far more than a kick to the nuts.

And still...

"I'll call a meeting," Sebastian says.

Now my stomach dips. A meeting? As in, a meeting to end this, once and for all?

Sebastian promised to let me go after this, but that was *before* I rejected him. Not to mention he lies almost constantly. If we try to break this curse, there's a good chance I don't walk away from it.

"I need more time," I blurt. "I'm not...I can tell I'm not strong enough. It's not going to work—"

Sebastian raises his hand, silencing me. I squirm where I stand, locking my gaze in the middle of his forehead. I can't meet his eyes, but I don't want him to think I'm cowering.

"Theo. Cora. You're dismissed," he says. He tilts his head, stepping toward me. "I'll return Grace to her quarters."

Sebastian waits until we're alone before speaking again.

"Do you want to practice?" he asks. He crosses the room, centering himself before me.

Without meaning to, I've lowered my eyes to his shoes. They're black and shiny, and I can make out my muted reflection in them. My blonde hair looks wild, and though I can't see my face, I'm sure it's red and sweaty and disgusting.

"Grace," he says. He doesn't come closer. His fingers twitch at his sides before balling into fists. "If you're still upset with me—"

"I'm the one who kicked *you*," I choke out. I'm talking to his shoes, and I realize how pathetic I must look. I swallow hard, forcing myself to look up.

He looks good today, and I hate that I notice. His light hair is tousled, his face cleanly shaven. I realize I don't know if hair grows on vampires. Oskar has a beard, but maybe he's always had it.

"I wasn't going to force you," he says softly. His Adam's apple bobs, and he ducks his head until his eyes are unavoidable. Deep green, framed by dark lashes. "Believe what you must, but that is the truth. I thought…"

He trails off then, finally breaking eye contact. He's not blushing. Another thing I'm not sure vampires can do. And yet, I feel like he's embarrassed all the same.

"You thought what?" I demand. Because I'm insecure, maybe, or cruel.

"I thought you wanted me to," he says through gritted teeth. His eyes meet mine again, almost defiantly. "You kissed me first."

"I know," I say. My voice breaks and I scramble for some sort of explanation. There isn't one though. I'd kissed him because he'd saved my life, because he looked at me like he cared. I kissed him because I wanted to, and though I'd barely admitted it to myself, I *still* wanted to.

"We don't need to discuss it again," he says. His voice comes down hard, like the period at the end of a sentence. "I am not going to harm you, not like that. So. Do you want to practice?"

"No," I say shakily. "Can you take me to my cell?"

He watches me for a moment before nodding, jaw tight again. We walk in silence, and he leaves me in my room without another word.

Sebastian and his inner circle surround the stone table in the courtyard once more. Like last time, I sit to his left, ignoring the six pairs of watchful eyes. Oskar likes me, I think, but he's the only one. Beatrice scowls whenever I look at her, and Theo visibly flinches, like he's worried I'll hold him captive again.

The other three are ambivalent, shooting me occasional glances, but mostly studying the artifacts on the table. I'm doing my best *not* to look at said artifacts. There's a bushel of grain, tied with thick twine. An abnormally large feather. A clear vase, filled with a cloudy liquid. A small pile of miscellaneous teeth, yellowed but not decayed. Those are all fine.

It's the rest that make my stomach turn.

I was never great with biology, but I'm pretty sure there's a liver and an oversized heart near the opposite end of the table. Even those are better than the dead rat and a human ear. It's covered in soft hair, like maybe it's the ear of a caveman.

One can hope. It feels better, for some reason, that the ear is centuries old and not fresh like the organs are. Those still have blood collecting beneath them, like they were harvested this morning.

"Sorry I'm late," Cora calls, stealing my attention from Milas's macabre collection. He keeps looking between the items and his handwritten list, as if only now verifying he has every-thing he needs.

"This stuff stinks," Beatrice says. She flicks the human ear, and it rolls into the misshapen teeth. I've decided they're from multiple animals. Some sharp and long, others short and blunt.

"Careful," Milas chastises. He delicately returns the ear to its original spot. "You have no idea how hard that was to get."

"I'd be happy to get you another one," Beatrice says, flashing him a broad smile.

"I'm sure you would," he says. He rolls the sleeve of his dark button-up, revealing a nasty scar. It's coated in yellow-green pus and goes from wrist to elbow.

"Hells," Oskar mutters.

"Maybe *that's* what stinks." Beatrice leans away.

"You should have mentioned," Cora says. She rolls her eyes as she takes the seat on my other side. "I would have brought an ointment. You're going to die if you let that fester."

I'm looking between the ear and Sebastian's inner circle,

trying but failing to understand. Just when I decide it doesn't matter, Oskar speaks from the opposite head of the table.

"It's werewolf," he says, nodding toward the detached ear. "Taken mid-transition."

"Jesus," I say. Looking to Milas, I add, "You're lucky it didn't kill you."

"She was a bitch," he says with a shrug. He glances at Beatrice, a taunting smirk pulling at his mouth. "You would have gotten along, actually."

"All right. Enough," Sebastian says. He has a thick stack of paper in front of him, and he's spent the last ten minutes studying them, rather than paying us attention.

I haven't forgotten he's here though. I've been disgustingly attuned to his every movement. When he turns a page. When he reads something under his breath. When he shifts on our shared bench.

I've pushed all my energy into watching his inner circle, but my attention keeps snagging on him. The way he smells, moves, breathes. I've realized out here, they're different. All of them.

They're *breathing*, first of all. There's a flush to their skin. They're shivering in their coats.

They're human, I think. Out here, exposed in the sun, I think they're more human than I am.

"Cora," Sebastian says, nodding toward her. "Tell us where we're at."

She doesn't immediately respond. Instead, she leans across the stone table, taking a moment to inspect each of Milas's collected ingredients. Once she's done, she uses Milas's jacket to wipe the blood from her palm. His nostrils flare, but he otherwise doesn't react.

"This looks adequate," she says. "Between this, my own collection, and Grace here, I think we're ready."

"You're sure?" Sebastian asks. "We might only have one chance."

His voice is a smooth blanket over my racing heart.

"We're as ready as we're going to be," she says. "Grace has regular access to her magic. She's not strong, but she doesn't need to be."

I want to ask what I *will* need to be. Despite the months I've been here, I still don't know exactly how breaking a curse works. They need my blood. I need to have magic. But obviously they'll need something more, right?

My heart thunders again, and I tap my foot in rhythm.

Though Sebastian's face doesn't change, he presses his hand to my knee. There's nothing sexual or flirtatious about the movement. He only holds my leg still, like a weighted comfort.

"We're ready," Cora says again. She looks between us. "There's a full moon next week. We'll do it then."

They go over more details, but it's things that don't really matter.

Where? The same ballroom where the Nectoa tried to kill me.

Who? Just us. Sebastian, the inner circle, me.

When? Right before midnight, when the moon is at its most powerful.

I'm fidgeting, spiraling, losing myself so completely I don't realize Sebastian has moved his hand from my knee to my shoulder until he squeezes it. His hand lingers there, rubbing softly, as Cora finishes her spiel.

I'm going to vomit.

I'm going to *die*, and I feel it with such certainty I'm not sure how I haven't felt like this every moment of every day. Maybe Cora has placed some sort of soothing spell over me. Or maybe I've been living in a state of complete denial.

Jesus fuck. I am going to *die*. There's no way that hasn't been the plan all along. And I've just been sitting here, waiting for them to be ready. For them to prime me for the slaughter.

What else could you have done? I ask myself silently.

Escape, is my stubborn response. I'm too overwhelmed to care I'm arguing with myself. *I never even tried to escape.*

There's still time, I decide. It's desperate, unrealistic. But if the full moon isn't until next week, I have time to figure this out.

"Change the location to the auditorium," Sebastian says.

I come out of my thoughts enough to register those words.

"The ballroom is better," Cora says. "More windows. Better for the moon to—"

"The auditorium," he interrupts. "Or the courtyard, if we must. Not the ballroom."

Cora and Beatrice shoot me identical, accusatory looks. I haven't said a single word, and they're still looking at me like this is my fault.

None of this is my fault! I want to scream. *You are the monsters, not me!*

I stay silent. I already know they won't care.

"Fine," Cora says eventually. She collects the dead and dried and decaying items from the table before nodding to Milas. "Carry the rest, would you?"

He obliges, and the others depart just as quickly. Then, it's me and Sebastian, alone in the courtyard.

I can feel him staring.

"Thank you for moving it from the ballroom," I say without turning my head. I'm staring at the center of the table, where moments ago, a werewolf ear sat bloodied. Milas had carved it off a woman's head, and everyone had made jokes about it.

Where was the woman now? Still alive? Or did he kill her to get that ear?

"Grace," Sebastian says. His voice is low, smooth and gentle, and I hate it. I want to scream and thrash and have a meltdown until he's forced to drag me to my room, kicking.

I push from the bench and start for the door. He's soon at my side, but not with the unnatural speed I've come to accept. I'm right, I decide. He's human. It's not just in his movements. It's in the faint color beneath his cheeks, made brighter by the wind.

"Once it's over," he says, "I'll take you wherever you want to go."

"I'm not going to survive," I say. My voice doesn't sound like mine. It's disconnected, far away. "Don't lie to me, Sebastian."

He forces me to stop, grabbing my chin, making me look at him.

"You are *not* going to die," he says. "Understand? I am not going to let you die."

"The ritual might need it," I say. "It might be the only way—"

"Then I will find a different way."

"You can't honestly expect me to believe that."

"No, I guess I can't," he says. He releases my chin, looking behind me at the statue of himself. After a lengthy pause, he looks back at me. "It's still the truth, Grace. I am not going to let you die."

Maybe he's telling the truth. Maybe he's lying.

I need to leave before I find out.

19

DON'T RUSH ME

GRACE

Over the next three days, I make my plan. It's not the most elaborate, but that's what I get for puttering around, refusing to acknowledge the truth. My days here at the manor are limited, and no amount of training with Cora will keep these vampires from draining my blood if that's what it takes to break their curse. I should have been planning from the day Sebastian dragged me here.

If I was smart, I would have the manor layout memorized. I would have made friends with the servant who brings my food. I would have learned Sebastian's weaknesses.

Instead, I've been too caught up in proving myself and not losing myself in a pit of depression.

Whatever. There's no use stressing about it now. I've got a week until I'm sacrificed for their ritual, and that means I'm running out of time. I don't have the luxury of feeling like an idiot.

On the computer Sebastian gifted me, I jot notes on a blank document. I start with any useful information I know. People's names, and which ones Sebastian trusts the most. The Echo, and any details I remember from when we traveled to the Flight

Realm. The spells I've seen Cora conjure, and which ones I think I might be able to replicate.

As I draft a timeline in my mind, I lay in bed, hands in my lap. All the while, I call magic to my fingertips, feeling it spark beneath my skin. It's impossible to explain *how* I cast, and only now that I *can*, do I understand why Cora couldn't give better instructions.

It's more about feeling than logic.

Without touching it, I move my laptop from the foot of my bed to a spot on the floor. Back and forth, until my arm muscles pulse with overuse. I might not be moving, but my body is working hard. I'm sweating, breathing rough, my tank top sticking to my abdomen.

I practice and plot my escape, only stopping when Oskar walks me to Cora's for the day. Then, after a long day of training, and once I've eaten an overflowing bowl of pasta, I get back to work.

I practice late into the night, even when my body begs for sleep. There's too much to do...and honestly, I'm not ready for tomorrow to come. If I sleep now, I will wake with not seven days remaining, but *six*.

I swallow the thought, sitting upright in bed. It creaks as I rise to my feet, crossing the room as quietly as I can manage. With my ear pressed to the door, I listen for movement in the hallway. I know someone is out there—most likely Oskar—but I can't hear him through this stupidly thick door.

I lean back. Running my hands over the frame, I study its simple design. Four hinges, all made of heavy black metal. I crouch to the lowest one, studying its elongated pin. The metal is too small, too delicately carved into the hinge for me to pinch with my fingers. Still, if I could just bend it and find a way to pull it—

It doesn't matter. Escaping from my bedroom isn't a good

idea. Even if I got through the door, I wouldn't make it far before my guard captured me.

I'll have better luck if I ask for a bathroom break. Any time Oskar walks me, he keeps his distance. To be respectful, I'm sure. Got to be a gentleman when you're keeping a woman prisoner.

That plan is better, but I still find myself reaching for the metal again. Before I touch it, the door flies open. It crashes into my side, knocking me against the wall. I let out a pathetic squeak and scramble to my feet.

It's not Oskar tonight.

"What are you doing?" Beatrice asks. Sebastian only brought her back on my guard rotation a couple nights ago, but *of course*, she has to be here now. She stares at me wordlessly, her dark eyebrows jetting toward her forehead.

"I was going to ask to go to the bathroom," I say. My voice is shaking—can she tell? "I was about to knock, and then you nearly killed me."

"You're a shit liar," she says. She scoffs a laugh, leaning against the doorframe. She studies me, and I fidget under her heavy gaze.

I want to beg her not to tell Sebastian, but I keep my mouth shut. It's her word against mine, and so long as I don't admit to anything...

"You realize vampires have superhuman hearing, right?" she asks. Her lips tick with a mocking smirk. "We can hear *everything*."

Once again, I don't respond.

"Taking the door apart by the hinges," she says. She pats its wooden face, letting her hand settle on the doorknob. "Terrible plan, Gracie. This thing weighs four times as much as you do. It'd crush you long before you got out. Not to mention I'd knock you on your ass if you did manage it."

"I wasn't—"

"Save it," Beatrice says, rolling her eyes. "I'm actually relieved you tried to escape. Stupid method, but at least you're not totally dead in there."

She taps my forehead, and I swat at her hand, stepping deeper into my room. I'm terrified she'll follow, but she only grins at me.

"Still," she says, drawling. "It's been a week, Grace. It's kind of embarrassing you haven't figured it out by now."

"Figured *what* out?"

"It's not nearly as hard to get out of this room as you seem to think," she says.

With that, she closes the door. It settles against its hinges with a heavy slam, and I glare at the space where Beatrice stood moments ago.

What a bitch.

Easy for her to say. I'm sure this room would be easy to escape. You know, if I was a freaking vampire with unnatural reflexes and superhuman strength.

Still, I find myself moving toward the door. I've studied every inch of this room over the past few days. There's no vent. No cut-out in the ceiling for an attic. No pieces of bed frame that can easily be unscrewed and used as a weapon. This place is a blank, useless room.

I stand before the door, glaring at it, as if it's responsible for Beatrice's mockery.

Once again, I run my hands over the wood and the metal hinges. My fingers dance along the stripes of iron before finally landing on the doorknob. I hold my breath tight in my chest.

Since arriving at this manor, I've checked this door a hundred times. It's been locked every single time.

But that was months ago, I think. *You haven't checked in months.*

It felt stupid to try. Not to mention dangerous. If Sebastian knew I was trying to escape this room, I'd surely be punished.

I grip the doorknob harder.

I already know Beatrice is just on the other side, grinning at the door and waiting for me to try. She can hear everything, and I'm sure she'd love nothing more than to hear me struggle. She obviously *wants* me to think it's unlocked, and I'm lining myself up to be humiliated and mocked.

I push against the handle as quietly as I can. Where every other time, I met resistance, the door now opens effortlessly into the hallway.

Beatrice stands across from me, arms folded over her chest. She's grinning, just like I expected, eyes glimmering with amusement.

"Why?" I ask.

Beatrice shrugs. "I was told you had a deal."

If you can prove you can handle yourself, I'll grant you free reign of the manor.

I hadn't forgotten the deal...I just didn't think he'd ever follow through. Especially after I'd nearly gotten killed in these very halls.

"He didn't tell me," I say, as if that wasn't already obvious.

Heat flares in my chest, but I can't decide if it's a pleasant warmth or a scalding burn. Sebastian held his end of the bargain. That's good. That's *nice*. And yet, he *also* didn't tell me.

"Where's his room?" I demand.

I expect Beatrice to deny me. Instead, she sets off down the hall, gesturing for me to follow.

"Do vampires sleep?" I ask as we hit the bottom of the spiral staircase. Beatrice glances at me, eyebrow arched. She doesn't slow though, pushing through the door and into a narrow hall. It looks like any of the others, but I don't think I've been to this part of the manor.

"Most do," she says. "It's not something vampires need. They do it mostly out of boredom. It's far more common with the sun curse. If you're asking if *Sebastian* sleeps, the answer is no. He'll be awake."

My pulse quickens at the idea. We've been walking too long, and now, my thoughts have muddled. I can't decide if I have a right to be pissed. I'm not sure whether I should yell at Sebastian when I see him or if I should thank him.

"This is him," she says. She stops abruptly, not flinching when I crash against her side. She nods toward the door, plain and unmarked.

"Am I supposed to knock?" I ask. My stomach dips with embarrassment, and I realize how stupid I'm being. I'm literally seeking him out in the middle of the night, as if this couldn't have waited until the morning.

And what am I meant to do? Tell him I've only now realized he unlocked my cell door? That he kept his end of the bargain and I was too stupid to notice?

Beatrice doesn't reply, but it turns out she doesn't need to. The door swings open, revealing a shirtless Sebastian.

Before I can resist, my eyes sweep over his toned chest and abs. His hair is messy. It's not from sleep, which means it's either from his hand running through it or someone *else's* hand. I lean, peeking into the room behind him.

It's simple but nice, and though he supposedly doesn't sleep, there's a four-poster bed against the center wall. A plain dresser across from it. A wardrobe to the side. A magnificent rug at the center

Zero naked women.

It wouldn't matter if there was, I chastise myself. He can have all the mistresses he wants.

"What's wrong?" he asks. His words come out sharp, and his eyes match their intensity, flicking between me and Beatrice.

"My door is unlocked," I finally say. I sound like a moron.

I *am* a moron.

"And?" he asks. Another flick between me and Beatrice.

"Never mind," I say quickly. Blush burns my cheeks, as I turn to Beatrice. I'm sure everyone can hear the desperation in my voice. "You should take me back to my cell."

Sebastian looks between us, a slow smirk taking over his expression. He clears his throat roughly before nodding at Beatrice.

"You're dismissed," he says.

Beatrice returns his nod, and then has the audacity to wink at me before disappearing down the hallway. She's gone in a flash of dark hair, leaving me alone with Sebastian and my own stupidity. I force myself to look at him. My spit tastes like acid.

"I didn't realize you unlocked the door," I say finally. I shift on my feet, my eyes once again drifting down the hall. "I asked Beatrice to bring me here so I could..."

I trail off.

"So you could..." he prompts.

"Yell at you?" I finish. It comes out more as a question, and quietly enough I barely hear it.

Sebastian does though. Of course he does.

"Yelling is typically much louder," he says. His mouth unleashes into a grin, so painfully beautiful I can't look away. He leans a shoulder against the doorframe, and my eyes snag on the deep V that disappears beneath his slacks.

"Thank you," I say. I force my eyes back to his. He's already watching me, grin in place, but eyes darkening with familiar intensity.

"We had a deal," he says. He doesn't move, but his hands loosen and tighten at his sides, as if he's resisting the urge to reach for me.

"I didn't expect you to keep it," I tell him. "I assumed it was a lie."

He doesn't respond. He tilts his head, waiting.

"You mean it, don't you?" I ask. "What you've said about keeping me alive, about letting me leave after it's done?"

"Yes," Sebastian says. "I swear it."

"I was going to try to escape," I tell him. I'm not sure why I'm honest, but when his jaw tightens, it relieves pressure in my chest.

His emotions are so clearly visible on his face. Frustration. Annoyance. Anger. Maybe even fear. And yet, he keeps it carefully contained. He doesn't move beyond that flicker in his jaw, that strain in his expression.

"I won't," I tell him. "If you truly mean what you say, I'll stay. I swear it."

Sebastian's green eyes darken again, and his attention lowers to my mouth. It's brief, but I see it, the way he's forcing himself to hold back. I'm standing before him in thin shorts and a small tank top. He can most likely see the outline of my nipples, hardened, desperate for his touch.

"Good," he finally says. His voice is deep, gravelly, calling me toward him like a siren's song.

I step closer. My hands shake as I press them against the naked planes of his chest. I curl my fingers against his collarbone, pulling him across the threshold of his room, into the hallway.

"Are you going to kick me?" he asks, the question a barely-there whisper.

"Kiss me," I say. In the morning, I might be embarrassed at the neediness of my own voice.

Right now, I'll do anything to close the gap between us.

So, while he's still cautiously watching me, gauging my words, I close the distance myself. I surge into him. Crash my chest against his. Let the cool press of his skin surround me.

I kiss him like I've only allowed myself in my mind, as if we're not captor and prisoner, but star-crossed lovers. I'm overeager, messy, frantic. His lips are soft, and his tongue tastes like cinnamon. He takes either side of my face, tipping my jaw up, opening me to him. Our teeth clank, fighting for control.

I don't realize we've moved until his door slams shut. Then I'm pressed against it, his wide palm tracing my curves from the hollow of my throat, over my breasts, settling on my hip. His other hand is still on my face, tight over my jaw. He crowds against me, slowing the kiss to a tortuous stop.

My hands claw down his back. He's as close as he can physically be, but it's still not enough. I dig my nails into his shoulders. I tip my hips toward his and let out a frustrated yelp when he shoves me back against the door.

"Don't rush me," he says. His lips trail from the corner of my mouth to my jaw and over my pulse, disappearing as quickly as they land. They're already moving back up, gently nipping the bottom of my ear. He pulls back, eyes flickering over my face. "I've dreamt of this, Grace. Let me savor you."

Then his mouth is on mine again. He sweeps a hand into my hair, twisting it around his wrist. With a sharp tug, he lengthens my throat. His tongue trails down, down, down.

I squirm, too desperate to feel embarrassed. I'm moaning, honest-to-god whimpering as he teases me.

"So fucking sweet," he whispers, just before tugging my tanktop down, exposing my breast. He runs his thumb over my nipple, staring intensely.

"Please," I whimper. "Sebas—"

He captures my nipple between his teeth and traces it with

his tongue. I'm a shivering, panting mess. I can't think. Can't speak. Can't do anything other than moan as he lavishes my breast with attention. I sag against the door, watching as he moves to the opposite side.

His hands roam down my body, sliding my tank top and shorts off, leaving me completely bare before him.

"Perfect," he says. He's on his knees before I can ask, before I can beg. "So fucking pretty, little witch."

His lips brush my clit, and my hips instinctively jerk. He smiles, kissing one side of my thigh and then the other. He kisses everywhere except where I'm desperate for him. I can't take it. I won't—

I grab his hair, tangling my fingers to the root, and shove his head where I want it. He could easily resist me, but he doesn't. He smiles against my center, deep green eyes studying my face.

"Whatever you want, Grace," he says. His hot breath tickles my clit, has me digging my fingers tighter against his head. "Take whatever you want."

He sucks my clit into his mouth, and my eyes roll back.

I gasp, writhing as his hand slips between my thighs. He fucks me with his finger, incessantly, unrelenting, matching the same punishing pace as his tongue. He's devouring me, and I'm bucking into him, hoping he will.

My orgasm strikes without warning. I come, muttering incoherently, my body sagging against the door. My limbs feel rubbery, so blissfully spent, I can't stand on my own. I'm ready to fold onto the floor, but Sebastian holds a heavy palm against my hip, pinning me in place.

"Give me another," he says. He kisses my thigh, biting it softly.

"It's too much," I say immediately, even as my body screams *please, more.*

"You can do it," he says. He pumps his finger lazily, curling with every stroke to hit my inner wall. His pupils are so dilated they look more black than green. "Come on Grace, I've been so good. Don't I deserve another?"

The few times I allowed myself, I imagined Sebastian would be rough and unrelenting in the bedroom. I was right. But I didn't expect this. For him to look submissive beneath me. Begging for another taste.

I toss my head back in silent answer, guiding his head back between my legs. This time, I can feel his smile against my skin. He trails his tongue up the inside of my thigh until it meets his finger, still moving rhythmically inside me.

"I want to hear my name," he says. He fucks me faster, pulling back to watch my face. "When you come this time, let me hear exactly who's making you feel this good."

I should tell him to go fuck himself.

I don't.

I let the orgasm build until it rips through me, until I'm too sated to care who hears me. I cry Sebastian's name, and for just a moment, I pretend he's not my enemy after all.

20

SO PRETTY WHEN YOU BEG

SEBASTIAN

Grace is on my bed. Naked. Sprawled out. Perky breasts on display. Blonde hair in a messy halo around her head. I'm never going to get her scent out of my sheets, no matter how many times they're washed.

Good.

If this is the only time I have her, let it be ingrained in this room, in my brain, so I remember every detail for as long as I live. I study her as she props onto her elbows. She smiles, soft and shy, watching me with pretty blue eyes. She brings her legs together, crossing them slightly, hiding her cunt from me.

A growl curls from my throat, raw and animalistic. I lean over her, spreading her legs, wider than they were before. Grace gasps, and I pause. She's surprised though, not hurt. I gently trail my fingers up her inner thigh, smiling as she squirms beneath me. I haven't been with a human since turning, and I've never been with a witch. Much as I'd like to lose control with her, I have to be careful. Patient. If she feels anything other than the purest pleasure, I'll never forgive myself.

"Don't hide from me," I whisper. With her legs spread, I pull her to the end of the bed and kneel before her. I'm still wearing my pants and my cock strains against the zipper. I've gone dizzy with lust, surrounded by the scent of her blood and her over-whelming arousal. Her taste lingers on my tongue, branded into my tastebuds. And still, I want more.

I press her knees down and spread her wide. She's glisten-ing, soaked, desperate for more, even as she writhes. My lips are almost to her center, to the place they want to stay, when she grips my hair, stopping me.

"No," she says.

"No?" I repeat, looking up at her.

"No more torturing me," she whines. She tugs my hair, pulling my head away from her thighs. "Fuck me, Sebastian."

A possessive growl shudders from my chest. I breathe steadily, fighting for control, feeling it fade with each strained breath. With one hand on her thigh and the other on her wrist, I swipe my tongue through her folds, savoring her. I pull back, grinning at her startled expression. Before she has to ask again, I kick off my pants and climb into bed, settling above her.

Her blue eyes are indescribably bright. I don't know how to define them. They're not like the ocean or flame or ice. They're purely *Grace*, and they're the most beautiful thing I've ever seen.

I lower to my elbows, until her warm skin grazes mine. Her breaths are ragged, eager, pushing her nipples against my chest. A sharp flicker jolts beneath my ribs, as though my heart is trying to beat, despite not needing to.

"So beautiful," I murmur. I hold my weight off her, memo-rizing every inch of her skin. In my many fantasies of this moment, I assumed I would be tempted by the steady pulse in her throat. I'd gotten dangerously close when she was bleeding, but this is different. Right now, I don't want her blood. I want her arousal, her desire, simply *her*.

"Please," she says in a breathy moan. She lifts her hips, gasping when her pelvis meets my cock.

I lower, grinding my erection against her. Her arousal—and my spit—has made her skin slick. I could come just from this, from her nails digging into my back, her eager hips seeking mine.

I don't breathe as I rock against her, waiting until the initial urge to come subsides. If this is the only time I have her, I'm going to make it fucking count. I notch at her entrance, and her legs instantly wrap around my waist. When I look up, her blue eyes are on me, soft lips parted, breath unsteady.

"Tell me if I hurt you," I command. "I'm going to be careful, but—"

"Just fuck me, Sebastian," she says. She yanks at my hips, tightening her legs around them.

"Trust me, I'm going to," I say. I push forward, but instead of entering her, I tease her, slipping over the top. She lets out an impatient moan, and I lower my lips to her throat. I can feel her pulse, and I trail my tongue up to her jaw. "I'll fuck you as hard and as long as you want, little witch. But if it's too much—"

"I'll tell you," she says. She lifts her hips again. "Please, Sebastian."

"So pretty when you beg," I tell her. I kiss her jaw, her cheek, before finally claiming her mouth.

She kisses like it's the last thing she'll ever do, and if I have to die, this is the way I'd want to go. With her legs fastened around my waist, nails digging into my skin, lips wandering over my shoulder.

I line at her entrance again, and this time, I don't tease. I push into her tight heat, and we groan in unison. I thrust slow, shallow strokes as she adjusts to my size. For several seconds, there is nothing but her pure, blissful torture. My eyes flutter, and I let myself be wholly consumed by Grace Renolds.

"Oh god," she says. Her head falls back, eyes rolling, mouth gaping.

"Good?" I ask. Because for the life of me, I can't fucking tell. I'm too deep in my own blissful oblivion. She takes me deeper with each agonizing stroke, until I'm fully seated, and I can't think of anything else.

"So. Good." Her voice is soft, breathy, half in this world and half in another.

"Thank fuck," I say. Because if I had to stop now, I'd spend the rest of my life chasing this single feeling.

I thrust a few more times before I'm forced to pause. Fuck, I'm already close. I clench to keep from bursting inside her, grinding my teeth as I look over her. I've never seen such an erotic sight as Grace sprawled beneath me, her tight cunt squeezing me in a vice grip. Her eyes are glossy, hands cupping her breasts, mouth slightly parted.

I grab her hips, stilling her. She lifts her head, and her sated expression is only a fraction of how I feel.

"More," she begs.

"Give me a second," I growl. I duck my head against her shoulder, kissing up the length of her throat. "You have no idea how close I am to coming. I've wanted..."

I trail off, refusing to say more than I should.

"Then come," she says, and she says it like a command. "Come and then fuck me again."

"Hells," I mutter.

I wait another beat, until that instinctual urge subsides, before thrusting hard and deep. Again and again, until the room is a symphony of her moans and our hips meeting. Her head drops back, and she toys with her breasts, pinching her nipples between long, delicate fingers.

I'm jealous of her own fucking hands.

I replace her touch with mine, palming one breast and capturing the other with my mouth. She comes like that, my name on her sweet lips, her back arching from the mattress.

I fuck her until she's gone limp, until she's spent and bone-less. Only then do I let my own urges take over. My thrusts grow sharp and reckless, and without my realizing, I've fucked her halfway off the bed. When her head hangs over the edge, I yank her back to me, pulling out to flip her onto her stomach.

She lets out a surprised yelp as I pull her ass into the air. Before she says a word, I shove back into her pussy in a single, hard thrust. Her moan fills the room, and I hold her firmly in place as the urge flares again. I don't want to come yet. I'm not ready for it to end. I'm determined to make this ecstasy last the rest of my fucking immortal life.

"Sebastian," she moans. She pushes her hips back, seeking friction.

And that's all it takes. Instinct takes over, and I manage two violent thrusts before I come on a roar. I collapse against her, filling her until my seed drips down her thigh. My vision spots as I lay atop her, kissing the heated flesh of her neck.

"Perfect," I whisper against her shoulder. "Fucking perfect, Grace."

I lay for a prolonged moment, savoring the touch of her naked body, before finally pulling away. She groans as I disappear from between her legs. She rolls onto her back and settles into the pillows, watching me with a sated expression. I study her in return, checking for any sign of remorse or pain. I find nothing but blissful exhaustion.

"Stay." It comes out as a command, one I hadn't planned to make. I've never asked a woman to stay the night, but I can't bear the thought of her leaving. Of her going back to her room and finding a reason to regret what we've done. "Sleep here tonight."

"You won't eat me in my sleep?" she asks. She waggles her eyebrows, making sure I don't miss the double meaning.

I don't, but also...

"I am not going to hurt you, Grace," I say. "I promise."

She watches me warily, long enough I feel uncomfortable. I slide off the bed to retrieve a towel from the bathroom. I wipe the mess from myself and then from between her legs, much as I'm tempted to leave it there. To stake my claim, even if it's only in this room.

"Okay," Grace says finally. She scoots higher in the bed, working her way beneath the covers, still naked. "I'll stay."

I crawl into the space behind her, pulling her ass against me. I wrap my hand over her, fingers grazing her chest, her throat, everywhere I can reach.

Soon, she's asleep in my arms. I lay perfectly still for the rest of the night, feeling her steady heartbeat against my palm.

21

MORTAL EMOTIONS

GRACE

The next morning, after Sebastian makes me come twice—once with his tongue, and once with his cock—we leave the sanctity of his room for the far less welcoming auditorium. His inner circle is already there by the time we arrive. They stand against the far wall, their backs pressed to the wood paneling. Opposite them, the drapes are drawn to reveal three narrow windows and the early rays of sunlight.

Cora was right.

If this ritual relies on the full moon, the ballroom is a better location. The windows are larger, and there are twice as many of them. I should tell Sebastian it's fine to do it there. Instead, I don't say a word.

While Sebastian fed downstairs this morning, I gave myself a much needed pep-talk in front of his mirror. I can hope he cares for me. I can have hot sex with him and believe his intentions are better than they once were. But I can *also* prioritize myself and not cave to his circle's every demand. Right now, that means learning how this ritual works without being reminded of my time as spider bait.

Sebastian's hand claims the small of my back as he leads us through the auditorium. My body relaxes against his touch, and for once, I don't fight the instinctual pull. I only step closer to his side and study the surrounding artifacts. They're staggered throughout the room, each one balanced on a short wooden stand.

The werewolf ear. The unidentifiable feather. The vase with cloudy liquid. The mismatched teeth. The bundled grain. The liver and the heart and the long-dead rat. At the center of it all, a tall podium stands with an empty glass bowl and an intricately-carved dagger.

That's where Cora stands. Dressed in her typical baggy black dress, she leans against the podium and smiles. It's meant to be reassuring, I think. It doesn't matter. There's nothing to calm the realization that the glass bowl is meant for *me* and that it looks equipped to hold *gallons* of blood.

"All right," she says. She pats the podium, drawing every-one's attention. And still, I see the faces of the inner circle as they look from me to Sebastian and finally to Cora. Their expressions shift, trying to hold back smiles. They're fidgeting like high schoolers with juicy gossip, and entirely too late, I realize what I should have long before I arrived.

They can scent me.

They know exactly *what I've done.*

A violent flare of shame courses through me. I've always strived to be sex positive, to allow myself to enjoy sex, even if it's a one-night stand. This is undoubtedly different. I let Sebastian fuck me, only days before he uses me as a sacrificial lamb. And now, his followers are absolutely judging me for it.

I dig my fingers against my bare thighs. *Oh god.* How pathetic. I suck a breath through my teeth, feeling the edges of my vision blur.

"And Grace, you'll stand here," Cora says, gesturing in front of her. She holds the dagger as nonchalantly as a pencil, twirling it between her fingers. "I'll get the spell started, and at my word, you'll slice your palm or wrist or what-have-you. Then, you'll give me access to your magic. There's a chance you'll lose consciousness at some point, but I'm fairly confident we can finish this before it kills you."

Cora moves on to each of the artifacts and their respective roles in the ritual. I should be paying attention, but my mind can't focus on anything but blatant humiliation. I only come back to attention when Cora claps her hands together, as if closing a book. She looks from Sebastian to the inner circle.

"Any questions?"

Amelia asks something, but I don't register a single word. My mouth has gone dry, and I'm staring absently in front of me.

Fairly confident.

They're *fairly confident* this isn't going to kill me. They *think* they'll finish before I die.

"Grace," Sebastian says. I startle as he touches my face, gently cupping my jaw. He tries to steal my attention, but I can't bear to look at him.

He promised. And he meant it. He's not going to let me die. He's not...

I close my eyes, fighting off a rush of tears. When a pathetic sob breaks from my lips, I cover my face with my hands.

"Grace," he says, voice soft, urgent. "Look at me, love."

It's that word—*love*—that has me opening my eyes. He's looking at me entirely too gently, like he cares. Like he's truly concerned, and not just trying to get me to calm down.

"I'm not going to let anything happen to you," he says. His thumb strokes my cheek, brushing away a stray tear. "Forget everything else. You have my word, little witch. I am going to keep you safe."

I'm nodding, even when I know it's foolish to believe, to trust.

Sebastian doesn't look away though. He doesn't show an ounce of hesitation or deceit.

The momentary flicker of warmth in my chest is shattered by Beatrice's animalistic snarl. She's moved from her place at the wall, surging closer until she's only feet from us.

"Master," she says. Her dark brows slant, mouth twisting into an ugly grimace. "Whatever mortal emotions you think you feel for her now, they are temporary. This darkness—this *curse*—is forever, unless she stops it."

"And she will," Sebastian says, keeping his eyes steady on me. "But not at the expense of her life."

"Master—"

"Does everyone understand?" he shouts. "We will break this curse, but not at the expense of her life. Repeat it back!"

The room is silent for a horribly strained second, until finally, six voices repeat Sebastian's words back to him. By the end, the inner circle stares at their leader in a mixture of horror and disbelief, except for Oskar, who looks only at me in pure wonder.

I DON'T REMEMBER the rest of the meeting. I blacked out everything following Sebastian's speech, and I'm still in a daze as we leave the auditorium an hour later. We don't speak as we walk. He doesn't tell me where we're going, but a rush of relief courses through me as we turn not for my cell, but his bedroom.

As soon as we're locked in his room, Sebastian crashes against me. He presses me against his closed door, lips trailing open-mouthed kisses across my throat. I arch into him, clutching his shoulders to keep from floating away.

"They're angry," I say. I force the words out, much as I'd like to fall into Sebastian's sudden affection. "Your circle...They're going to—"

"They're not going to do anything," he interrupts, lips not leaving my skin. "They're going to do as they're fucking told."

He nips at my jaw, letting his hand slip up my shirt and beneath my bra.

"They're scared," I say. "And they're—they're right—everyone is depending—"

Sebastian drops to his knees, yanking my shorts to my ankles. My words break away on a gasp as he presses his lips to my clit.

"On me," he says. "They're depending on me. You've agreed to try, and you're going to do what you can. All right? That's it. You're not going to die to clean up my mess."

"But you said—"

"That was before," he says roughly. He sucks my clit into his mouth, humming as he slips a finger between my legs.

"Before you realized how good I am in bed?" I ask. It's meant to be a joke, but it comes out as another needy gasp.

"I don't know," he says, pausing again. He looks up at me, somehow looking both savior and sinner. "Maybe before I met you. Before I realized..."

He trails off, but he doesn't look away. His eyebrows crinkle, mouth twitching silently with words he can't seem to say.

"I can't explain it, Grace," he says finally. "Just...just shut up and let me—"

I use my magic to move him.

For the first time, it's not to hold him down or to put him on his knees. It's to bring him to his feet. He yells out in surprise as I slam his back against the door. Before he can say another word, I'm knelt before him, hands frantically undoing his belt. He might not understand what's happening between us, but I finally do. And while I'm not ready to tell him either, I can certainly show him.

"Take off your shirt," I say without slowing my movements. He does as I say, not bothering to undo the buttons. They fly off his shirt, scattering across the floor. If I weren't a jittery, wanting mess, I might laugh.

As it is, I'm too focused. I yank his pants down, letting his cock spring free. It's long and thick, straining for me. It's too big to take all at once, but I stroke the shaft with one hand, leisurely, if only to watch Sebastian at my mercy. He stares at me like I'm his salvation, and I smile up at him, because I think he's right. His hips jerk, thrusting him harder into my fist.

I wet my lips, slowly, teasing him. Until finally, Sebastian snaps, wrapping my hair around his wrist and tugging my head back.

"Give me your mouth," he says roughly.

I consider making him wait, but I'm desperate too. I run my tongue over his length before wrapping my lips around him, taking him as deep as I can. As soon as his cock hits the back of my throat, a heady growl rumbles from his chest. And then, his cautiousness is gone. His hips snap hard and fast, until I'm gagging on him. He fucks my mouth like he owns it, like it's only ever belonged to him.

I shouldn't love it.

I do.

I grab his hips, falling into rhythm with his frantic thrusting. Spit trails from my mouth, and my eyes water. He's too big, too much—and I can't get enough.

"Holy fucking hells," he says. He curses, dropping his head back as he unloads into my mouth.

I swallow every drop, and when I'm done, he wipes the tears from my face.

"That was..." he trails off. "You're perfect, Grace."

I sit back on my heels, dabbing the corners of my mouth. Satisfaction hums through my chest, building me up until I feel nothing but pride.

"Tell me I was a good girl," I say. When he lifts a surprised eyebrow, I continue. "I've got a praise kink. I want you to be rough. Take what you want, and then tell me I did a good job."

"Praise kink," he repeats. His gaze darkens, mouth ticking into a smirk, but there's nothing mocking about his expression. "Is that a human thing?"

"I don't know. I guess," I say. "I just...I like when guys tell me I was good for them."

"Only me," he says sharply. He presses his thumb against my lips, until I open for him. "You're a good girl for me. All right? No one else."

"Only you," I repeat. I close my lips around his thumb, sucking softly. My center aches, and I shift on my heels, seeking relief.

"Good girl," he says. The words tumble easily from his lips, and he tightens his fingers around my chin. "My only girl."

Now, I'm the one surprised. I didn't expect him to say those words, let alone this quickly.

"I'm going to fuck this mouth for the rest of my life," he says. "Understand?"

I pull back, letting his thumb fall out of my mouth.

"The rest of your life is a very long time," I say carefully.

I try to control the fluttering warmth in my stomach, but I'm afraid it's too late. I've stood on the edge of this cliff for too long, and now that I've jumped, there's no going back.

"Yes," he agrees. He cups my jaw again, applying pressure until I open my mouth. He feeds his rapidly hardening cock between my lips. "Now be a good girl and swallow."

22

SAY THE WORD

GRACE

On the night of the full moon, Sebastian and I walk to the auditorium, side by side. I'm a nervous, fidgeting mess. My fingers bounce against my thighs and I keep wetting my lips, only for them to immediately turn to dust. My mouth is so dry it hurts to swallow.

Sebastian wears a carefully blank expression. We spent the entire day, isolated in his bedroom. He'd wanted to spend the time practicing my magic, but he didn't protest when I turned him down. He laid in bed beside me, toying with my hair, while I binge-watched my favorite movies and he memorized every line of Cora's planned ritual.

I'd done my best to block out tonight, but now, it's impossible to ignore. After this, the curse will either be broken or it won't. I will either be free or...

Sebastian stops just beyond the auditorium. The doors are open, exposing the layout we saw days ago. I can spot a few members of the inner circle, and Cora flits between the different artifacts, adjusting them on their stands. In less than an hour, the moon will be at its highest, and I'll be placing my literal life in Sebastian's hands.

Somehow, I know I can trust him with it.

"You don't have to do this," he says softly.

I startle, turning to look at him. His green eyes are already on me, and an undeniable panic swims within them.

"What?" I ask. My stomach lurches at the words I was sure I'd never hear. The words I've been desperate to hear since arriving. No matter how hard I look, I can't find anything but pure sincerity in his gaze.

"Say the word, Grace," he says. "We won't do it. I'll buy us more time. I'll find another way—"

"There isn't another way," I say. It's true. He *knows* it's true.

"Even if there's not," he says quietly. "Say the word, Grace. I'll get you out of here. I promise."

I swallow. It's everything I hoped he would say, and yet, it's no longer what I want. I've spent months training, learning. And while there are many things I would change about my time in this manor, there are certain things I wouldn't. I am stronger now than I used to be, and despite everything else, I know I can do this. I can break this curse—not just for Sebastian, but for every vampire in this strange world.

"When I break the curse," I say. Ignoring his surprised expression, I take his hand in mine. "I want you to turn me. I like who I am here, Sebastian. I'm important. Smart. Capable."

"You have always been those things, Grace. You always will be," he says. "You don't need to be here for that to be true."

"I mean it," I say, shaking my head. "If you'll have me, I want to stay."

"I have never wanted *anything* quite like I want you, Grace Renolds," he whispers.

"Is that a yes?" I ask. "You'll bite me? Make me one of your own?"

"We turn people with venom. Make them ingest it," he says, swallowing. His eyes flicker to my lips, pupils expanding. "I'll feed you my venom, if that's what you want, Grace. I'll turn you. I'll do whatever you want."

I kiss him, knowing his inner circle can see us. Knowing they're judging us and not caring that they are.

"Let's end this," I say, finally pulling back. I even manage a teasing smile. "You can give me everything I want after it's over."

Sebastian kisses me again, and together, we enter the auditorium.

THROUGH THE AUDITORIUM WINDOWS, the full moon shines between wispy clouds. I stare at the glowing orb, bright as any sun, while Sebastian and Cora go over the ritual once more. The inner circle left shortly after we arrived, and now, they stand outside, beneath the windows, surrounded by multiple unfamiliar vampires. They're all watching, all serving as a reminder. This ritual doesn't just affect me or Sebastian or his favored followers. It affects an entire species.

They're all desperate for change, and I'm the only one who can give it. Once I do, my life will officially be my own again. Now, I just have to survive the ritual, break the curse, and find my new beginning.

"I'm ready," I say. My voice shakes, but I'm more confident than I've felt in weeks.

I am strong, I remind myself. *I can do this.*

"Then let's begin," Cora says. She gestures for Sebastian to join her outside of the circle, but he doesn't move. His hand tightens over my shirt, as if anchoring himself to me.

"If she says to stop, you do," he says, looking at Cora. "Immediately. Do you understand?"

Cora lifts an unimpressed eyebrow.

"Fine," she agrees. Her dark eyes shift to mine.

I bite down, grating my teeth together. I can feel my heartbeat everywhere, radiating through my organs and veins and bones.

I will keep you safe.

I let myself believe the words.

I nod at Sebastian and step out of his hold. He takes the dagger from the podium, holding it for me like an offering. I take it wordlessly. My pale face is reflected in the blade, and I have to look away before my nerves consume me whole.

"Say the word," he reminds me. Then, he's gone in a flash too fast for me to follow. He stands at Cora's side with an unreadable expression, eyes locked on me.

"Focus on your magic," Cora says. "Once I signal you, cut your wrist, but keep casting. I should be able to channel your power as long as you're conscious."

"Got it," I say. My head is dizzy, riddled with nerves, but I force myself to look at the watching vampires again. I know all too well what it is to be trapped in this manor. If I succeed, I won't be the only one finding freedom.

"And you," she says, glaring at Sebastian. "Stay out of my way and out of this circle."

A solemn nod. He's still looking at me.

Cora lifts her hands. She's always made magic look effortless, so I'm surprised by the way her fingers tremble. Her eyes glaze as she speaks a string of unfamiliar words. They're of another language, I realize, one I don't recognize.

The air pulses as if electrified. I waver on my feet, gripping the table as magic presses over me. It surges from Cora's hands and surrounds my skin, choking my every breath. The surrounding artifacts twitch on their stands, as if coming to life.

Cora's voice grows louder and louder, until it's all I can hear. My brain feels heavy and foggy, the magic seeping into me, overflowing through my pores. There's no pain, but the pressure is all-encompassing, making it impossible to move.

She pauses, and the magic pulses around us. For the briefest of moments, my head clears enough to look at Sebastian. He stands at Cora's side, his hand lifted as if reaching for me.

I'm okay, I want to tell him. I don't. My mind may be clear, but the magic has done something strange to my voice. I'm not sure I remember how to speak, whether I could if I tried.

"Now, Grace," Cora says.

Her voice is stale, detached. Beneath it, however, her breath is ragged, as if she's clawing each inhalation from the bottom of her lungs.

"Now!" she repeats, louder.

I clench my jaw until it hurts. I'm hoping it's enough to distract the pain of slicing through my own skin. It's not.

In one swift motion, I slice my wrist, and blood pours from my veins. I stare in shock as dark red pools from my skin and into the glass bowl. Pain erupts across my palm. I drop the dagger, letting the blood-stained metal clatter across the floor. My attention remains on the bowl, watching as it fills unnaturally fast.

As soon as Cora resumes chanting, the pressure of magic is back, like it never left. Only now, it brings with it a scalding heat. I scream, knees buckling as pain scours through me, devouring me from the inside out. I don't know how I remain upright, if it's magic or my own stubborn will.

I look at Cora. There's nothing human about the way she looks now. Her eyes have rolled back, until there's only hazy white. The foreign words stream from her lips, voice lowering as if powered by something demonic.

Almost done, I tell myself. *Keep going. You're almost there.*

I don't know if it's the truth.

I'm desperate enough to believe the lie.

In the back of my mind, I wonder if this is a vampire's death. Is this how they felt after the witches' curse? Did they feel like they were being boiled alive? Like someone was shredding their insides and reducing them to ash?

I try to find Sebastian, but there is only this violent light, devouring me whole.

Until I'm dizzy.

Sick.

Dying.

I finally find him. Staring at me. Blank. Emotionless. Uncaring. His mouth moves, but I'm too gone to hear it. Or, maybe, the only voice I can hear now is Cora's.

She's staring at me too. Her eyes are black, hands still lifted.

"It's working!" she screams. "We've got it!"

My knees buckle again, just as my hands burst with inexplicable heat. I loll my head to the side, searching for them, as if they're not attached to me. They are, but they don't look right. They're coated in something red or orange or—

Fire, I realize. I'm on *fire*.

It's my last thought before everything goes dark.

23

I WARNED YOU, MASTER

SEBASTIAN

I shouldn't be here. There's too much to figure out, and yet, I can't tear myself away from this room. Grace is still unconscious. She lies on my bed, wrist bandaged but still bleeding. It's under control now, at least. She's not going to bleed out. She won't die.

Too close.

It's the only thought in my head. I can't focus on anything beyond the way her eyes shifted, the way her soul seemed ready to vanish from this world completely.

She almost died.

I almost let her die.

I pace my bedroom, pausing to evaluate her wrist again. Cora should be here to stitch her up, but obviously that's not possible. I don't trust anyone else to try, and I never learned how to do it.

"Come on, little witch," I whisper. "I need you to wake up."

I run the back of my knuckle down her cheek. She doesn't open her eyes, but her face twitches, as if she senses my presence. As if she wants to get away from it.

Another twenty minutes pass. The room is silent except for

my footsteps as I pace the room. Back and forth, back and forth. We're nearing twelve hours since the ritual, and still, she sleeps.

It isn't until hour eighteen, when I'm checking her bandage for the hundredth time, that her eyes open. She blinks, taking in the room, before settling on me. She's confused, disoriented.

It's the only reason she smiles at me.

It's a punch to the gut anyway.

"Grace," I whisper.

Her eyes close again, and her mouth falls slack.

"No," I say. It comes out harsh, like a command, and her eyes struggle to open once more. "Come on, Grace. Stay awake."

I dip into bed beside her, carefully tucking her against my chest. Without a moment's hesitation, I bite my wrist, roughly tearing the skin. Dark blood pools from my wrist and onto her shirt. I press it against her mouth, cupping the back of her head when she instinctively rears back.

"Be a good girl," I say. "Swallow for me."

Whether she hears me or she's too weak to fight, Grace relaxes against me. She nestles her head against my shoulder, those warm lips latching onto my wrist. She drinks from me as if by instinct, as if she's done it before. Between each swallow, she lets out a tiny, satisfied moan.

It's the most beautiful sound in the world.

Vampire blood is healing, but I've only ever allowed one person to drink from me. It was Cora, as a child, when she was so beaten and bruised, she would have died without it. It was necessary, and yet, I vowed to never do it again. It made me feel weak, like a lowly animal, as if I'd fallen down the evolutionary chain.

Now, I'm glad to give it. I pull Grace closer, urging her to drink more, to take every drop she needs. There's an unfamiliar sensation in my chest, one deeper than lust, fuller than joy. It's a sensation I thought didn't exist—that I'm now determined to keep.

Two days later, Grace opens her eyes for real. She blinks at me, and there's nothing hazy in her expression. She's *here*, eyebrows scrunching as she takes in her surroundings.

"How are you feeling?" I ask.

The words are too sharp, more like a command than a genuine question. I don't correct myself. I'm too busy studying her features, looking for any sign of distress or lingering injury.

Tell me you're okay.

Tell me you'll be fine.

"Did it work?" she asks.

There's a streak of my blood on her throat. I've done my best to keep her clean, but it's stained her shirt, creating a collar of dried blood. She's been feeding off me for days, and while I haven't felt tempted by *her* blood, I know I'm being reckless. I should have fed by now, and yet, I can't bring myself to leave her.

"No," I say. I swallow, keeping my gaze steady on hers. "It didn't work."

"Oh," she says. With that single word, her entire body deflates into the mattress. She sags against the pillows, letting her attention drift from me. Her eyelids seem to grow heavier, as if she's ready to go back under.

"But you survived, Grace," I say. "*That*'s what matters."

"Yeah, sure," she says, scoffing. Tears fill her eyes, but she quickly blinks them away. "Did I...I don't remember how it ended. Was I close before I called it? Would it have worked if I didn't—"

"You didn't," I say, interrupting her. Part of me wants to lie. It'd be easier to say she stopped it, that it would have worked if she hadn't called it off. But I can't force the words from my mouth. "It was working. It was going to work."

Grace doesn't respond, but her throat bobs as she swallows.

"I stopped it," I say. "Cora said you would make it, but you were in so much pain. I was sure...I was terrified you were going to *die*."

Her attention flickers from mine again. She's still holding her wrist, staring blankly toward the corner of the room.

"Thank you," she finally whispers.

"I'm sorry," I repeat. "I'm sorry I made you go through it. I thought it would work, that you'd be able to handle it."

Another scoff.

"That came out wrong. I didn't mean—"

"Stop, Sebastian," she says through a snarl. "Stop acting nice, like you care. You're pissed, and you know it. You were so close to getting what you wanted, but you'd made a stupid promise and had to stick by it. And unfortunately for you, you forgot just how pathetic, how weak—"

I press my mouth against hers. It's barely a kiss, too firm to do anything more than shut her up.

"I am not bound by my promises," I say. My lips brush against hers as I speak, and I tighten my hands over her jaw. "If I didn't care whether you died, I would have let you die. If I didn't care, I would have risked it. I didn't stop it because I think you're weak or because I'd told you I wouldn't let you die. It was because, for the first time, I feared something more than my own mortality."

She swallows, and I trail my thumb down her throat, letting it settle over her pulse.

"I feared *yours*, Grace," I whisper. "I had to choose between the curse and you, and I chose you. And no matter how many times I have to choose, that's not going to change."

I pull back, studying her expression. She's impossible to read, her eyes staring just past me.

"Okay," she says finally. "We can try again later."

Rather than respond, I claim her mouth, kissing her until she makes a soft sound of protest. When I pull back, she's not looking at me but the front of her shirt.

"Is this mine?" she asks, plucking at the blood-stained fabric.

"No. It's mine."

"How did it get here?"

"Vampire blood is healing," I say.

Her eyes widen.

"That was *real*?"

My lips tick into a smile without permission. I'm still half draped over her.

"That should be gross, right?" she asks. Her nose crinkles, and I kiss her again. I don't know what's wrong with me, but I can't seem to stop. I'm obsessed, so desperate to consume her, I can think of little else. Kiss her until she's moaning. Fuck her until she's thinking of nothing but me.

"It was hot," I say.

"Yeah?" she asks. Her eyes sparkle, even if only slightly. She's still weak, still tired. But she's still *here*, and that's what matters.

"Yeah," I confirm. I press my lips to her throat, her jaw, her cheek. "Now, can I please fucking kiss you?"

Before she answers, her stomach lets out a low rumble.

"You're hungry," I say. It comes out more like an accusation than a statement.

"It can wait," she says immediately. She presses her hands into my hair, flinching when she bumps her bandaged wrist against my head.

I'm off her before she can even think of wrapping those legs around me.

"Food first," I tell her. "I'll make it up to you after."

"Sounds like *I'm* the one who should be making things up," she mumbles.

"It wasn't your fault," I say. I pinch her chin, angling her head until she meets my gaze. "You don't owe me—or anyone else—a single thing."

I swallow the sudden knot in my throat. I'm being too honest, revealing too much.

"Is Cora angry?" she asks.

I hesitate. Before I can decide whether I want to tell her the full truth, Grace sits up straight.

"She's furious, isn't she?" she asks. "Is Milas going—"

"I haven't seen Cora since that night," I admit. "I imagine she's furious, but I'm not sure. The last time I saw her, she was unconscious at my feet."

"You didn't—"

"I did," I say, cutting her off with a growl. "She ignored my orders. She was going to let you die."

"Maybe she knew I wouldn't," Grace whispered.

"Maybe," I admit. Surprise flashes over Grace's features. I hold my hand out to her and help her off the bed. "I wasn't willing to find out."

Grace blinks at me, eyebrows scrunching like she's searching for a hidden meaning.

I stare right back, letting her find the same truth I already have.

"Come on, little witch," I say finally. "Let's get you something to eat."

AT GRACE'S REQUEST, we're in the courtyard. She's eating a fragrant bowl of pasta, humming to herself between bites. I lean against the statue of myself, watching her without bothering to pretend otherwise. It'd be smart to use this time to feed, but I still don't trust anyone else alone with her.

A soft knock sounds at the courtyard entryway, and I turn to find Oskar watching us. Damn him. All these years, and he's still the only one to surprise me.

"Master," he says.

We've only spoken twice since the failed ritual. First, when he updated me on Cora's recovery—and fury—from my hit. Second, when he asked what plans I had to try again. I didn't have an answer for him then, and I certainly don't now.

"Oskar," I finally reply. My attention flickers back to Grace. She has her electronic in front of her and a pair of headphones over her ears. She glances our way, offering a shy nod, before turning back to the movie.

"How is she?" he asks. He steps into the sunlight, breathing deeply as the warmth hits his face. He stands with relaxed posture and a soft smile, staring at me like a father would his son.

"Better," I say, even though that much is obvious. The last time he saw her, she looked like a bloodied corpse. "The food should help."

"Looks like food might help you too," he says. "When's the last time you fed?"

"I'm fine." I look at Grace again. Not long ago, I stared up at the sun, hating its violent light. For so long, I believed it was the only force strong enough to contain my kind.

Now, I realize Grace is far more powerful. Her violent light is the only thing capable of containing *me*, and if I'm not careful, she'll consume every last piece.

Oskar claps a hand on my shoulder, and I force my gaze back to him.

"She would have died," he says. His expression is soft, with something unrecognizable just beneath the surface. "You could have broken the curse, but you chose her life instead."

"We don't know it would have worked," I say. "It might have failed. And if she was dead, we would have been fucked."

"Perhaps," he says.

We both know the truth.

I hold my breath, hoping Oskar will let it go. Instead, he lets out a soft laugh and lowers his voice for only me to hear.

"I warned you, Master," he says. "Love has driven people to madness."

I turn, ready to deny it, only to find him already gone.

24

IT'S A RELIEF, TRULY

GRACE

"**W**hat's the plan, Sebastian?" I ask.

He takes a moment to meet my gaze. He looks up from between my legs, pausing to lick my arousal from his lips. His eyes are hazy, as if he's only partly here. Rather than respond, he looks back to my center. He trails his finger up my thigh, and without warning, thrusts it inside me.

My back arches, and a breathy moan breaks from my lips.

God, he's insatiable. In the week since the failed ritual, we've spent most of our days like this. Lost to each other in his bedsheets, naked and sated. If we're not actively fucking, we're watching one of my movies or talking about his plans for the Night Realm's future. We've done a bit of everything, so long as it's happened within this room.

"My plan is to make you come another time like this," he says, adding another finger. I moan again, and he smiles, pumping leisurely. "Once you have, I'll fuck you with my cock. After that…"

He trails off. He's fully focused on my pussy now, staring at it in wonder.

"Sebastian," I force myself to say. "What's the plan with the curse? Have you—"

I break off in another moan. He's impossible. I let myself ride his hand for another minute before grabbing his wrist. He looks up at me in surprise, his typical, arrogant smirk still on his face.

"Sebastian," I say. "Hold on."

He withdraws from me but remains between my legs. His eyes scan over me, as if gauging how serious I'm being. When he realizes I'm not going to drop it, his shoulders deflate.

He pulls himself away, rotating until he's sitting beside me. He sweeps his comforter over us, pausing to pull it over my chest. He tucks the blanket beneath my chin.

"Can't think with those things on display," he mutters. He runs a hand through his hair. "I don't know what the plan is, Grace. I've been in this room almost as much as you have."

"Don't you think..." I trail off.

"Yes," he says. Now his hand slides over his face. "I know we have to figure something out, Grace, but I don't want to fucking think about it. Every time I do, I'm imagining you bloody and pale and screaming and...I don't want to think about it."

I blink at him, unable to hide my surprise. It's more honest than he's ever been, and his gaze flits away from me, as if he's realized that too.

"Well, it's going to end up like that if we don't make a better plan," I say. "Maybe there's something with my bloodline that could be useful. Maybe if we found something that once belonged to my dad or..."

I trail off, realizing how stupid I sound.

"Keep talking," Sebastian commands.

"I have a whole box of my dad's things back home," I say. "There's a good chance Tessa threw them out, but if she didn't...I wonder if they'd help strengthen my magic. Or at least my connection to the original spell?"

Sebastian doesn't reply right away. He stares up at the ceiling, winding his fingers through my hair.

"Maybe," he says finally.

"You don't think it would work," I say, turning to look at him.

"It's not that," he says. He doesn't return my gaze. "It's just…I think we need to look at other options. Ones that don't involve you."

"Sebastian—"

"I know, Grace," he says. "I know. But I'm not ready, all right? I need—"

He doesn't get a chance to finish his thought. A heavy knock pounds against the door.

"What?" Sebastian snaps.

The person knocking doesn't respond. They only keep knocking and knocking and—

Sebastian growls and climbs out of bed. He slides into a pair of slacks and glances to make sure I'm covered.

"What do you want, Cora?" he asks before he's even opened the door. Once he has, I still can't see her from my position in the bed. I can only hope that means she doesn't see me either.

Everyone knows we're having sex, but still…

"We have three weeks until the next full moon," she says. "As much as I know you two would like to fuck for that entire time, I'd appreciate a *little* help here. I'm fine, by the way. Nice of you to check on me, Sebastian. Only one of your oldest friends, risking her life to do this for you. And what do I get? A fucking punch to the face and a week of silence. Real. Nice."

"Hells," Sebastian mutters. He rubs his hand over his face again. Part of me expects him to yell, to shove her out of his doorway. Instead, he releases a heavy breath. "Tonight, all right? We'll talk about it tonight. Grace has an idea that might help."

"Is she here?" she asks. Even without seeing her face, I can feel the accusation in her question.

"None of your business," Sebastian says.

He's already started to shut the door, but Cora is quick to catch it.

"In case you've forgotten," she says. "*Everyone* is counting on you. If this fails, if you choose her over them, you're dooming your entire species. *Again*."

The door slams. Sebastian crosses the room, kicking out of his pants when he reaches the bed. He presses a hand over his mouth, and without saying a word, I can tell he's moments from breaking.

Cora isn't wrong. We *do* need to figure out a plan, but maybe, it's okay to put off the world for another half hour.

"Need a sex break?" I ask.

"Is that a human thing?" he asks. He lowers his hand, mouth tilting into a mischievous smirk. Even if it's temporary, I feel a stroke of pride.

"Sure, why not?" I say. I flip the covers back, revealing the full length of my naked body.

Sebastian swallows, eyes falling to my center. He strokes himself as he crawls onto the bed. He touches the soft spot between my legs before notching his cock there, and with one hard thrust, he presses into me. We groan in unison, and I wrap my legs around his waist, anchoring him to me.

"I won't let anything happen to you," he whispers as he moves. "You're mine. You feel that, right? You're mine, and I'll keep you safe."

Before I can respond, his mouth is on mine, tongue claiming every inch of it, until I'm not sure where he ends and I begin.

THAT NIGHT, I lie in Sebastian's bed with the covers tucked to my chin. He left over an hour ago to meet with Cora and Oskar, and though he invited me to join, I decided to stay. I already know the next few weeks will be crammed with hard training and endless brainstorming sessions. Before anything else, Sebastian and Cora need to get on the same page.

I *did* ask him to pass my idea onto Cora though. If she thinks my dad's belongings might strengthen my magic for the ritual, I want to try. Sebastian and I have spent the past months as enemies, so it's thrilling to imagine what we might accomplish as *allies*. I'm pathetically eager to contribute something more than my witch blood, and this feels like the perfect opportunity.

For now, I'm happy to snuggle in his bed and watch *Legally Blonde* for the millionth time. I've almost drifted to sleep when a heavy knock comes at the door.

I groan and pause the movie. Much as I'm tempted to ignore Beatrice, who's standing guard in the hallway, it feels like a jerk move. I straighten my clothes as I cross the room, only to startle when I open the door. It's not Beatrice. Oskar stands in the doorway, and he offers his standard, soft smile.

"Oh," I say, raising my brows. I glance at the empty space around him. "Where's Beatrice?"

"I relieved her shortly after the meeting," he says. He pauses, craning to peer in Sebastian's room. "Are you ready?"

"I didn't realize the meeting was over," I say. Then, "Ready for what?"

"Apologies. I assumed Sebastian told you," he says. "We're to collect your father's belongings in the human world."

"Wait...Cora thinks it will help?" I ask. I can't keep the smile off my face, and I immediately bounce onto my toes. "We're going to do it? And *I* get to go?"

"Apparently," Oskar says, chuckling. "Sebastian and Cora have business to attend though, so they're sending me to accompany you. I hope that's all right."

"Yes, of course," I say. I bob my head and try to tame my

smile. I'm terrified he'll retract the offer if I seem too eager, but I can't help myself.

I get to go. Sebastian is trusting me to go.

"All right," Oskar says with a nod. He steps back, sweeping his arm into the hallway. "Well, if you're ready, let's go."

I don't give him any reason to hesitate. For the first time, I get to be an active part of the team. I'll break the curse with more than just my blood. I'm actually contributing an idea. Something to break the curse *and* save my life.

I snag my jacket from the dresser and follow Oskar into the hall, making a mental list of everything I'll take from Tessa's apartment. Beyond Dad's box of letters in my closet, I can get my phone and my favorite perfume and Mom's old sweatshirt. If Oskar isn't paying attention, I'll grab some lingerie too.

By the time we exit the manor, I'm beaming. I spent months terrified I'd never see Aberlena or the human world again. Now, I can't wait to say my final goodbye.

OSKAR RUNS through the Night Realm with me in his arms. He's noticeably slower than Sebastian, and yet, I end up retching once we reach the neutral territory. I fold over, hands on my knees, and breathe through the lingering nausea. It feels like we just ping-ponged across the Echo, and my brain is struggling to find steady ground.

"You all right?" Oskar asks, roughly patting my back.

"Fine," I say.

I wipe my sleeve across my mouth, blinking down at the blackened ground before us. The burnt soil spreads all throughout the neutral territory, from what I can tell. I make a mental note to ask Sebastian about it later, but for now, I'm just trying not to hurl again. I squeeze my eyes, grunting when Oskar slaps my back again, harder.

"I'm wearing weird clothes," I say when I finally stand up. I glance at Oskar, and his outfit is no better. He's wearing black slacks, a buttoned shirt, and a medieval-looking coat. "We're going to stick out in Aberlena. The humans will probably notice."

It's the first time I've said that. *Humans*, as if they're something I'm not.

I swallow and refuse to let myself dwell. Instead, I focus back on our surroundings. I haven't seen the neutral territory since Sebastian first carried me through it, and I'm surprised how ordinary it seems. Aside from the startling black ground, it's far more like the human world than the Night Realm.

The buildings are simple and painted dull shades of brown, grey, and white. In the distance, an evening market is starting. There are colorful booths with lush bouquets of flowers and silken scarves, dried meats and assortments of strange weapons. People mill throughout the streets, and even from here, I can tell they aren't human.

As Oskar leads us into the neutral territory, I struggle to absorb the endless sights and smells and sounds. This place is filled with obvious signs of poverty: overflowing garbage and boarded windows and the distinct smell of waste. And still, the partygoers hoot and holler, clearly ecstatic for the escape.

"How are they outside?" I ask as we approach them. "It's nighttime. Shouldn't vampires be out hunting? It feels like they should all be hiding."

"This is the neutral territory," Oskar says gruffly. He moves closer, keeping his hand on my shoulder as we merge into the crowd.

We're surrounded by too many strange creatures for me to process them all. There are women with papery wings and short, wrinkled goblins. Children with animal horns over their brows and a woman with misshapen gills on her throat. Down a nearby alley, a group of teenagers play with a ball between them. It floats, untouched by gravity, as they shout and laugh.

We've already passed them before I realize what they are. Witches. *Like me.*

Only they seem as foreign, as strange as any other creature we pass.

"I don't understand," I say, clearing my throat. I glance back at Oskar, stumbling when he hurries me along. "Why is the neutral territory different?"

"Any physical harm attempted here happens to the attacker instead of their victim," he explains. "The whole neutral territory is protected. That's why the ground is black. Nasty spell."

I start to ask another question, but Oskar tightens his grip and urges me faster. We press through the overbearing crowd, until finally, he veers down an unmarked side street and then another. I steal a final glance at the celebration before we turn a corner and it disappears from sight.

Oskar doesn't slow his pace, and we navigate through a twist of sleeping neighborhoods and empty streets. Before long, even the melodic festival music fades, and we're left with only our quick footsteps and my embarrassingly heavy breathing.

"I'm glad the master found you," Oskar says as he finally loosens his hold on my shoulder. "I feared he would never love anything other than himself. It's a relief, truly, that he found you."

I sputter out a surprised laugh, even as a pleasant warmth spreads through my chest.

"I'm not sure Sebastian loves me," I say carefully. He's certainly never admitted it, and yet, the idea doesn't feel as preposterous as it should. Whether he loves me or not, I'd be lying if I said I haven't *felt* loved these past few days.

"He does," Oskar says. He finally eases his steps, coming to walk at my side. "It might not be clear to you, but I've known him a long time. He looks at you like I looked at my wife. My Freja."

"I didn't know you were married."

"I was. She passed years ago."

"I'm sorry," I say, my stomach dropping. I've never been good with sad stories. It doesn't matter that I never knew Freja. I know Oskar, and the look on his face now is enough to make me cry.

"Shortly after Sebastian betrayed the witches, they decided to punish him," Oskar says. "To punish *all* of us. The witches cursed us to burn in the sun. No warning. No time to prepare. My Freja...she died that first day. Burned to bone and ash in the courtyard Sebastian now uses to house his statue."

It's the first time Oskar has sounded bitter toward Sebastian, and I look at him, unable to mask my surprise.

"Oskar..." I say finally, voice cracking. "I'm so sorry."

Rather than reply, Oskar offers his arms to me. My stomach lurches at the thought of running again, but I'd rather vomit than hear more of this heartbreak. I ease into his arms, tucking my head against his shoulder as he jolts into a run.

After what feels like hours, and is likely only minutes, Oskar staggers to a stop. We're surrounded by the same blackened earth as before, but all signs of civilization have disappeared. It's painfully dark and quiet. We've stopped far enough away that the impoverished city and its lively festival are nothing more than an outline of buildings in the distance.

Oskar releases me, and I crash to my knees. I dig my fingers against the black rock, blinking through the darkness. Even with the moon hanging overhead, I can barely see my friend's pale face. An endless expanse of shadows closes around us, as if the night has swallowed us whole.

"This isn't the Paragon," I say. I force myself to look at him, at his pale face, silhouetted by the moon.

"No," he agrees. His voice is as steady, as soft as ever, and yet, it steals any lingering warmth from my body.

Something is wrong.

Very wrong.

"Oskar," I whisper. "What's going on?"

I rise to my feet, keeping my movements carefully slow. Still, every inch of my body is trembling, and I'm sure Oskar can tell. I'm sure he can hear each erratic and reckless beat of my heart.

"He killed the only thing I've ever loved," Oskar says. He steps closer, and I mirror his movement, taking a step away. He doesn't lunge like I expect. Instead, he pauses, tucking his hands into his pockets and smiling sadly at me. "There is no worse pain to suffer, Grace."

"Oskar," I repeat. My mouth bobs, but I can't find any other words. Every nerve in my body fires at once, begging—*screaming* —for me to run. Whatever I thought I knew of Oskar suddenly feels untrue.

"For what it's worth, I am sorry," he says.

I lift my hands, and the moonlight shines over them as they tremble. I channel every ounce of magic I can muster, but I don't strike. Not yet.

"Please don't make me hurt you," I say. I take another slow step back, fighting a sob even as tears streak down my cheeks. "I'm sorry about Freja, but that has nothing to do with me."

Oskar doesn't move. He remains perfectly motionless, hands tucked away, head tilted in thought. He smiles at me again, soft and genuine as ever.

"She would have liked you," he says.

My mouth gaps silently. I'm still scrambling for something to say when an unseen person grabs me from behind. There's not even time to scream. A pair of hands latch over my shoulders, and seconds later, another person grabs my legs. Before I comprehend what's happening, I'm on the ground, paralyzed by the familiar press of magic.

It's unlike anything I've ever felt, stronger than I even knew to fear. The force hangs over me, violent enough I can barely expand my lungs. I stare up at the star-speckled sky, gasping for breath.

"He'll come for her," Oskar says. He looks not at me or my two attackers, but at someone unseen beyond us. "Don't give him the chance."

"Final offer to join us, Oskar Duluth," a cold, feminine voice says. "I imagine you won't survive a reunion with your *master*."

She says Sebastian's title like it's an insult.

"Survival was never the goal," Oskar says. He dips his chin, looking over me one last time. "*This* was the only thing keeping me here."

"He doesn't love me," I say. My words are so strained, they're barely audible. "Sebastian doesn't—He's not going to care, Oskar. Don't do this!"

If Oskar understands me, he doesn't react. He only tilts his head to the sky, smiling to the heavens. It's the last thing I see before my vision goes black, and I lose sense of everything.

25

THE MOST BEAUTIFUL THING IN THE WORLD

SEBASTIAN

We have a plan, or at least, the beginning of one. I met with Cora and Oskar in the courtyard to explain our new challenge: breaking the curse without risking Grace's life. Oskar understood immediately, as I hoped he would, but Cora was more difficult. She had endless questions and dozens of hypothetical consequences if we failed the ritual a second time.

Eventually, Oskar retired for the night, promising to inform the rest of the inner circle of our changed plans. Cora hounded me for another two hours after he left, and it all came back to her earlier sentiment.

If you choose her over them, you're dooming your entire species. Again.

Cora was right. It was my recklessness that caused the sun curse, and this is my only chance to repair the damage...but sacrificing Grace isn't saving my people. It's making the same mistake of selfishness, all over again. This time, I'm not choosing Grace over the vampires.

I'm choosing redemption over revenge.

The future over the past.

Our love over my pride.

By the time Cora and I left the courtyard, I felt like she understood. I can only hope the others will feel the same way. We don't need to risk Grace to save ourselves. We can break the curse—and we will—but we'll do it the right way. The witches don't realize Grace exists, so we have nothing but time to—

"Beatrice?"

My brain stutters as I enter the blood letting room. There are dozens of feeding vampires, but my eyes immediately lock on the brunette at the center table. Beatrice sits across from a human man, his wrist pressed to her ruby lips. Her eyes are hazy as she pulls back to wave at me. She uses the back of her wrist to wipe her mouth, expression shifting when I don't move a single muscle.

I'm sure I must be hallucinating, and I blink, desperate to make the vision disappear.

"Is everything okay?" she asks. She breaks away from the bloodletter, snapping to attention. Without taking her eyes off me, she strides across the room to my side.

"Where is she?"

Beatrice freezes, jaw tensing, teeth grinding. She studies me silently, as if decoding a complicated riddle.

"Grace?" she asks finally.

"Did you leave her alone?" I ask.

Without waiting for a response, I spin out of the room and take off in the direction of my quarters. I don't let myself run, much as I'm tempted. I need to understand, because Beatrice wouldn't abandon her post without reason. Something must have happened.

"Is she hurt?" I ask.

Without turning, I know Beatrice has followed me. She keeps pace at my side, our shoulders brushing.

"She was fine when I left," she says. Her voice wavers. "Oskar came to replace me."

I stop, turning abruptly on Beatrice. She stumbles, back striking the wall, eyes widening as I crowd her against it. I breathe her in, searching for even the faintest hint of Grace's blood.

There's nothing.

Beatrice shudders where she stands, neck tense as she leans away from me. I can smell the fear radiating off her, but there's no sign of deception or guilt. She's telling the truth, but no matter how hard I try, I can't make sense of it.

"Why?"

"He said you'd sent him," she says. "This was two hours ago. He said—"

I don't hear the rest of her sentence. I take off, tearing through the halls so fast I can barely track where I am. I'm up the stairs and down a twist of corridors and standing in front of my closed bedroom door.

He's not here.

The hallway is quiet, and so are my quarters. There's nothing, not even a hint of breathing, coming from my bedroom.

I already know.

With my heart in my stomach, I shove the door open, revealing an empty room. My bed is unmade. Grace's shoes are gone, and so is her coat from the dresser. Everything else is as I left it.

There's no sign of her, but there wasn't a struggle either.

Beatrice flies into view, shuddering to a stop inches from me. Her head whips one way, then another, before she lunges into the room. She's cowering as she turns, dark eyes growing large.

"I didn't..." she starts, lower lip trembling. "I swear, I am telling the truth, Master. Oskar came, and he told me to leave, and I—I did. But I swear..."

Her words break into hysterical sobs as falls to her knees. She dips her head, resting it on the floor between us.

"Please, Master," she says, her words muffled. "Have mercy. I didn't—"

"Did he say anything?" I demand. "Did he give any indication he was taking her somewhere?"

"No, I swear," she says. She stares up at me, makeup running down her cheeks. "He said he was taking over until you were done with Cora. That's it. I promise."

I don't know if she's telling the truth. Right now, it doesn't matter.

"Get up," I say. "Round the others. Bring them to the courtyard."

Without a word, Beatrice launches to her feet and disappears around the corner. I grab Grace's electronic from the bed and make my way through the manor.

Cora can use it for a locating spell. If Grace is gone, if she's been stolen from me, these will help bring her back.

Unless she wasn't stolen at all.

Unless she ran, and he helped her.

I shove the thought out of my head. There isn't time to consider it.

"No one speaks," I command. I stand at the head of the table, looking from each seated member of my inner circle. They all face me without a speck of remorse or guilt, as if they're all as determined to find Grace as I am.

Is it possible they're all innocent?

It doesn't make sense for any of them to betray me. Outside of Cora, they're all vampires. They *want* to break this curse as desperately as I do. I glance at our resident witch as she adjusts

Grace's electronic on the table. No, it's impossible to imagine Cora sabotaging this.

"Is it ready?" I ask, nodding toward her set-up. Three brightly-colored herbs surround the electronic, forming a loose triangle.

Cora nods and closes her eyes. With her hands spread over the table, she mutters a foreign spell beneath her breath. The air shifts with magic, and the herbs slowly begin to twitch against the stone. As Cora works, the rest of us alternate between watching her and watching the courtyard's entrance.

Beatrice and Amelia sit on the far side of the table, and Theo sits across from them. I stare at the opposite head of the table, where my oldest friend usually sits.

"Master," Milas calls.

I turn, chest tensing. Milas strides into the courtyard, hand on Oskar's shoulder. The old man isn't fighting him off. He doesn't look riddled with guilt or fear. His expression is as gentle, as steady as ever. He walks with his hands loose at his sides, a soft smile lighting his face once he reaches me.

"Oskar," I say, searching his eyes.

If Beatrice is telling the truth, he was the last to see Grace before she disappeared. He would be guilty of something terrible—and I should be able to sense it. Looking now, there is nothing but gentle warmth and a familiarity deeper than my own reflection.

"Everyone sit," I say, forcing myself to look away. My voice is hard, teeming with overflowing tension. I can feel every muscle in my neck, in my back, in my legs. It takes all my effort not to lunge for Oskar's throat.

Careful.

The fastest path to Grace is with the truth. Until I know what happened, I can't know where to look. Or who to punish.

"Beatrice, tell me your truth," I say. "Be brief, but don't leave anything out."

All eyes turn to Beatrice. She swallows, placing her trembling hands on the stone table. She keeps her eyes locked intently on me as she wrings her fingers together.

"I was posted outside your door," she says. "I'd been there for about an hour when Oskar arrived. He said I was being dismissed and that he would take over watch. I went straight to Amelia's quarters from there, and I remained until I left to feed. That's when you found me."

I shift my attention to Amelia.

"True?"

"Beatrice arrived about twenty minutes after sunfall," Amelia says. "She mentioned she'd been relieved by Oskar. She was with me until the second hour, when she said she was going to feed."

"Oskar," I say.

The old man, my longest friend, sits on the opposite end of the table at his usual place. He sits with relaxed posture and his eyes keep flicking to the heavens. In the moments before he speaks, I scan over his entire appearance. Where I had to search for Beatrice's emotions, Oskar's are written plainly over his face.

He's confident, comfortable, unbothered.

Innocent, I tell myself. *He's clearly innocent.*

"Beatrice speaks the truth," he says finally.

Something jolts in my chest, sharp as a wooden stake through the heart.

"After our meeting, I went to your quarters," he says. His eyes are on mine, steady and unrelenting. "I dismissed Beatrice. I told Grace she was to retrieve her father's belongings from the human world."

Something violent and scalding crashes through my insides. It's impossible to think, to feel, to do anything but stare at my oldest friend. He'd taken the words from our meeting and used them to mislead Grace. My Grace. I want to lunge across the table and rip his head from his body.

Instead, I force myself to swallow, to take a deep, heaving breath.

"Why." I meant to ask it as a question, but it comes as a sharp command.

"I told her Cora believed it would help the curse," he says. His face remains soft and warm, but something in his eyes flickers with darkness. With cruelty. So brief it would have been easy to miss.

At some point, it seems Oskar started a game, and I'm at the center of it. How many times did that flicker of evil cross his expression, and I was too naive to notice?

Whatever his plan, it's clear he wants to relish this moment. He'd like to drag it out, make me beg for each parcel of information. He's going to hold his words close, so I must do the same.

I tuck my emotions into a careful box in the back of my mind and harden my stare.

"Where is she now?" I ask.

All the other members have fallen perfectly still at the table. Beatrice's eyes have fluttered shut, and a tear streaks down her cheek. Amelia has her hands pressed to her temples. The two younger men are silent, but their eyes flick from each other to me to Oskar. Cora is too deep into her spell to realize what's happening around her.

"Hard to say," Oskar says.

He smiles. He fucking smiles at me.

It's not mocking or taunting. It's gentle and kind, as if he's done nothing wrong.

Maybe he hasn't, I remind myself.

It's a useless, pathetic hope.

"Oskar," I say. My voice booms through the silent courtyard, and his eyes spark. I'm giving him exactly what he wants, but I can't control myself for another second. "Tell me where she is or I'll rip your fucking head from your body."

"Go ahead then," he says. He rests his elbows in front of him, leaning toward me. "Rip my head off, Master. See where it gets you."

I suck air into my lungs, clenching and unclenching my fists.

"Oskar, if you don't—"

"See, but that's your problem," he interrupts. "Your only way to threaten me is with my own life. You can torture me, starve me, kill me...but that's where your options end. I have only ever loved one person in this world, Master, and you stole her from me."

"This is about your fucking wife?" I ask. I'm seething, vibrating with coiled fury and tension. "She died by the witches' curse, not my hand, and it's been twenty years. It's too late for petty revenge."

"Not revenge," Oskar says. He shakes his head, drawing a deep breath and closing his eyes. The final word is spoken on a breath of relief. "Justice."

"So what, this curse kills your wife and now you're damning us all?" Beatrice demands. Tears leak down her face, and her fangs extend as she glares at him. "Ruining *all* of our lives, just because you've suffered. As if we *all* haven't—"

"It is not about you," Oskar says gently. He speaks as if she's a selfish, petulant child, as if she's too young to understand. "It is about *him*."

His eyes are back on me. I search them, searching for each splinter of evil within the grey.

"His selfish behavior took my one love from me," he says. "And now, my selfish behavior will take his from him."

"Where is she?" I roar.

I'm on the other side of the table before he can blink.

Before anyone else so much as moves, I have him pressed to the glass window, my nails digging through the flesh of his throat. Blood leaks over his pale skin, but Oskar only smiles at me.

"Horrible, isn't it?" he wheezes. "You found the most beautiful thing in the world, and someone else stole it away."

I close my fist, slowly crushing his windpipe. The life drains from his eyes, but he loses consciousness with a smile on his face.

~

"She's alive," Cora says.

She sits in Oskar's usual place at the stone table. The other inner circle members remain in their seats. I don't think any of them were involved in Oskar's treachery, but I'm not letting them leave. They'll stay here until we know what happened. Where she is. How to find her.

I glance over my shoulder at Oskar. He's tied to my statue, rope tight enough he won't be able to move. For now, he's still unconscious, crushed windpipe healing with agonizing slowness. I wish he was awake to feel it.

I focus on the table again. Cora has one hand over Grace's electronic. The other clenches a fistful of amber herbs, hand pulsing in steady rhythm. She's exhausted. It's been an hour of this, and her eyes keep rolling back, skin paling every time she attempts a spell.

"It's getting less cloudy," she says after some time. "Now that I can sense her..."

"Where?" I demand. "Tell me where."

I stand with one leg on my bench, shaking it so hard the cobblestone beneath it cracks. I can't stand still. I can't do anything but imagine what he's done to her. Is she beaten?

Bloodied? Left for dead in one of the far-reaching vampire clans?

Cora goes back to muttering, her eyes rolling to pure white. I pace the courtyard as she works, only pausing to kick Oskar in the shin. It's not the first time I've done it, and even as his throat heals, I make sure his legs don't. Lest he gets any ideas about trying to run.

A heavy thump sounds behind me. By the time I've turned, Amelia and Milas are already knelt at Cora's side. She's prone on the ground, blinking absently toward the darkened sky.

"Did you find her?" I ask, shoving the others out of my way. I crouch beside Cora's head, tilting her so she's resting against the stone wall, rather than the floor.

"Yes," she says. Her words tremble as she looks at me. "She's with them, Master. My people."

I stagger backward. My heart seizes, pulsing too fast, squeezing like it might explode. I clutch my chest, as if to hold it in place. I'm being shredded from the inside out, and I don't know how to stop it. I don't know how to *fix* it.

"No," I whisper. My voice is hoarse, cracking like a child's.

Oskar has doomed us all. He is punishing our entire kind for showing him and Freja mercy. For giving them a chance.

I am back in front of him, kicking his shins until both legs are shattered. Blood trails from his pant legs, and still, I don't stop. I scream as his body breaks at my touch, as a piece of my soul shatters for the man I thought I knew.

I force myself to stop. With a hand on my statue, I take ragged breaths and close my eyes. I'm wasting time—time Grace doesn't have.

"Don't let him leave," I say, turning back to my followers. They stare with wide, stunned expressions. "Restrain him by any means necessary."

"Yes, Master," Beatrice says. Then, "What are you going to do now?"

I look between them, but I don't know who to trust. Before tonight, it would have been Oskar. He was always the easy one. The loyal one. Understanding, dedicated, reasonable.

A fraud. A fucking fraud.

He always did have a way of surprising me.

"I need to negotiate a deal," I say. I step toward Cora, holding my hand to her. "Will you come?"

Her dark brows lift in surprise. She hasn't returned to the Day Realm since crashing into me all those years ago. She's made it clear she doesn't want to. I've made a point to never ask...until now.

"Yes, Master," she says, dipping her head. "Bring Milas. He knows the Echo better than we do."

It's a logical choice, unless they're secretly against me. Then it's a trap.

"No," I say. "We'll take Beatrice and Theo. Amelia and Milas, you stay here. Keep Oskar alive. Grace alone deserves the honor of killing him."

26

MAYBE OSKAR WAS RIGHT

GRACE

I may have been a prisoner in Sebastian's manor, but here, I am less than human. I'm kept in a literal cell, with iron bars and no furniture. I'm forced to sit on the cold stone floor, exposed to frigid air that filters through a gaping window. While it was too dark to see much of anything when I arrived, I know I'm in some sort of village. This building is small, closer to a shack than anything else. From what I can tell, I'm the only prisoner here.

I decide that's not a good thing.

Perhaps witches don't have the patience for prisoners. Perhaps everyone who interferes with their laws is slaughtered.

"How long have I been here?" I ask.

It's still too dark to see. Morning has not come, but I am sure of little else. It could be close to midnight or in the final stages of this blackened sky. I hope there's still time. As soon as the sun breaks, Sebastian won't be able to come until evening.

If he comes.

Just because Sebastian didn't want me to die, doesn't mean he's willing to risk his life to save me.

The curse, I remind myself. *He needs me to break the curse. He'll come. He has to come.*

I sob against my knees, pulling them tight to my chest. It's too cold. I don't know what the temperature needs to be for someone to freeze to death, but I'm sure I must be near it.

"Hello?" I call.

I know someone else is here, if only because he keeps shifting his position near the door. His boots crunch against the gravel, and he occasionally lets out an exasperated sigh, as if my imprisonment is a terrible inconvenience for *him*.

"Are you going to kill me?" I ask. My voice falls now, even as I try to keep it steady, strong.

The man appears in front of my cell. He's one of the men who grabbed me from Oskar, as if I am nothing but cattle for trade. He is young, a few years younger than I am. Despite his cruelty, he looks soft. Rounded features and wide eyes. Is that fear I see in his expression, or is it only wishful thinking?

"I can't tell you anything," the man says. His gaze drifts over me before finally settling on my eyes. "You know who you are —*what* you are to us—don't you?"

"I am *no one* to you," I snap. "If you were smart, you'd send me right back where I came from. Sebastian doesn't like sharing his toys."

"Is that what you are?" the man asks. He crouches into the only sliver of moonlight, letting the light shine over his face. He's handsome, in a plain sort of way. "A toy, Grace?"

"You have no idea what I am," I say, propping onto my knees. I flex my fingers, both surprised and offended they didn't bother binding my hands. "But I assure you, if you keep me here, you're bound to find out."

A slow, easy smile crosses the man's face.

"That's exactly what we're hoping."

He starts retreating, back to his place on the other side of this tiny prison.

"Aren't you at least going to give me food?" I ask. I'm sure he can hear the desperation in my voice—it's *all* I can hear. "Or let me go to the bathroom?"

"You're welcome to piss in there," he says mockingly. The snarled grin on his face transforms his look entirely. Forgotten are those boyish features, consumed by the demonic spark in his eyes. "As for food, there's no point, is there? You're a walking corpse, Grace Pruce, and in a matter of days, you will be nothing but ash."

With a parting sneer, the man returns to his side of the prison, and I press my face against my knees. I do my best to keep my sobs quiet, so he doesn't get the satisfaction of making me cry.

I DON'T MEAN to fall asleep, but I am woken by a violent scream. By the time I'm to the bars, hands clasped over the rungs, knees pressed to the stone, my guard and I are no longer alone. A second guard collapses through the doorway, his throat torn out, leaving his head barely attached to his body.

"Don't—"

That's the only word my guard manages before Sebastian has him against the wall. I strain to follow the action from my cell, but it's too shadowed to see much of anything. There is only my smarmy guard, kicking his feet in the air, and Sebastian's back. He's wearing his usual slacks and a stark white shirt, bright enough he almost glows through the darkness.

"That should be all of them," Beatrice says. She enters the room, followed by Theo and Cora.

There's a horrific tearing sound, and moments later, my

guard's head bounces to the gravel. Through the darkness, his wide eyes are frozen open, staring at me.

"I'm here," I say. My voice is shaking, and I start crying before I can stop myself. "Over here! I'm—"

Sebastian is in front of the bars. He reaches for them, only to stop when Cora grabs him forearm.

"Careful," she warns him. This close, the moonlight shines over them. I can see every detail. The thick blood coating Sebastian's chin and shirt. The way Cora's hands are trembling. The desperate, wild look in Sebastian's eyes.

Maybe Oskar was right, I think. *Maybe this man* is *terrified, not just to lose the curse, but to lose me.*

"Sebastian," Cora snaps.

He ignores her. He's looking over my cell, silently calculating. When he reaches for the bars again, Cora flares her palms at him. He's thrown backward, smacking hard against the stones. My eyes widen, and Beatrice instantly lurches for Cora.

She flicks the vampire away with an easy twitch of her wrist.

I raise my eyebrows. I can't help it. I assumed Cora was powerful...but this is a different level.

As if sensing my surprise, she flashes a cat-like grin at me.

"They didn't condemn me for nothing, Gracie."

Sebastian growls and pushes to his feet.

"You're going to kill her," Cora snaps, placing herself between Sebastian and the bars. "They've got this riddled with magic. If you pull her out, she's going to die. So stay the fuck over there."

Sebastian's eyes are one me, and I feel it then. No doubt in my mind. No second thoughts.

Love. He looks at me with pure, tortured love.

"I didn't run," I tell him. It's not one of the many things I'd considered telling him while rotting on this cell floor. And yet, right now, it feels like the most important. "I didn't try to escape. I don't know what Oskar told you, but I swear—"

"I am going to get you out," Sebastian says, ignoring me. "All right, Grace? I'm going to get you out."

"It's going to be difficult," Cora murmurs. "I need time."

"Then get started," he says. He jerks his chin at Beatrice. "You, stay here with them. If Cora needs anything, you fetch it immediately. Understood?"

"Yes," Beatrice says. She bows her head, slipping behind Cora. My mentor is already muttering under her breath, eyes rolling back as she works.

"Theo and I will be back," he says, looking at me. He steps forward, touching the bars with forced caution. I grab his wrists, as if anchoring him here.

"Where are you going?" I ask. "Can't you—"

"I'll be back," he says, rather than answer. His wild eyes roam my body before settling on my face. He brushes my lower lip with the pad of his thumb, pulling back far too soon.

"Thank you for coming for me," I say. My voice cracks, and already, the tears are back.

"You underestimate the things I'd do, little witch," he says.

"To break the curse?"

"To keep you." He swallows as he stands. "Now, help Cora if you can, all right?"

He doesn't give me the chance to respond. He's already gone, and Theo has disappeared with him.

"You two better work quick," Beatrice snaps. "Or we'll all going to die for nothing."

"Is it working?" I ask.

I collapse against the back wall, so covered in sweat my

clothes are wet. We've been at this for nearly an hour. Cora is doing most of the work. I'm only sending magic her direction, casting it for her to channel. She leans forward, pressing her head against the iron bars.

"Not well enough," she says. She gasps for breath, each one coming ragged and slow. Her skin has lost all color, and her balance is starting to waver.

"You have to stop," I say. I choke out a sob, and I can't bear to look at her. "You're going to kill yourself, Cora."

"We have our direction," Beatrice snarls. She's glaring at me, and I can't bring myself to be annoyed. She's hated me since I arrived at the manor. I'm only surprised she's here at all.

"Cora," I say, ignoring Beatrice. "If you keep pushing, you are going to die. You said it yourself, this isn't working well enough. We need a different plan."

"There isn't another plan," she says. There's no bite to her words. There's only bone-deep exhaustion and those heavy breaths. "This. Is. The. Only. Way."

I run a hand through my hair, tugging at the roots. This is impossible. Cora isn't saying it, and Beatrice won't either, but I still know. I can feel each of Cora's attempts getting weaker. She's withering away before my eyes, and I'm sure I'm doing the same.

Cora lifts her shaking hands, palms facing me.

"No," I say. I lurch forward, snatching her hands in mine. She's too dazed to be irritated. I tug her close. "You need to go, Cora."

"I was in this cage once," she whispers. "Did you know?"

I glance at Beatrice, who looks away.

"Three months," she goes on. "Beaten and starved and treated like an animal. I was too dangerous for their liking, and they hoped to break me until there was nothing dangerous left. Do you know what I did?"

I shake my head, lips parting.

"I broke for them," she says. Her eyes are staring past me, as if she can see herself standing in this very position. "I became small and harmless and weak. I convinced them I was different now, that I was nothing to fear."

She blinks and pulls back, her hands falling from mine.

"And then?" she says. "When they let their guard down, I killed them all, just like they once feared I would. I ran through sleeping town after sleeping town, until finally, I ran into a man I was taught to fear. He had sharp teeth and a black heart made of stone. He was a monster, Grace, and finally, I felt safe. Like I belonged."

I swallow. Out of my peripheral gaze, I notice Beatrice has fallen as still as I have.

"You have cracked his untouchable heart," Cora says. "I owe it to him to save you, as he once saved me."

Cora lifts her palms, brows scrunching as she closes her eyes.

"Now, give me everything you have," she says. She starts chanting before I get the chance to protest.

Within seconds I'm gasping again, tears streaming down my face as I give her every ounce of magic I contain.

Be enough, I beg. *Please, just be enough.*

The door to the prison slams open, striking the stone wall. We all turn, and Cora's magic snaps. We keep our arms raised and ready, only to lower them when we realize it's not a witch.

It's Theo.

He's covered in more blood than before, and now, some of it appears to be his own.

"We have to go," he says. "Now."

"Buy me more time," Cora snaps. "We're close."

We're not, and we both know it.

"Master's orders," Theo says. He smacks the door, holding it open. "Let's go."

Cora looks back at me, and for the first time, I think I understand her. Harsh and blunt and at times cruel. She was raised in a world where there wasn't another option, and she'd done her best to prepare me for the same.

"Go," I say. I'm surprised at how level my voice sounds, as if I'm not telling them to leave me here to die.

"We'll be back," she promises.

"Go!" I scream.

Beatrice doesn't give Cora the choice. She grabs her, and together, they disappear. The wind howls through the gaping window, and I am alone once more.

I curl into the corner, sobbing as I wait for the witches to arrive.

27

SACRIFICIAL LAMB
GRACE

When I wake, it's to sunlight on my face. Night has officially passed, the sun has risen, and any hope of Sebastian coming back disappears. My bones ache as I shift into a seated position. A steady pulse beats against my skull, and my mouth is so dry it's impossible to swallow.

I hope you all made it, I think distantly. *I hope you killed as many of them as you could.*

"You're awake," a voice says.

I startle, craning my neck to look at the doorway. Now that it's daylight, I realize this building is even smaller than I originally believed. The stones are old and decrepit, with vines growing between the gaps and through the opened windows. Down the way, a cell identical to mine sits empty.

At the doorway, an older witch stands with exaggerated, stiff posture. She reminds me of an old-timey headmistress, the kind who'd make her students walk with books on their heads.

I don't even know if that's a real thing. If it is though, she fits the bill perfectly.

"Yes," I say, stating the obvious, if only because she did first. "Who are you?"

"Your new guard." She's wearing bright and layered clothing, the colors of a vibrant autumn day. I always imagined Cora's people—and mine, I guess—were dark and bleak like she is. I expected black clothing and neglected hair.

This woman is colorful. Full of personality. Of life.

"Brave," I say. "Considering what my friends did to the last one."

I want to smirk at her, to make it clear I'm taunting her, testing her. To show her they haven't broken me like they hoped. Instead, I can't muster even the barest amusement.

I slept for hours, and yet, I feel emotionally and physically drained. I think I gave away part of my soul last night, trying to escape this hellish place.

"Well, unfortunately for your friends, their greatest enemy is here to protect us," she says. She walks the length of the room, planting her heeled boots in front of my cell. She's pretty, for a miserable hag. She looks past me, out my window and to the glaring sun. "By the time it's safe for them to return, you'll already be dead."

I suck in a hard breath. My last guard refused to tell me anything, and though I suspected this was their plan, I hoped it wasn't. Suspecting something and having it confirmed are entirely different beasts.

Especially because this horrible woman is right. If they kill me now, there won't be a thing Sebastian can do to stop it. He's mortal in the sun. His army will literally burn in it. And Cora, powerful as she may be, can't take down these people on her own.

She'd be suicidal to even try.

"What are you going to do to me?" I ask.

I expect her to give me a mocking smile as her predecessor did. At the very least, I assume she'll waltz back to her post at the door. Instead, she sits in the gravelly dirt, curling her bare legs to sit on them. Her bright orange skirt flows over her lap, and she smooths it with her manicured fingers.

"What the Mother wants," she says. She looks up at me, hazel eyes drifting over my clothes and undoubtedly wild hair. "It is She who decides, not us."

"The Mother?" I repeat. This sounds like something out of a cult documentary, and my stomach sours at the thought. Only now do I realize how little I know about witches. Everything I saw from Cora aligns far more closely to the vampires than... whatever the hell these people are.

"Yes," she says. She tips her nose up slightly. Rather than elaborating, she continues. "The Mother keeps our world in perfect harmony. Through her, and only her, we achieve balance, love, unity. Peace, Grace. Do you understand?"

"Does your Mother's harmony often involve the death of an innocent?" I ask. I ignore the way my heart races, the way my muscles twitch, begging me to run. They don't understand I have nowhere to go, that I cannot fight what is about to happen.

"I do not expect you to understand," the woman continues. She speaks as if I'm a child, too naive to understand her grand knowledge. "But I thought you deserved to know. It is not your death we seek, but the harmony it will bring. The safety for all in the Echo, not only our coven's."

"You're crazy," I say. I move from the bars to slump against the nearest wall. My adrenaline is pumping too hard for me to feel tired, but I decide to trust Cora's advice. I need this woman to believe I'm exhausted, that I'm nowhere near a threat.

I need her to leave me alone. I can't think, let alone cast magic, with this psychotic woman staring at me.

"You look like your father," she says. She gives me a soft smile, and I'm sure she thinks it looks like the perfect combination of empathy, sadness, and selflessness. Crazy. She looks freaking crazy. "Your father was a good man, Grace. I truly believe he would have understood our decision."

"Clearly not enough to ask him," I say. I tip my head back, looking at the cracked ceiling instead of her. "The dead seem to forgive far easier than the living."

When I look back, the woman gives me a tight smile.

"You should rest," she says. "This will all be over soon."

She rises to her feet, moving swiftly for her post.

"How long?" I ask. She pauses, looking over her shoulder at me with a lifted eyebrow. "How long before you slaughter me like a sacrificial lamb?"

This time, she doesn't answer. She turns away and slinks into a corner I can't see. Apparently, she's told me all I deserve to know.

As it turns out, my sacrifice is scheduled for the early afternoon. It's long enough I can practice my magic, but nowhere near enough time to feel ready. My best chance at escaping is to make my move while they're taking me to wherever I'll be sacrificed.

Murdered.

I swallow, forcing the thought from my mind. There's no time to be scared. I'll only get one chance to escape, and if I miss it...

Do not think about it, Grace. You cannot think about it.

It's like standing at the edge of a cliff and trying to keep your balance. If you look down, the fear of falling might make you stumble. If you don't look, you don't know to be scared. You'll stand perfectly still, as easily as anywhere else.

"It's time," my guard says. She approaches me, flanked by two men. One is short and thin, the other tall with lean muscles.

None of them look like they'd win a fight, but I know better than to judge a witch by their size.

The three work to undo whatever magic they've cast over my cell. They each hold a different herb and chant in eerie unison. I wonder, had Cora had those herbs, would her spell have worked? It's useless knowledge now, but I try to memorize the way they look and smell all the same.

I shift on my feet, stepping back as the door opens. My cell reeks of pee, and despite everything, I'm tempted to apologize. I don't let myself. I exit the cell with my chin lifted and my jaw clamped tight.

My plan isn't elaborate, and it's certainly not foolproof. There are a hundred things that could go wrong, but as far as I'm concerned, I'm dead either way. Let me at least fight. Let them all know I was outnumbered and overpowered, and that I still tried.

We walk from the dingy prison, out into a sprawling field of neatly trimmed grass and a path of square stones. The woman follows behind me, and the men flank me on either side.

I blink against the sun's brightness. It feels too hot against my skin, and I'm reminded just how rarely I've been outside since coming to the Echo. If by some miracle I survive, I am going to stand in the sun every day for hours. I'll soak up the warmth until it's embedded in my pale skin, until I can feel it even when I'm indoors.

After twenty minutes of fast-paced walking, we reach the top of a hill. On its other side, a small town winds between a thick forest and a slow-moving river. The streets are filled with witches, all wearing clothes and hairstyles as bright and lively as the three surrounding me. Some, like my female guard, wear oranges and reds and golds. Others wear cool shades of grey and white and dark blues. Then more are lavender, pale pink, and pastel yellow. And finally, sky blue and bright green.

The seasons, I decide. They dress by season, and if that doesn't show exactly how much of a cult these freaks are, I don't know what would.

Few of them look at us, and I get the feeling they've been instructed to keep their distance. I look away from the town, studying the river and then the forest. I don't know which direction leads back to the Night Realm. It was too dark last night, and my fear was too great to pay attention.

All those years of Dateline for nothing.

The men walk for the river, and I fall into step between them. We're going to avoid the town altogether, it seems. I take another glance at the trees. Whether they lead toward the Night Realm or not, they seem like a safer bet. There are many places to hide in a forest, and I'm not a great swimmer.

A large bird flies overhead, momentarily blocking out the sun. I look up. The bird is gone, but I realize my guards have looked up too. They pause, turning toward the woman guard.

"Was that—" the short man asks.

"Let's move faster," the woman says from behind me. "We don't want to keep the council waiting."

Perhaps it was not *a bird at all.*

A spark of hope pulses up my spine. The vampires might not be able to help me now, but that doesn't mean *no one* can. I scan the skies again, searching but there is only clear blue and wispy clouds.

The woman presses between my shoulders, urging me along. It's the only confirmation I need: I am not alone out here.

By the time we reach the base of the hill, we're jogging. I'm already covered in sweat and my limbs are shaking. I haven't eaten in over a day, and my body is running on fumes. If we keep this pace, I'm going to pass out long before we reach our destination.

I gasp for breath as we move, keeping my eyes on the river

and the forest and the sky. Constantly waiting for a moment, even a split-second of opportunity. Before I find my chance, the ritual comes into view. A raised platform stands in the center of a barren patch of dirt. The wooden structure is weathered and water-damaged, and it's clearly older than I am. I wonder if this is where they kill all their prisoners, if Cora ever feared this stage as I am now.

My mouth turns sour with the taste of my own bile. I fall to my knees and puke across the grass. The men yank me back to my feet, and the woman shoves my shoulders again.

"Keep moving," she demands.

But she doesn't understand. I can see it. The lifted stage, the dozens of witches standing before it. The same macabre artifacts Cora had during our attempt to break the curse. And there, in the center of it all, is a large rectangle of glass.

It's deep and wide. Too large to be considered a bowl or even a container. It's a freaking kiddie pool of glass.

For my blood.

Every last drop.

"Don't make me," I say, falling limp in their grip. They easily hold me between them, straining my shoulders at the joints. I'm crying so hard I can barely speak. "Please, don't!"

"If you comply, we will make it quick," the woman says. She pauses the men, whipping to come in front of me. "Look at me, Grace Pruce. If you comply, it will be over before you realize it's happening. We'll make it painless. If you don't—"

It's the perfect opening, and I force myself to take a deep breath.

"Did you make my father's death painless?" I ask. My voice shakes, but I glare at her with every ounce of hatred I've built over the last few months.

They made my mother look crazy.

They stole my father from me.

He tried to protect me.

When he could have exposed my existence to save himself, he died silently, so they could never find me.

"Yes," the woman replies. She speaks the word with more conviction and self-righteousness than should be possible. So arrogant, so superior as she looks down at me.

"You didn't though," I say. I blink, letting tears roll down my cheeks. "Death is never painless. My mother felt the pain of losing him for the rest of her life. I've felt it too. And even once I'm gone, my brother will feel it still. Except worse, because now he's lost his father *and* his sister to you monsters."

The woman stills. I'm only looking at her, my expression carefully twisted. Still, I feel the guards' shock. All three of my captors have stopped moving.

I play the part I've mastered for years. The dumb blonde. The ditzy girl who's oblivious to the world around her.

I have a brother, I chant inside my head. *What? Is that a problem for your curse or something?*

I blink innocently at the woman, showing only the anger and terror I still feel. I bury the fact I'm lying as deep as I can. For all I know, these witches can sense deception, so I can't give them an ounce of uncertainty or guilt.

I have a brother, I repeat to myself. *He's Walter's son too. He has Pruce blood too, and so long as he's alive, your curse will be threatened. If you kill me, you'll have no way of finding him.*

"Brother," the woman finally repeats. I don't know if she thinks she's being subtle, but she's not. I can taste the panic radiating off her.

"Don't you even think of touching him," I say. "You already have me. So use me for whatever stupid magic you need, but don't you dare think of hurting him."

I bend my fingers, then straighten them. My magic may be

weak, but if they don't buy my lie, I'm ready to throw whatever I've got.

"She's lying," the man to my left says.

I pulse my fingers again. I don't let myself react, too terrified I'll give something away. If this man has some supernatural ability to catch lies, I'm screwed. But if not...

"Take her back," the woman snaps. "Let me consult with the council."

"Madam," the other man starts.

"Not another word," she snarls. She strides toward the ritual, waving her hand again. "Take. Her. Back."

They do, and I'm shaking with too many emotions by the time I'm locked in my cell. I curl into the corner, facing away from them as they replace the trapping spell over my door. Soon enough, they leave.

I hear the men whispering about me, trading theories over whether I'm full of shit. I don't engage. I just wait, trembling and hoping the woman doesn't return before nightfall.

28

THE GREAT AND FEARSOME
SEBASTIAN VULCE

SEBASTIAN

"Alive?" I ask. It's not the first time I've asked Cora for an update, and it's far from the last.

"Yes," she says without looking at me. Her eyes are closed, but I'm pretty sure she's not casting.

"Don't placate me," I snap. "Check. Make sure—"

"I am not going to check," Cora interrupts. She opens her eyes, her stare unwavering. "I don't wish to defy you, Master, but I can't waste energy on checking. She's alive. For whatever reason, they're keeping her alive. She's in her cell, and according to Nicasi, the council hasn't left their meeting room."

I force myself to remain still, to not lash out like I'm desperate to. Not only because she's right, but because I knew better than to ask to start with.

"They were clearly going to kill her," Beatrice says from my opposite side. "What could have changed their mind? Did they realize they were missing an ingredient? Or that they wouldn't be strong enough to complete it? Or..."

I tune Beatrice out. We've been sitting in this forest since leaving Grace last night. It was our best option in the moment, but I'm not sure I'll ever forgive myself for making the call. I'd had us retreat, and I sent Theo to get backup.

He'd found it from random sources. Nicasi and a few of his brothers from the Flight Realm. A couple of Beatrice's acquaintances from the Float Realm. All of our servants who were desperate to be turned. If they survived this mission, they'd finally get their wish.

We're spread throughout the coven's settlement. The harpies took to the sky hours ago, and they watched over Grace whenever she was out of our sight. Just as we were readying to storm the ritual and make the most reckless rescue attempt imaginable, they'd taken her back to the prison. The ritual crowd had dispersed. The council had gone into a meeting and have yet to reappear.

"She must have convinced them," Beatrice says. "Maybe offered herself as some sort of sex slave. She's pretty. They'd probably agree—"

"Stop," I say.

"Yes, please do," Cora agrees. "The last thing we need is for Sebastian to think they're torturing Grace and go ballistic. Right now, the best thing we can do is stay calm and wait."

So we do.

We sit in the treeline, clinging to the shadows as well as we can. Aside from an occasional update from Nicasi, we wait for nightfall in silence. The sun dips behind the horizon, turning the sky brilliant with hues of orange and purple and red. I count to one million and beg nature to move faster.

The sun lingers, but I rise to my feet anyway. The others follow suit, and I order the humans back to the manor. Their presence seemed helpful when it was our only option, but now, they're nothing more than obstacles. My followers will arrive soon enough to replace them.

"The leader is returning," Cora says. She frowns at me as she climbs to her feet. "Just got word from Nicasi."

I'm still unclear how their mental communication works, but I couldn't care less right now. All that matters is he's our eyes where we don't have them, and Cora is his mouthpiece.

"Dammit," I mutter. "It's fine—it was bound to happen. Just hang back here, and let me go in first. It will be more believable if I'm alone."

"Nothing about this plan is believable," Beatrice hisses. "We should just slaughter her too."

"Not unless we have to," I say.

I expect Beatrice to argue, but thankfully, she doesn't. Killing the witch leader is too dangerous for a number of reasons. Not only is she likely armed with a horrific protective curse, but killing her would wage war between the Night and Day realms. It's the last thing we need.

"Everyone know their place?" I ask.

I've already started walking before they can respond, but their footsteps behind me are the only answer I need.

By the time night rises and my vampiric army arrives, twelve witches stand guard outside the prison. They're eerily still and violently bright in their ridiculous, flamboyant clothing. They glow through the darkness, but there was no point in trying to hide. Their rancid blood makes it easy to locate each of them. Just beyond the hill, dozens more stand in wait. They haven't broached the forest, which tells me they already know we're here.

I linger at the treeline, waiting for a final signal from Beatrice.

And there, three sharp sticks cracking in the distance, echoed by a short bird call.

"Windward!" one of the witches screams. He's nearest me, and his voice lights the area like a siren.

It's better than I could have hoped. Twelve witches twist in Beatrice's direction, all aiming their palms toward the darkness. Theo and a pair of men are arrows in front of me. They slice through the pasture, picking off three witches in a matter of seconds.

The witches twist, blasting magic and sputtered curses. Their magic is invisible, but the force is tangible. It hangs in the air as I break from the trees, eyes locked on the prison door.

There are too many vampires and witches to count now. My men burst from the forest, and endless witches pour over the hilltop, hands raised. I'm surrounded by falling witch heads and obliterated vampire hearts, by the sound of frantic screams and desperate moans.

Through it all, I strain my ears for the prison. Three voices come from within its walls. Two men. One woman. Grace is silent, and I can only hope it means she's been left alone.

Just as I reach the door, a wave of magic blasts against my back. It immediately coils around me, squeezing my chest until my ribs ache. I don't let myself fight it. I force myself to wait, and within seconds, the magic disappears. A man's head rolls past me in the dirt, and Beatrice drops his body at my feet. She's gone before I say a word.

I return to the door, expecting it to be locked, but it swings easily at my touch. Madam Lyrie stands before me, one man a shadow at her side. The other isn't visible.

With Grace, then.

"Madam," I say. I stroll into the room, kicking the door shut behind me. "You've aged terribly."

The last time I saw this woman in person, we shared a stage

together. It was meant to be a peace treaty of sorts. They wanted vampires to stop hunting humans and supernaturals, and in return, they'd help fund bloodletters for us. I made a show of agreeing, only to turn on them as their people watched. I grabbed Lyrie by the throat and showed the council exactly what I thought of their treaty. I drank from her until their previous leader knocked me unconscious.

It was meant to be a show of power, a reminder to Walter Pruce and his council that we could not be leashed. It had worked. Until, of course, Madam Lyrie rebelled, cursing my entire species.

Twenty years later, Madam Lyrie's brown hair has turned gray. Her skin is soft, wrinkled. Years of frowning have left deep brackets around her mouth. She's wearing her usual colors: orange and yellows and other autumnal hues.

"You haven't aged a day," Lyrie says. She keeps her hands at her side, but the tension is clear in her neck. "You're as hideous now as you were then."

Even all these years later, I can still see the faint puncture marks I left on her neck. She could have used magic to remove the scars. It's intentional that she's left them, a reminder to her people, I'm sure, how monstrous my kind is.

"I want to see her," I say. "I know the whole place is warded. I know she'll die if I try to steal her."

"And yet, you've risked your life to see her?" Lyrie tilts her head. "Either you're as impulsive and foolish as ever, or you're lying."

"Am I wrong?" I ask. "Is it not warded?"

"I assure you, it is," Lyrie says. "But seeing as your men have just slaughtered mine to give you this opportunity, I'm not particularly compelled to indulge you."

"Everything you believe about me—that I'm a horrible monster, a selfish creature—is true," I say. "I stole that woman from the other side, hoping to undo your curse over my people. But I am standing before you, begging you not to punish her for my sins. I will get on my knees if I must. We can make a new agreement. Please, at least hear me."

She quirks an eyebrow, as much of an invitation as she'll give me.

"Keep her alive," I say. "Figure out a way to separate her from the curse. Certainly the Mother has punished you for killing Walter Pruce. You cannot tell me she wants you to kill another of her children."

"Do not use my faith against me," Lyrie sneers. "It will *not* end in your favor."

"Find a way to separate her from the curse," I repeat. "I won't try to break it. I won't try to steal her from these walls. Just...find another way. She is too good to die."

"Look at you," Lyrie says. She tsks her tongue like she's disappointed. "The great and fearsome Sebastian Vulce, enamored by a half-breed. A *witch* half-breed, no less. You must be disgusted with yourself."

I glance toward Grace's cell. I can hear her heart beating too fast, the way she keeps holding her breath. I want to call out to her, but I force myself to look back at Lyrie.

"As touching as your proposition is," she says. "I learned my lesson long ago to never trust a bloodsucker. Now, I suggest you leave before I add to the curse. Perhaps I should make vampires flammable in moonlight, as well?"

She says it as a threat, but I can tell, it's already in motion. *That's* what they were planning with their ritual. They were going to use Grace, not just to seal the curse, but to worsen it.

As much as I'd love to kill them for it, I don't let myself react. This only works if I keep my composure.

"Lyrie—"

"Go," she says, voice booming.

I lunge, not for the exit or for Lyrie's throat, but for Grace's cell. None of them are expecting it. By the time they realize I've moved, I already have the man nearest Grace in my grasp. He's shorter than I am by several inches, and I hold his back to my chest. With my hand wrapped around his neck, finger pressed to his jugular, I glare at Lyrie.

She glares right back, raising her hands as her guard does the same.

"Let me say goodbye to her," I say. It's a demand, my voice ragged and reckless. "We all know I can't steal her. So just let me say fucking goodbye."

Strained silence falls over the room. It's gone quiet outside too. The slaughter has paused, but I extend my fangs, making it clear I'm happy to continue.

"To be clear," I say. "If you refuse me, I will kill you all, consequences be damned. As you said, Madam, I'm known to be impulsive."

Her throat bobs as she swallows. The man behind her looks ready to bolt for the door, whether she gives her blessing or not. The one in my grasp strains against me, trying to escape my hold over his hands. It's useless, and he must know it. Still, he tries.

To my right, a flicker of movement catches the corner of my eye. It takes every ounce of self-control not to look.

"Fine," she says after a long silence. "Two minutes. And before you ask if we'll give you privacy—"

"You can stay," I say. I make myself as small, as humbled as possible. Advice from Cora. Dipping my head, I add, "Thank you, Madam. It will not be forgotten."

She stares at me, and I keep my hold on the man's throat.

"Theo!" I call. Looking to Lyrie and the other guard, I say, "Just to ensure you don't kill me once I've turned my back."

The prison door opens. Theo enters, his hands held in a gesture of goodwill, of pure intentions.

I shove the man away from me, and he staggers to Lyrie's side, between her and the wall. Coward.

Only once Theo nods do I turn.

And there.

Grace.

Beautiful, radiant, fucking flawless. She's been here two days, and they've been the worst of my life. Two days, and she already looks different. Thinner. Paler. So fucking sad it makes me want to burn this entire realm to the ground.

Maybe someday.

Right now...

"Are you okay?" I ask. "Did they hurt you? Have you eaten? You look—"

"They know about my brother," she says. Her words come in a babbled rush as she stumbles to the cell door. Her trembling fingers twist around the rungs, and she presses as close to me as she can. Her smell—decadent and alluring—wraps itself around me.

Good. Let it fucking stain my clothes, my skin, my hair.

Her words finally catch up to me. Her brother?

"You can't let them find him," she says. She widens her eyes and gives me a knowing look. "They're going to kill him, just like they're going to kill me."

Smart, cunning little witch.

This is how she escaped, how she convinced them not to murder her.

I cup the side of her face, running my thumb along her cheekbone. She closes her eyes, and a tear races down her cheek. A heavy sob rattles her chest, and she falls against the bars, crying until her entire body shakes.

"You'll be okay," I tell her.

"If only you were fae," she whispers. "I might believe you."

She tries to smile through her tears. She's spoken those words before, an echo of my own monstrosity.

I catch her tears with my thumb.

"I may not be fae, Grace, but you can trust me."

With one hand still on her face, I tangle the other through her hair, pulling her close. Our lips meet between the bars, and I kiss her the way I've dreamt of for days. I allow myself one moment longer, and then, I do what I came here to do.

Her eyes widen in shock, but I kiss her through it, holding her still.

As soon as I'm done, I pull back, using my hands to keep her jaw shut.

"Be a good girl," I tell her firmly.

I stare at her, praying to every god the Echo has that she understands. That for just this once, she listens without hesitation.

I watch as her throat bobs, as she swallows.

"Good girl," I whisper.

I release her and step back.

"Two minutes are up!" Lyrie calls. "Now keep your word for once and *go*."

"I will," I say. I grab the cell door by its frame, pulling as hard as I can. It snaps off like it's made of parchment. Magic swirls around me, violent and hungry, biting against my skin. "But I'm taking her with me."

"You'll kill her!" Lyrie screams.

"That's the plan."

Grace's eyes widen as I lunge into the cell, grabbing her by the shoulders. She lets out a tiny yelp as I force her through. And then, she collapses. A puppet with cut strings, she falls limp in my arms.

Those pretty blue eyes stare up at nothing. Lifeless. Gone.

Just like that.

"Let's go!" Theo shouts. He lunges for the nearest guard and rips his esophagus from his throat.

I force myself not to look at Grace. I cradle her to my chest and brace myself for the inevitable. The curse has again been altered, and the vampires must pay. I tense, only making it a few steps before the pain hits. Stronger than ever. A heat equal only to the sun's surface flares beneath my skin. I push myself forward, determined not to fall into agony. My legs shake, my arms struggle to keep hold on Grace.

Two enemies and Theo stand at the exit, and I force myself to reach them, one step at a time.

This is the first time the curse has truly and wholly closed. Grace's life weakened it, even if no one—not even the magic itself—knew she existed.

Scalding heat rages through my body, dousing my organs with boiling, wretched pain. My knees buckle, my arms shake, but I refuse to fall. This pain is temporary, but my chance of getting Grace home depends entirely on this moment. If I crumble now, we'll never make it.

"Fuck," Theo cries.

He has the remaining guard's neck in his hands, and it takes all his effort to break it. The witch manages one final spell as he falls. It strikes Theo's side, tearing a massive hole through his stomach. Blood darkness his shirt and drains toward the floor.

Theo screams as he slouches against the wall. One hand clasps his wound, but the other grabs his chest.

"Go!" I scream.

It's too late. Lyrie's shock has finally worn off, and she finishes what her guard started. She throws both palms in his direction, and like a blade through water, her magic slices through Theo's chest.

His heart flings to the ground, and seconds later, his body follows.

Lyrie's attention shifts to me.

My chest rages with heat, but already, I can feel the curse shifting, the pain softening each breath. I drop Grace to the floor, stepping over her body. Lyrie watches as I approach, hands lifted but expression hesitant, confused.

"Careful, Sebastian," she says, lips curving in a taunting smile. "You never know what killing me might do."

"Only one way to find out," I snarl.

Her magic strikes my chest, exactly where it's charring on the inside. I push forward, knees shaking, head spinning. But as much as I would love to end Madam Lyrie, she's right. Killing her might very well be the last thing I do.

I shove forward, knocking her against the stone wall, hard enough to break her spell. The force of her magic leaves my chest gaping and bleeding, only slightly smaller than the wound she left in Theo. I can't afford another hit.

Lyrie lifts her palms again, the sadistic grin already curling her lips. I lunge. Fangs drawn, I bite as hard as I can over one wrist. Then the other. When I pull back, her hands are bloodied, flesh torn and veins exposed. Lyrie screams as blood pours over her palms and to the stone floor.

It won't kill her, but it should make casting impossible.

As she screams, I dart back to Grace, pulling her into my arms. Her body already feels cold and stiff, like she's been dead for hours, not minutes. I tuck her against my chest, and the burning finally ceases.

It ends. Finally, and for the last time, it ends.

"You better hope we find her brother before you do," Lyrie says. The bloodied leader glares at me from where she's collapsed to the ground. She's bleeding heavily, her arms hanging limply at her sides.

Though she's not casting, I can still sense her magic. It hovers around me, as if it might surprise me yet. I don't give it the chance.

"Until next time, Madam Lyrie," I say. I don't say a word about Grace's supposed brother. Let her chase Grace's imagination for the rest of her miserable life.

Then, I'm gone. Past Madam Lyrie and her dead henchman. Past Theo's mutilated body and the graveyard outside the prison. I scan the dead, looking for familiar faces. Witches and vampires alike surround me, too many to count, but Beatrice, Milas, and Cora aren't among the lost.

Only once I reach the forest, do I find my retreated people. They're alive and covered in rancid witch blood. Beatrice scans the space behind me, but Cora's eyes are locked only on me and the woman in my arms.

"She's dead," Cora says.

"Yes."

"You're lucky it didn't kill *you*," she points out. Then, "Let's hope it works."

"It worked," I say, because I refuse to consider the opposite.

"Where's Theo?" Beatrice asks, pulling my attention back to her. By the tone of her voice, she already knows. When I shake my head, she dips her chin, eyes closed.

"You've got Cora?" I ask.

"Yes, Master," she says softly.

I nod, adjusting Grace higher in my arms.

"If we make it back to the manor," I say, managing a smile. "You'll never have to call me that again."

"Thank the heavens," Beatrice drawls. It's forced and sad, but it's a seed of hope all the same. "I've always hated it."

"Let's go," I say, rather than reply. "Don't stop until we reach it."

Both Beatrice and Cora nod, and then, we run.

29

THAT'S IT, LITTLE WITCH

GRACE

Something is very wrong.

I wake with a strange coldness running through my body. There's something wrong with my skin, with my insides, with every single piece of me. I blink up at the ceiling of Sebastian's bedroom.

It takes me nearly five seconds to realize I must be dreaming.

I'm not in the manor. I'm in the witches' prison. I'm up for slaughter.

I blink again. Snippets of last night filter through my brain, but they're foggy. The woman interrogating me about my fictitious brother. Sebastian bursting into the prison, demanding to see me. The unexpectedly sour taste of his spit when he kissed me.

Be a good girl.

Venom. He'd spit venom into my mouth, instructed me to swallow. And I—I had done it. I knew what it would do, what it meant, and I still...

It was a dream. It had to be. There's no way—

I sit up slowly. My head spins at the movement, and my stomach growls louder than I've ever heard it. When I look to the side, I'm surprised to find Sebastian lying next to me. He's *asleep*. I've never seen him be anything but awake and sharp and scheming.

He looks beautiful like this. Peaceful. Young and innocent.

My stomach growls again, this time accompanied by the inexplicable urge to...

I don't mean to move. It just *happens*. One second, I'm staring lovingly at this monstrous man, and the next, my teeth are in his neck. His blood is cold and oddly reminiscent of room-temperature beer. It's not the satisfying heat my body craves.

And still, I drink. I gulp his blood into my mouth, as if it's something I've always done. To call it instinct feels wrong, and yet, I'm devouring him in his sleep. I didn't wonder how to find the vein. I didn't worry about hurting him. I just lunged and took and drank...

And what the hell am I doing?

I throw myself backward, falling off the bed and crashing onto his hardwood floors. His blood drips down my chin.

"Oh my god," I say. I'm already on my feet, and though my head should blur from the sudden movement, it doesn't.

Sebastian is in front of me, awake and seemingly undisturbed by the fact I was just *eating* him.

"It's okay, Grace," he says. He strokes the side of my face, too loving, too calm for what I've just done.

"I was...I don't know why I did that," I say. I take a deep breath, but it doesn't feel right. It's as if the air doesn't reach my lungs, doesn't fill them like it should.

"Yes, you do," he says. He's still touching my face, his expression far more anxious than his words. "You know, Grace. And I'm *sorry*. I didn't see another option. I was terrified—"

"Am I..." I trail off. Then, "Did you kill me?"

Sebastian flinches.

"It was the only way," he says, closing his eyes. "That vile woman was guarding you. Cora wasn't going to have another chance to break the ward. And if daybreak came, I feared…"

He trails off, swallowing.

He feared they wouldn't be able to save me. He feared they'd kill me.

But if he killed me…

"What about the curse?" I whisper. "If you killed me, if I'm a vampire, can it still be broken?"

"No," he says. His eyes are heavy on me, his attention as strong as physical touch. "You're no longer a witch, Grace. No longer *alive*. Your witch blood doesn't exist."

"No," I say.

My heart should race, but it doesn't. I don't feel anything, and it's not until now that I realize how *alive* I used to be. All the pieces of me I never noticed, simply because they were always there. I don't feel the need to breathe or blink or go to the bathroom. There is only ravenous hunger in my gut, not for food, but for *blood*.

Without permission, my attention flickers back to Sebastian's throat.

"You're hungry," he says. He takes my hands, and for the first time, his touch isn't cold.

Or maybe rather, mine is not warm.

"What do you mean 'no'," I say, pulling out of his touch. "Just like that? It's over?"

He stares at me with an unreadable expression. I wait as long as I can, but he can't just stand there, looking at me. As if what he's done is nothing of significance.

"Sebastian—"

"It's done, Grace," he says. This time, his hands are on my face, pulling me so close our foreheads touch. I close my eyes, leaning into him despite myself.

"So you'll all be trapped, forever, because of me," I whisper.

If I were still human, I'd be crying. I don't know if vampires *can* cry.

Oh my god. I'm a vampire.

Sebastian is quiet for a long moment. He strokes the sides of my face, his eyes closed as he touches me. If he's feeling any of the turmoil I am, he doesn't show it.

"You know," he begins, voice soft. "When I discovered you were gone, I had something of an epiphany."

"Yeah?" I ask. My voice is as quiet as his. I'm scared to break this moment, scared to be pulled out of his touch and forced to face this new reality.

Right now, I can pretend things are normal. That he is touching me simply because he wants to, and not because he's trying to hold me together.

"I realized, if I had to choose between sunlight or *your* light, I'd choose yours, Grace," he says. "Every single time."

I study him, even as his eyes remain closed. Despite everything he's just lost, he looks at peace, maybe for the first time since I've known him.

"I'm in love with you, Grace Renolds," he says. He pulls back to look at me. His hands are still on me, trailing down my throat, over my sides. His green eyes open, impossibly bright. "I *love* you, and that's something I didn't know was possible."

I kiss him then, with his blood in my mouth and his hands touching every inch of exposed skin. The kiss is violent, messy, and before long, we're back in his bed, clothes discarded on the floor.

He kisses down my throat, and I arch into him, wrapping my legs around his back. He notches at my entrance, but I stop him, hand pressed to his chest.

"Do I smell different?" I ask.

It's a stupid question, and probably the last thing that should be on my mind. But I am suddenly, inexplicably horrified at the thought. Sebastian *craved* the way I smelled. It fucked with his head, made him desperate for me. If I'm a vampire, that has to be gone.

"Yes," he says.

He kisses my collarbone before looking up at me. He grabs my hand, pressing it against his hair, until I tangle my fingers through it. Then, he licks my jawline, my ear, and the skin on my neck. He sucks the soft spot where my throat meets my shoulder, hard enough it should leave a hickey.

Vampires probably don't get hickeys.

"Is it..." I trail off, too afraid to finish the question.

"You smell divine, Grace," he says. He trails open-mouthed kisses down my arm, pressing a final kiss to my wrist. "Now, I'm just not tempted to kill you for it."

I huff out a laugh, but it's forced. Sebastian pauses, tilting his head to look at me.

"I am in love with you, Grace," he says. "I fell in love with you because you are kind and beautiful and *good*, and because you make me want to be good too."

He gently presses his hand against my chest.

"You are not tied to anything," he says. Something unreadable flashes across his expression. "I know I chose this for you. I know you might have chosen differently. And I'm *sorry* for that. My promise from earlier stands. If you want to go somewhere else, even if it's far from me, I'll take you anywhere."

I study his face. He means it.

"That would be a shitty trade for you," I say, swallowing against the lump in my throat. "No curse. No girl."

His hand spans higher, until it's a collar over my throat.

"It would be miserable," he agrees. "But if that's what you decide, I still wouldn't regret it. I would still choose your light, again and again."

I smile despite myself.

"I don't believe you," I say. A full grin takes over my face, and I don't try to hold it back. "You'd miss me too much. You'd spend the rest of your immortal life trying to win me back."

Now, it's his turn to smile. A crooked, mischievous grin.

"Maybe," he admits.

"Luckily for you, there's nowhere else I'd rather be," I say. I tug at his shoulders, drawing him upward until his face is level with mine. "Now fuck me, Sebastian."

He doesn't need to be told twice.

He hooks my legs around his waist and thrusts deep with a single stroke. I cry out, surprised that there's still pain mixed with pleasure. Now that I'm not human, I expected to feel nothing.

Instead, it's somehow *more* of everything. More pain, more pleasure.

He fucks me harder than he ever has, and I only now realize how much he's been holding back. With one hand gripping my shoulder, and the other on my hip, he pounds into me until my head strikes the headboard.

"Fuck," he says. He rotates us, dangling my head over the edge of the bed, without missing a thrust.

"I'm coming," I say, more in surprise than anything else.

I've no more than spoken the word when pure bliss tears through me. It's beautiful, erotic, addicting.

"You can take more," he says without slowing. My center feels sore already, but Sebastian doesn't ease his brutal pace. He dips forward, capturing my nipple in his mouth. I cry out, arching into him, and he pulls back to look at me. "Prettiest fucking thing I've ever seen. You know that? You look perfect, taking my cock. So fucking good for me, Grace."

That's all it takes, and I'm coming again. It's as if my nerves have been restructured to draw every ounce of pleasure from his cock. And I let my head fall back, taking everything he'll give me.

"I'm going to fuck you until the end of time," he growls in my ear. "Until you can't think of anything but this cock inside you."

I'm already there, I want to say.

My ability to do anything other than mumble incoherently, a mixture of his name and curse words I rarely use, disappeared a long time ago. I don't even try to respond. I just dig my nails into his back, surprised to feel his skin break.

Rather than feel horrified, I let instinct take over. I pull Sebastian's head roughly down, latching my lips over his neck once more. I drink, and ecstasy takes over my every thought.

"That's it, little witch," he groans. "Take what you need. *Fuck.* I'm going to—"

He doesn't finish his sentence. His thrusts grow erratic, hips jerking as he empties inside me. He fucks me through his orgasm, and I come a final time, his blood coating my tongue.

30

ONE MONTH LATER

SEBASTIAN

"How sure are you that this worked?" Grace asks. She stands at my dresser—or rather, *her* dresser. She moved my weapons to a cabinet two days after officially moving into my quarters. One month as a vampire with free reign and my funds, and Grace has accumulated more clothes than she could ever possibly wear.

I roll my eyes whenever she comes home with another find, but I don't complain.

I never will.

"It worked, Grace," I say. "I promise."

I come behind her, wrapping my arms around her waist. I rest my head on her shoulder, slowly trailing my hands up her sides, until they reach her breasts. I've already fucked her twice today, and it's not even noon.

I'm insatiable. Now that's she's no longer breakable, I'm addicted to the point I'd be happy to do nothing but fuck her. It's probably for the best that I've stepped down as king. Not only because that's what it took to get my inner circle on board with Grace's rescue, but also because now, if I feel like it, I can ignore everything outside of these bedroom walls.

If only Grace was as easily tempted.

She whirls around, pushing my hands back to her hips. Despite having thirty days of her in this form, I'm still not used to her strength. So much of her is different. The way she moves, smells, tastes. Before I changed her, I was worried I wouldn't like it, that I'd miss her human softness.

I don't. I like that she's stronger now, that I can fuck her against the wall hard enough to crack stone. That I can skip a few feedings without feeling tempted by her blood. That I can tie her to my bedpost and do whatever depraved ideas enter my head.

"We don't have time," she says pointedly. She pinches my wrists, a smile sneaking through her feigned annoyance. "If you wanted to fuck me, you should have done it *before* I got dressed."

"I did," I say. I echo her smile, leaning in to trail my tongue up her neck. I curl my hand over her shoulder, roughly grabbing her braid. "Then you had to go and put on this dress. Now I need to fuck you in it."

Grace shoves me away. She rolls her eyes and turns back to the mirror. I expect her to fuss with her hair more, but instead, she leans over the dresser and lifts her skirt. She's bare underneath, and I raise my eyebrow.

"You have three minutes," she says. "You better make them count."

I'm inside her before she's finished speaking.

 Beatrice drawls as Grace and I enter the courtyard.

She's not wrong.

Our three-minute tryst on the dresser slipped into a final round on the floor, with her straddling my hips.

Grace moves slowly across the cobblestone. It's her first time being outside since Cora transformed her with the sun spell. She raises her arms, watching the sunlight bathe her bare skin.

"I missed this," she murmurs. She tilts her head back, closing her eyes. "It feels so good."

"Hells, man, get a hold of yourself," Milas laughs from his place at the table. Cora sits beside him and a stack of parchment is spread between them. He rests on his elbows, grinning stupidly. "You already fucked her. We can all smell it. Stop looking at her like you're about to take her again."

I glare at Milas, fists clenching before I can stop them. For all the shit I gave Oskar over the years, I never understood this feeling. I'd slept with dozens of women, and I never cared if someone made jokes like that. With Grace, it makes me want to rip Milas's tongue from his body.

Luckily for him, I'm distracted by Grace's laughter.

"I don't know," she says, giggling. "It might be fun. We've never slept together when we're *both* mortal."

Great. Now I'm getting hard, and there's an audience here to mock me for it.

"At least wait until we're done," Beatrice calls. "Then you two can consummate every room in this manor, for all we care."

"Now there's an excellent idea," I say.

Grace and I cross the courtyard, taking our place at the stone table. This area feels so much larger now. Shortly after escaping from the Day Realm, and while Grace was still adjusting to life as a vampire, I met with my inner circle one last time.

In exchange for ruining our chance of breaking the curse, I promised a change. And unlike the last time I made an agreement, I kept my word. I stepped down as king of the vampires, to let this group lead as a clan. Beatrice, Milas, Amelia, and I now have equal claim.

I offered a place for Cora, and she'd pretended to vomit.

I'm a witch, Sebastian, she'd said. *What would I want looking after a bunch of bloodsuckers?*

And yet, here she sits. In her baggy black dress, thick tights, and clunky shoes. She can pretend all she wants—we all know she belongs at this table as much, if not more, than the rest of us.

"Let's start with the worst of it," Grace says before anyone else has the chance.

I smile despite myself. Here for thirty seconds, and already taking charge.

"What did you do with Oskar?"

My smile falls.

Grace has her hands on the table, palms up and to the sun. She's staring at them, rather than me, so I'm sure she won't notice the way I pause. The way my fingers curl into fists.

Her hand finds mine instantly. She strokes her thumb over my knuckles, glancing at me with a reassuring smile.

"It's okay," she says. "Whatever you decided, it's okay."

When I told her I'd saved his murder for her, she had balked at the idea. When she realized I was serious, she actually *laughed.* She'd gotten laughing so hard she started crying.

Look at that, she'd said, still giggling. *Vampires* can *cry!*

After that, she told me to do what I wanted with Oskar. She made it clear *she* wouldn't be killing anything, and that she certainly wouldn't be killing Oskar.

If someone caused my death, I think you'd go crazy too, she said. *I'd want them to have mercy on you. But this isn't about me, Sebastian. Do what* you *need to do.*

I visited him that night. He'd been kept in the basement cell for a week at that point. He was wild with bloodlust, snarling like an animal from within his cell. It made me nauseated in a way I hadn't expected.

You were supposed to be my friend, I wanted to say. The rush of anger paralyzed me and twisted through my gut until I said something that surprised us both.

I'm sorry, I said. Oskar paused in his erratic pacing, glaring at me from between the rungs. *Truly, Oskar. I am sorry for what happened to Freja. For my part. I never meant for our people to get hurt. I'm sorry that they did. That* she *did.*

He didn't respond. He only stared at me, as though trying to decide if I was fucking with him

I wasn't. The truth was, I hadn't been a good friend to him either.

When I killed him, I was fast. He knew it was coming, but he didn't fight me. He stood proud, chin lifted, as I tore his head from his shoulders.

"Sebastian," Grace says.

I startle back into the present, blinking at her. Everyone else at the table is looking at me, waiting. They're not going to tell her what I've done.

Cora. Beatrice. Milas. Amelia.

So fewer than we used to be.

"Dead," I say. Grace flinches, but I don't let myself look away. "I made it fast. I promise."

I expect her to cry, to look disappointed. She only nods, and her thumb resumes its strokes over the back of my wrist.

An hour later, we are deep into discussions of a new Night Realm. How we'd like to lead, how we'll balance power, how we'll continue to fight for our people.

"Maybe we should find more witch allies," Cora says. "We can't break the curse, but we *can* make more sunwalker spells."

"Cora," I say, shaking my head. "You can't be serious. After everything—"

"It's just an idea," she says, cutting me off. "A lot to consider, obviously, but Grace and I can't be the only decent witches in this world. There might be others willing to help.

"I like it," Grace announces. "And not just because everyone hates me for *immediately* getting a sunwalker spell."

"Nobody hates you," I'm quick to say, and Beatrice howls from the end of the table.

"Hells, you've gone soft," she accuses. She glances around before pushing to her feet. "Can we go now? Their love is making me physically ill."

"Good with me," I say. I pull Grace to her feet, already tugging her toward the manor entrance. "We've got *a lot* of rooms to consummate."

"That's disgusting," Cora says.

"Blame Beatrice for giving him the idea," Grace says. Now, she's the one pulling *me*, giggling as she hurries us along.

Fuck. Yes.

"Love is peculiar," Amelia says. She scrunches her nose. "I'm not sure I'd like it."

"I certainly wouldn't," Beatrice agrees.

"You would," I say, but I don't stick around to argue.

Grace and I cross the patch of dirt in the courtyard's center. Not long ago, my statue stood there as a painful reminder of everything I lost, as a desperate hope of what I might find again.

We tore it down days after returning. Beatrice wanted to get statues of *all* of us, but thankfully the others put a stop to that idea.

"Every room?" Grace whispers as we disappear into the house. "That's going to take a while."

I spin her around, tossing her over my shoulder. She squeals but makes no attempt to get down.

"Don't worry. We've got all the time in the world."

The End.

ACKNOWLEDGMENTS

To my readers: Thank you for joining me on my first journey into the Echo! I hope you enjoyed Grace and Sebastian's love as much I did. Enemies-to-lovers will always be one of my favorite tropes, and their relationship proves why. Grace's bubbly and sharp personality, mixed with Sebastian's broken but redeemable character, was the perfect pairing to mend my heart after it was broken by a certain on-screen couple. On that note...

To the writers of *The Vampire Diaries* (TV show): Thank you for royally botching the most epic love story of all time. It fueled me to write a couple inspired by their romance. While the stories and characters are unique to *This Violent Light*, I used Klaus and Caroline's outstanding chemistry as inspiration for our main couple.

To HJ Nelson: Once again, thank you for being my person. The one I call when I can't decide if a character motivation makes sense. The one I text when I realize I have a disastrous plot-hole. The one I email my first draft, the moment I complete it. Here's to many more years of publishing torture together - there's no one I'd rather suffer with.

To my parents and Jonni: Thank you for your many hours of childcare while I'm frantically pursue my dreams. This book would not be releasing when it is without your support and encouragement.

To my ARC readers: Thank you for taking the time to support a little indie author like me, especially if you helped with *Between Smoke and Shadow*. It means so much to have a community of readers behind me, and I appreciate you every step of the way. I can't wait to hear what you think...and I hope you continue to join me for many books to come!

To my siblings, Brittany, Beau, & Dyston: I am so thankful for our group chat. Whenever I get a new piece of art or cover design, you're the first people I text. Thank you for your invaluable feedback and for always being available to brainstorm my crazy ideas.

To my husband and Ali Rose: Thank you for supporting me while I chase plot bunnies and moody characters at all hours of the day and night. I love you both, and I am so happy we get to do this life together.

To: Katrina, for always being my partner in crime (no matter how crazy the idea). Cooper and Tiegan, for always showing up at my author events (and for being wonderful sister-in-laws). Hannah, for being wildly supportive of my writing (and also for being endlessly funny...our husbands could never).

To Dyston: Thank you for the many designs you created to bring Grace and Sebastian to life. You are so talented, and any author would be lucky to work with you.

To Asterielly Designs: Thank you for the gorgeous book cover. You were wonderful to work with and made my fuzzy ideas shine. If any authors need a cover designer, be sure to check out her work here.

To Ink and Lore Maps: Thank you for the stunning map of the Echo. If any authors need a map made, I highly recommend her.

If you enjoyed *This Violent Light*, please take a moment to review this book on Amazon and/or Goodreads. It makes a huge impact for indie authors like me! If you want to stay up-to-date with my upcoming releases and bookish sneak peeks, join my newsletter! You can follow me on social media at @authorbreewilde.

ABOUT THE AUTHOR

Bree Wilde writes romance and romantasy books for adults. *This Violent Light* is her second novel. She lives in Idaho with her family and spends most of her time reading, writing, and yapping about books.

9 781945 860065